A PALETTE
FOR LOVE

Visit us at www.boldstrokesbooks.com

A PALETTE FOR LOVE

by

Charlotte Greene

2016

ISBN 13: 978-1-62639-758-3

THIS TRADE PAPERBACK ORIGINAL IS PUBLISHED BY
BOLD STROKES BOOKS, INC.
P.O. BOX 249
VALLEY FALLS, NY 12185

FIRST EDITION: NOVEMBER 2016

CREDITS
EDITOR: SHELLEY THRASHER
PRODUCTION DESIGN: SUSAN RAMUNDO
COVER DESIGN BY SHERI (GRAPHICARTIST2020@HOTMAIL.COM)

CHAPTER ONE

I'd been back in New Orleans only a few days now and wasn't sure if I could trust the cabs to pick me up on time. My interview was scheduled for one p.m., but paranoid I'd miss it, I got to the warehouse where it was being held almost an hour early. It wasn't in the best part of town, but I didn't feel as if I was in danger, either. Like many parts of the city, it was a mixed-income neighborhood. Nice streets with manicured lawns and new paint alternated with rundown streets with boarded-up windows and trash in the yards. This part of Mid-City had been undergoing gentrification for the last decade, and the yuppies were buying the cheap shotguns and Victorians in blocks at a time, fixing them up, and selling them to other yuppies for ten times what they'd paid for them. In a few years, the entire neighborhood would be expensive.

I grew up in New Orleans, living mostly with my Aunt Kate after my parents died. I'd attended Loyola on a full scholarship, commuting from the Bywater by bus and streetcar all five years I was there. When I was accepted to a graduate arts program in Paris, I'd been happy and excited but found myself missing my home city more every year I was in Europe. Four years away had been too long, and I was happy to be back home, newly minted PhD in hand. I didn't particularly love living with my aunt again, but what twenty-six-year-old would?

Because I was so early, I walked leisurely around the warehouse, which took up an entire city block. Artists around town had been hired to paint the outside of the building, and it was now a work of art on its own. Each side of the building was unique, sharing a different facet of the city's culture and history. On a shorter side facing one street, shadowy outlines of jazz musicians played visual music on Spanish-style balconies painted onto the building's metal siding. On the next side, antebellum ladies and gentlemen danced in front of a faux plantation, enjoying the ill-gotten wealth of a bygone era. The back of the building, however, was the most interesting and puzzling, and had apparently been painted in direct reference to the plantation scene. There, slaves stood near shanties and shacks, looking longingly in the direction of the dancing scene on the next side of the building. Why is this hidden back here? I wondered. Wishing I'd remembered to bring a camera, I made my way around a cluster of trashcans to the final side of the building and was surprised to see several people on scaffolding and ladders working on the last painting. They all looked over at me curiously, and I flushed under their gaze. Turning around, I returned to the slave scene and stood as far away from it as I could, trying to take it all in.

"It's beautiful, isn't it?" someone asked.

I jumped and then turned toward the voice, surprised to see an elegantly dressed woman standing near the trashcans. She was about my age, her dark hair pulled up in a severe, no-nonsense French braid. She wore pearls around her neck and at her ears, and the style and cut of her clothes suggested a former era. Her makeup was impeccable, and she wore square but flattering glasses. Standing by the rubbish and trashcans of the alley, with her smart clothes and refined looks, she looked altogether as incongruous in this setting as possible.

"It's incredible," I managed to say.

"You looked puzzled a moment ago. Is something wrong with it?"

"Nothing, and that's why I'm puzzled. I don't understand why it's hidden away back here. This is clearly the best mural. It's shocking and thought-provoking."

She shrugged. "That's exactly what I thought. Unfortunately, I had no say in the matter. If it were up to me, the entire building would be covered with this scene, all those accusing eyes directed at the city around them. The city commission decided otherwise."

"I supposed that makes sense. Few people like talking about this part of the city's past." I indicated the scene.

"Especially if tourists might see it."

We stood there for a while smiling at each other before she seemed to shake herself awake. "How rude of me." She walked closer and held out a hand. "I'm Amelia Winters."

Amelia Winters was the woman interviewing me at one. I swallowed, my hand trembling as I shook hers. "Clothilde Deveraux."

"Miss Deveraux—or should I say Doctor Deveraux—I'm so happy to meet you. We had a meeting arranged for later today, correct?"

"Yes. I got here early. So sorry to intrude. Oh, and Miss or Doctor, whatever you prefer."

"It's not a problem at all, Doctor. In fact, I'm rather relieved. An important client is calling from Paris this afternoon, and I was afraid it would intrude on our conversation later. Now we'll have ample time to get to know one another."

Still embarrassed that I was here so early, I wasn't certain whether she was being truthful or accommodating, and I blushed. "Thank you for being so obliging, Miss Winters. I wasn't sure how long it would take to get here, and I wanted to see the warehouse beforehand."

"Let's move inside, shall we? I'll ask one of the interns to prepare some tea."

I followed her around to a door into the warehouse, which doubled as the door to the plantation house on the painted scene. She entered a code on the keypad by the door, and it opened for us automatically. After my eyes adjusted to the dim light, I caught my breath. Inside was a treasure trove of artwork in various conditions. Several paintings on easels were set up around the room, some with serious-looking people seated before them, examining the work closely or working on it with brushes and feathers. Artwork hung on the walls, covering nearly every available space, and I recognized several contemporary French paintings mixed in with some unfamiliar work. Elsewhere, paintings were partially boxed as if waiting for shipment or further opening. In the far end of the room, statues stood on wooden platforms, some wrapped with packing materials and others open for viewing.

Seeing my stunned expression, Miss Winters said, "Feel free to explore for a few minutes while I get your file ready for the interview. I'll come get you when I'm ready."

"Thank you. I didn't mean to gawk."

"That's what you're here for, Doctor. I'll see you soon." She turned and disappeared into an office in one corner of the building.

I spent the next twenty minutes doing just what she'd suggested: exploring. As the time passed, I grew increasingly impressed by what I was seeing. Amelia Winters was one of the best-known art dealers in the country, particularly the South, but I'd had no idea the scale of her enterprise. Literally millions of dollars' worth of art was sitting around in this one room, and, I noticed, it looked like there was another floor of it above us. I watched some of the art restorers working on older paintings for a moment, shocked even further that this enterprise could afford to retain so many of them. At least ten people were restoring works of art, and other, unmanned paintings on easels were clearly undergoing restoration as well. What I took as her personal collection—the art on the walls—was also awe-inspiring. Besides the contemporary French painters, French masterworks from the eighteenth and nineteenth century were scattered here and there, restored to pristine condition. Looking longingly at the boxed work I had yet to see, I walked over to the lone security guard, curious.

"Hello," I said as I approached. "I'm sorry to bother you."

He stood up from his chair to greet me. "Not at all."

"I was just wondering about the security systems here. This place is larger than some museums I've interned in."

He smiled. "We have more security than you'd know just looking around, miss," he said. "We have state-of-the-art video surveillance in every corner of the building, as well as myself and another armed guard upstairs. Police monitor this building at all times, and we're never more than twenty seconds from a patrol car."

I nodded but found myself wondering if that would be enough. If thieves decided to come in here, they would find a treasure chest. "But surely more could be done," I said. "Everything in here is a priceless, irreplaceable masterpiece." I gestured around me.

"I wouldn't go so far as to say that," Amelia Winters said from behind me, and I jumped. She smiled when I turned toward her. "Some of the work here is true garbage, I would argue, but my clients asked me to get it for them." She looked over at the security guard. "Getting grilled, Henry?"

Embarrassed to be found criticizing her employees, I began to stammer. "I'm sorry—"

"Please don't apologize. I was concerned about security too, which is precisely why I hired the best security firm in New Orleans. You'll learn all about it soon."

I gave a great heave of relief as she said this, as it suggested that she meant to hire me. I smiled sheepishly at Henry. "I really didn't mean to imply—"

"Don't mention it." He winked.

"Now, Doctor Deveraux, if you'd be so kind?" Miss Winters said, indicating her office. "I'd like to begin the interview."

For its size, the office was nicely decorated, the furniture mainly art-deco antiques. Miss Winters indicated a chair a couple of feet from her desk. I sat and placed my purse on the ground, and she handed me a cup of tea before sitting on the front edge of her desk, gazing down at me. She was quiet for quite a while, just looking. After a long moment, I began to heat up with embarrassment under her gaze, unsure how to respond to her stare.

Finally, she smiled. "Please forgive me," she said. "I don't mean to make you uncomfortable, Doctor." She stood and went around the side of the desk, sitting in her chair. She opened a manila folder, which, I noticed, was one of many on her desk. My stomach dropped as I realized the other folders represented my competition. She flipped through my file a couple of times, nodding as she read, then returned to my C.V.

"Clothilde Deveraux." She looked up at me. "What a fantastic, old-fashioned name. French, right?"

Unexpected as it was, the question caught me off guard, reminding me, once again, of how long it had been since I'd been interviewed. "Yes. French Creole." I tried to swallow my nervousness. "Clothilde is a family name. My friends call me Chloé."

"Clo-ee," she said slowly, nodding. "And the name Deveraux is very common in New Orleans."

"Yes—I have a lot of close and distant family here and in other parts of Louisiana."

"I can imagine." She sat back and removed her glasses, revealing a pair of startlingly dark-blue eyes. "My family is also from here."

"Yes." The Winters family was known for its money, its reign stretching back as far as the history of the city. An area of mansions in the Garden District belonged entirely to the Winters clan.

"We're not Creole, of course. English interlopers, I'm afraid."

Not sure what response she expected, or whether she was making a joke, I smiled nervously in reply.

"Soooo." She put her glasses back on and looked back down at my file. "BFA and MA from Loyola University here in New Orleans, and a PhD in French Art History from the Sorbonne. Summer internships with museums including the Art Institute of Chicago, the San Francisco Modern Art Museum, and, most recently, the Musée d'Art Moderne in Paris." She took her glasses off again and looked up at me once more, obviously puzzled. "Doctor Deveraux, you are perhaps the most overqualified person I have ever interviewed for a position with my establishment. You make my experience and education look sad and paltry by comparison. Why on earth do you want to work for me?"

I swallowed. Although I'd spent several hours yesterday preparing for this interview, somehow the idea of justifying my application had slipped my mind. I'd been desperately trying to get back to New Orleans for some time now. Academic positions at New Orleans's universities were very difficult to come by, particularly with the current recession. None of this, however, explained why I'd applied, and it wouldn't be smart to say that the job I really wanted wasn't available right now. Thinking as quickly as I could, I came up with an idea.

"In Paris last year, I went to an exhibit of Jean-Claude Sasseur."

"Mmmm, I love his work. I was there myself."

"Exactly. I missed meeting you, but I saw the results of your meeting with him. You bought five of his paintings."

Miss Winters raised her eyebrows in reply but said nothing.

"Later that same month, I went to a photography exhibit by Madeline Allemand and the same thing happened, only there you nearly bought out the show."

She remained silent, her eyes unreadable.

"The same thing happened with Adrienne Bayle, Guy Montagne, Cerise Payan, and others. At every show I attended last year, you bought something."

Miss Winters sat forward, resting on her forearms. "Let's be frank, Doctor Deveraux."

I nodded, heart sinking because of her serious expression.

"You have been groomed to work in the academy or a museum. Every bit of information I have on you here suggests that fact. I see no work in galleries or art dealerships in your file whatsoever. If you had told me you were seeking a career change, I still wouldn't believe you. Not after all your hard academic work and training."

I swallowed and agreed.

"But you didn't say that. Instead, you suggested that my purchases impressed you, which is something altogether different."

I said nothing, realizing she had caught me.

"Do you want to know what I think? I think you wanted—perhaps desperately—to come back home, and you're willing to do anything to make that happen."

I was stunned. She was, of course, completely right.

"I think you want very much to work at Loyola or Tulane, or perhaps the state college, but with all of these hiring freezes, nothing is available for you in the schools here. Am I right?"

Ashamed and disheartened, I nodded.

Instead of getting upset, she said, "There's nothing wrong with that, Doctor Deveraux, and in fact, I would have liked to have known your motives coming in, as they work in my favor. You're not likely to leave until an academic position opens up for you here in the city, and in that regard, I believe I may be able to help you."

"Excuse me? What do you mean?"

She sat up in her chair. "The Winters family is one of the largest private contributors to Tulane University. My company is one of Tulane's largest corporate contributors. If I want you on the faculty there, it'll happen. Maybe next year, maybe the year after that, depending on what I can do. Do you understand me, Doctor?"

The realization that she might have enough influence to get me an academic position startled me. Stunned, I had no reply.

"That is, of course, if we can reach an agreement as to your tenure with me. And who knows—you might like working here more than you know." She leaned back in her chair, hands steepled beneath her chin, staring at me. Her gaze was probing, and I flushed with embarrassed warmth again, still not certain how to respond to her inquiring gaze. Finally, she said, "Yes, I think you'll do nicely. Very nicely indeed." She paused and then sat forward again, meeting my eyes. "Do you know what this job is?"

"The ad said I would be your assistant but contained no further details."

"Yes, my assistant. Let me explain. In that role, you will not act as my secretary. I don't know if you noticed, but I already have one. She takes care of my appointments, travel arrangements, and most of my paperwork, as well as billing and payroll for the other employees. The position I'm offering you is more personal. It involves a lot of things, Doctor, and again, I feel strange offering it to you, knowing your credentials. For example, I might one day ask you to do my errands around town. You took a cab here, so I'll arrange a company car for your use. Would you be willing to do such menial work?"

I nodded, my hopes rising.

"Another day, I might ask for your advice regarding an artist I might purchase from, so you would help choose the work we buy for my clients. Occasionally you might visit the homes of my clients in order to ascertain tastes, color schemes, etcetera. You should be very good at this task, even if you don't know it yet. How does that sound?"

"Very interesting." It did appeal to me. I'd never had enough money to buy artwork, and the idea of acquiring it in the quantities she tended to purchase excited me.

"On other occasions, you would accompany me to various functions both here in New Orleans and elsewhere, which could mean extensive travel. Are you willing to travel at least once a month with me, perhaps, at times, more often?"

"Of course," I said, though a little reluctantly. I enjoyed travel but had always been a wallflower at most parties.

"At said functions, you would act as my reference base for any possible clientele we might be able to acquire. This would mean researching attendees before these functions and coming up with ways to get them to buy art through us. Again, I think you will be very good at this skill with some practice."

I kept my face interested and calm, trying to cover my mounting excitement. It sounded more and more like she might hire me.

She paused, as if weighing her words. "Finally, as my assistant, you must dress and act in a very particular way in public. We will represent one of the most influential modern-art dealerships in the world, and I'm not saying that to impress you." She looked at me critically again, frowning slightly. "Do you usually wear clothes like this?"

I looked down at myself and frowned. In truth, I'd borrowed the outfit from my aunt. My own wardrobe was definitely casual. While I'd interned at several museums, I'd worked strictly behind the scenes, so I wore street clothes. I'd never purchased business wear in my life. "Not exactly."

"That's good, because they're terrible." Miss Winters chuckled. "Those clothes are designed for a much older woman and probably don't flatter her, either."

I laughed. "They're my aunt's."

"Thank goodness. That explains them. Well, that will be our first order of business, then—getting you new clothes."

"*Our* business? You mean you're going to help me shop?"

"Obviously you wouldn't even know where to begin." Seeing my expression, she laughed. "Please don't be angry. As I said, as my assistant you will be expected to look and dress a certain way at all times, and since it's my requirement, I want to help you. When you're here at the office, I expect business wear, and when we're at parties, I want you to look as if you belong there." She paused, her expression softening again. "You don't look very happy about this requirement, Doctor."

I made myself shrug, trying to look casual about it. Just think of the clothes as a uniform, I thought. "I'm sorry. I'm just surprised. I didn't know I'd get a new wardrobe, too."

She laughed again. "And a makeover." She paused. "So...are you interested in the position? Does the salary fit your requirements?"

In fact, the salary was one of the only reasons I'd even considered applying, as it was more money than I'd ever earned. "Yes, I'm more than interested. I'd be very pleased to work with you."

"We can negotiate commissions when you begin to sell on your own, but until then, I'll provide bonuses when I think you've earned one." She stood up and held out her hand. "Welcome aboard."

I jumped up and shook with her, the guilty weight of joblessness finally slipping off my shoulders. As I gathered my belongings and made my exit, I glanced back once more to find her watching me again. Her stare was as unflinching and unreadable as ever. While I was relieved at the idea of money coming my way again, I found her presence unsettling in some fundamental but confusing way. It would take a long time before I could feel anything but embarrassed around her.

Chapter Two

My Aunt Kate was gardening in our front flowerbox when I got home, and she looked surprised as she watched me climb out of the Rolls Royce owned by the Winters Corporation. The driver looked concerned as he got out of the car, obviously used to opening the door for his passengers. I waved at him and said, "Thanks for the lift, George. I've got it from here."

"You're welcome, mademoiselle." He gave me a quick salute and lowered himself back into the car, and I watched with my aunt as he drove away down our narrow, pitted street.

"What on earth was that?" Aunt Kate asked as the car disappeared around the corner.

"I got the job," I said. I put my clasped hands above my head in a gesture of victory, shaking them a few times as if I'd just won a race.

She shrieked and launched herself into my arms, and we jumped up and down a few times, laughing together. Her large sun hat fell off onto the ground, and she bent down to pick it up. I noticed then that her hands were covered in dark mud and wasn't surprised to see that she'd gotten it all over the outfit she loaned me. We both laughed at the mud on the sleeves and back of the jacket.

"So wonderful, honey," she said, smiling broadly as she tried to brush some of the mud off with her dirty gloves. "When do you start?"

"On Monday, technically, but I have to do some shopping with my boss this weekend."

"Shopping?"

"It's complicated." I shook my head. "Anyway, I'm starving. Want to walk over and get a bite at Tony's?" Tony's was the neighborhood dive bar. "We might catch Meghan there."

"Tony's? Are you kidding me? This calls for a celebration!" Aunt Kate was always one for celebrating something, which to her meant getting dressed up and going out on the town.

I shook my head. "I just want to do something low-key. We can celebrate in style some other time. Maybe after I get my first paycheck."

She looked disappointed and sighed in resignation. "Fine. Tony's it is. You should get out of those dirty clothes, though."

My friend Meghan was in fact working when we finally reached Tony's, and she squealed when she saw me. I'd been back in town for a few days now, but we hadn't planned to go out for the first time together until later tonight. She lifted the barrier between the dining room and the bar and ran over to me, enveloping me in a big hug.

Meghan, my oldest friend, had always been a rebel. We'd been friends since eighth grade, and even then, she was different from the other kids. She'd shown up for school the first day in solid black, her hair dyed purple, half her head shaved, and a ring in her nose. Her difference had probably drawn me to her, as I always felt like something of an outsider too. While I was never as funky as she was, the weirdos at school had still accepted me, mostly because of my friendship with Meghan. Now she was the manager of Tony's bar and sang with a bluegrass band a couple nights a week.

"What are you doing here?" she shrieked, holding me at arm's length and looking me up and down. "And why do you look so thin? I thought Paris had the best food in the world."

I laughed. "I barely lost any weight, Meghan," I said, "and Aunt Kate and I wanted to get a drink to celebrate my new job."

Meghan clapped her hands and hugged me again. "That's great news! I'll make you both my newest cocktail creation." Turning to my aunt, she hugged her, hard. "I hardly ever see you anymore, Aunt Kate. Is Tony's not good enough for you anymore?"

Aunt Kate shook her head. "I'm sorry, dear. I do mean to get over here more often, but I've been...a little distracted."

Meghan raised an eyebrow at me and I laughed. "Aunt Kate has a new beau."

"Ahhh, that explains it. You've been too busy honeymooning." Aunt Kate reddened and then slapped Meghan's arm playfully. "Oh, hush. I don't want to talk about that with you girls."

Meghan, Aunt Kate, and I linked arms, and the three of us made our way over to the bar. Though considered something of a dive, Tony's was actually a lovely place, with a long, wooden bar and wooden walls and booths. With a little more money invested in it, it could easily become an elegant hangout, but most of the locals preferred to keep it as it'd always been: homey and cheap. Like most of the bars in New Orleans, you could smoke inside, and a faint odor of cherry hung in the air from someone's recent cigar.

It was three thirty in the afternoon, which meant we had the place to ourselves. Aunt Kate and I sat in our favorite seats on the corner and watched Meghan mix our cocktails. Though she'd outgrown her solid-black clothes, Meghan still displayed some of her punk beginnings. Her hair was her natural dirty blond now, but it was styled similarly to the way it had been in her younger days, with bits and pieces longer and shorter, her head shaved on one side. Over the years, she'd gotten more and more tattoos, and the outline of several magnolia flowers traced up and down both of her arms. She was delicate and cute, and never stayed single for long. Her tastes in men were as eclectic as her style, and when we were younger she used to go through boyfriends almost monthly. Because I'd been finishing my degree last spring and my last internship over the summer, I hadn't seen her in almost a year, and I was relieved she was looking so happy.

"Here you go," Meghan said, delivering our drinks with a flourish and a bow. Aunt Kate and I laughed and took a small sip.

"It's wonderful," Aunt Kate said. She licked her lips.

"It is. What do you call it?"

"It's our new Bywater Hurricane." She held her hands out as if presenting us with something remarkable.

Aunt Kate and I groaned together. While Pat O'Brien's had been serving the world-famous hurricane cocktails in New Orleans since the 1940s, ever since Hurricane Katrina, the drink had been popping up in various new formulas around the city. The Category-Five Hurricane was served downtown in the Quarter, as were the Uptown Hurricane and others. The cocktail personified the macabre sense of humor most of us had adopted since our city's most recent tragedy.

"It was only a matter of time before someone started selling it in the Bywater," Meghan sniffed, feigning hurt feelings. "I decided it should be Tony's since we've been here the longest, and people around here love it."

As we drank, we chatted about Paris, and I told them both about my new job and my possible duties.

"I still can't believe you want to work for a gallery," Aunt Kate said, shaking her head. "Especially after all your schooling. You could have gotten a job there with your BFA."

I shrugged. "Still, I think it could be interesting, at least for now." Seeing their disbelief, I laughed. "Listen, my boss is really nice. I get to travel, I get to be around great artwork all day, and I'm being issued a company car for personal use, too. The job will be fine for a while. Anyway, Miss Winters promised she'd help me get a position at Tulane later. She and her family have a lot of sway at the university. She told me it might take a year or two, but she could help make it happen." They both stared at me, clearly as stunned as I was at the influence this offer suggested.

"So what is the famous Amelia Winters like?" Meghan asked. "I read about her in the paper every once in a while. Is she the ball-busting bitch everyone claims she is?"

I shifted uncomfortably in my seat, not sure how to answer. In truth, the woman had completely charmed me, though she also intimidated me. She was beautiful, elegant, and rich, and obviously thought very highly of my qualifications. "She's not exactly what you'd expect."

"What do you mean?" Meghan asked.

"She was actually very nice. Warm even." They both looked skeptical and I laughed again. "Anyway, we're going shopping this weekend, so I guess I'll know more about her soon."

"You mentioned that before." Aunt Kate frowned. "What kind of shopping?"

I blushed, not sure how to explain. "Clothes, mostly. She told me I need to look the part of her assistant. Oh, and she's taking me to get a haircut at some fancy salon in the morning."

Aunt Kate shook her head and looked away, obviously miffed, and Meghan stared at me, one eyebrow lifted. "You gotta admit it's kind of weird, Chloé," she finally said.

"How so?" I asked, my face warming with anger.

Meghan and Aunt Kate shared a glance. "Haven't you heard the rumors about her?" Meghan asked.

"What rumors?"

"That she eats girls like you for breakfast," Aunt Kate said, looking anywhere but at me.

"Sounds like she's grooming you to be the next meal," Meghan said, her expression serious.

I stared back and forth at them and then laughed out loud. "You must be kidding. Are you seriously saying you're afraid she'll seduce me?"

Meghan appeared less certain now, and she and Aunt Kate shared an amused look. "I guess it does sound kind of stupid," Meghan finally admitted.

Aunt Kate's face softened and then she laughed. "You're right, Chloé," she said after a moment. "I guess you're smarter than that. You have such a great head on your shoulders."

"Aside from the fact that I'm *not* a lesbian," I added.

Meghan and Aunt Kate laughed, and then Meghan asked Aunt Kate about her new boyfriend. As they chatted about him and a recent trip Aunt Kate had taken with him to Key West, I tuned out a little, thinking about Amelia Winters. I tried to reconcile what I'd just learned about her and my meeting with her this afternoon. While it was true she'd disarmed me a couple of times during the interview, and I'd caught her staring at me several times, at no time had I suspected she was hitting on me. She'd simply seemed like a curious employer, hoping to hire the best person for the job. She was beautiful and intimidating, but she wasn't interested in me in that way, I was sure.

"So...tonight," Meghan finally said, pulling me out of my reverie.

"Yes. Tonight," I said.

"I'm picking you up at eight and have a whole evening of debauchery planned."

I groaned. "I'm not sure I'm up for that. I'm still not over the jetlag."

"I won't take no for an answer, sourpuss. I haven't seen you in ages, and I bet you haven't had a single night of fun that whole time."

"Well, your kind of fun, no," I admitted.

"Anyway, I want you to meet someone."

I groaned again and Aunt Kate and Meghan laughed. "Please don't set me up with one of your friends again, Meghan. They're never my type."

"You haven't met this guy, Chloé," Meghan said, eyes excited. "He's actually not even one of my friends. He's my drummer's brother, and he'd be perfect for you. Good career, tight body, tall, dark, handsome—the whole nine yards."

I laughed. "Really, Meghan. I'm not up for a double date."

"It won't be a double date. A bunch of people will be there, so it'll be totally casual. If you don't like him, you don't even need to talk to him. It won't be awkward at all."

I rolled my eyes. This was a losing battle. "What should I wear?" I finally asked.

❖

The bar was dark and intimate, and I was surprised to find that I was having a good time. Meghan and what I took as her beau-of-the-week were currently wrapped up in each other (literally), and Charles and I shared an awkward glance as we tried not to watch them make out. Despite what Meghan had promised earlier, the night had turned into a double date, with all of the people Meghan invited as filler cancelling at the last minute. In fact, I'd begun to be afraid that I would be the third wheel all night until Charles finally showed up, apologizing for his lateness.

He was handsome, with chiseled features, a fit body, gorgeous black hair, and piercing gray eyes. He was just getting off work when he joined us, still dressed in a suit. He hadn't had time to freshen up, and his face was darkened with a sexy five-o'clock shadow. The four of us shared a nice late supper before walking over to the bar where we were now sitting, waiting for the band to start. We were here to listen to a trombone player Meghan wanted to recruit for her band, that is if she managed to detach her face from her boyfriend long enough to hear him play.

"So tell me about Paris," Charles said, gazing directly at me.

I blushed under his gaze and looked away. I'd forgotten how direct most American men could be and wasn't used to meeting anyone's eyes.

"I spent a lot of time working, really," I said, not sure what he wanted to hear.

"I've only been there once," he said. "I did a year abroad in London during high school, and we got to go to various cities during our breaks. I spent about two weeks in Paris when I was seventeen."

"Oh?" I asked, sipping my cocktail. My hands were shaking slightly, and I set the drink down on the bar to avoid sloshing it all over myself. It had been a long time since my last date, and my nerves were making me feel clumsy and dumb.

"We did a lot of the museums, of course, but my favorite part of Paris was the Left Bank. All those bookstores and antiques. I wanted to move there, live in a dirty loft, and write poetry all night while I drank cheap wine." He laughed. "I was kind of a romantic then."

"And you aren't anymore?" I made myself meet his gaze.

He chuckled and moved closer. "Not in the same way," he murmured.

My heart rate picked up and I glanced away again. Luckily the band began to play, and all four of us spent the next thirty minutes listening to the first set. As we listened, I glanced over at Charles a few times, enjoying the view. He was, in fact, stunning. For once, Meghan had set me up with the right guy. He nodded in time to the music, seeming oblivious to the fact that I was staring at him.

The band took a break and Meghan stood up, grabbing my hand. "Come with me to the ladies', would you?" she asked. She raised her eyebrows at me, clearly trying to tell me something without words.

I touched the top of Charles's hand and then slid off my stool.

Meghan and I were soon inside the dark bathroom. "So…what do you think of Charles?" she asked. She looked positively gleeful, proud that she'd set us up.

"Well, he's certainly a beautiful piece of manliness, though we haven't had much time to get to know each other."

"What's to know? He works for the city, he's drop-dead gorgeous, and he likes you. What more do you need?"

"I'm not the kind to jump into bed with the first guy I meet, Meghan." I shook my head. "I have to know someone better before I can do that."

"Oh, and I am?" Meghan said, her color rising.

"That's not what I meant—"

"I think that's exactly what you meant." Meghan spat out the words. "And I'll have you know, Zach and I went out for three weeks before we started sleeping together. We've been together for almost three months."

I sighed. "I'm sorry, Meghan. I didn't mean it that way."

She nodded. "And I'm sorry to jump down your throat. I guess I'm still kind of sensitive about it. I don't want to be that person anymore, that's all. I know I used to sleep around a lot, but you've been gone for a long time. I've been trying to change."

I grabbed her hand and squeezed it. "Really, I'm sorry. It was rude of me to make assumptions."

She seemed to shake off her anger. "Anyway, back to Mr. Gorgeous. Do you think you'll go home with him?"

I shook my head. "That's just not me. I wouldn't feel right. And anyway, I have to get up early in the morning."

She shrugged. "Don't wait too long, Chloé. Guys like that don't hang around forever."

I shrugged in response. "He'll wait or he won't. That's not up to me."

"Well, he certainly seems to like you." She winked. "He can barely tear his eyes away from your ass."

I swatted her arm and laughed.

When we returned to the bar, both of the men got to their feet as we approached, and I smiled at Charles shyly, pleased with his gallantry. He really was a catch. As we listened to the rest of the next set, he reached over and grabbed one of my hands, and my stomach flipped with excitement. He rubbed my knuckles with his thumb and my face warmed with pleasure. It had been an incredibly long time since I held a man's hand. Too long.

Charles and I decided to excuse ourselves after the next set ended, and Meghan pouted. "It's only midnight!"

"I have to get up early tomorrow, Meghan," I said. "I need to get going or I'll be a zombie all day."

"And I've been up since five," Charles explained. Turning to me, he said, "May I drive you home, Miss Deveraux?" He held his hand out for mine.

I giggled stupidly and took it, turning to wish Meghan and Zach good night before letting him lead me outside.

The night was still oppressively hot. The summer never seems to want to give up its grip on New Orleans, and autumn had only technically just begun. Just outside the door to the bar, Charles turned toward me.

"Instead of taking you home, we could stop by my place for a nightcap," he offered "I live just around the corner."

My stomach dropped, but I managed to shake my head. "I'm sorry, Charles. I really do have to get up early. Some other night?"

His face flashed with anger for a second, but the expression cleared so fast I thought I might have imagined it. "Completely fine, of course, and yes, I'd love to see you again." His eyes seemed to darken, and he stepped closer. I unconsciously backed up but bumped into the wall behind me. He came even closer, and I caught a whiff of aftershave and sweat.

He suddenly kissed me, his mouth hard on mine, and my head slammed painfully against the wall. For a moment I let it happen, and then I pushed on his chest as hard as I could. He continued to kiss me, jamming his tongue into my mouth, and I could taste the bourbon he'd been drinking. For a moment, I thought I might gag and managed to wrench my mouth away. His lips moved to my face and neck, and his unshaven face scratched first along my chin and then downward as he pushed into me. One of his hands started to sneak across my chest, and I struggled harder, panicking. Finally, I managed to slide out of his grip and jump away.

He laughed, but he was panting slightly, staring at me, eyes hungry. Seeing my expression, he seemed amused. "What's the matter?" he asked.

I backed up a few more steps, keeping my eyes on him to watch for movement. "I-I think I'm going to get a c-cab," I explained, trying to keep my voice steady. "Thank you for dinner and the drinks."

He chuckled, shaking his head. "Oh, come on. It wasn't that bad, was it?" He took a step closer.

"It was, Charles, and I think you know it was," I said quietly. "Don't come near me again." Steeling myself, I turned and walked in the direction of the police station, hoping I could get there fast enough to get away from him.

"Oh, give me a break! You can't be serious!" he called after me.

Luckily, he sounded farther away, which meant he wasn't following me, but I wouldn't take any chances. I kept walking, not responding. As I turned the corner, doing everything I could to stop myself from breaking into a run, I heard him yell again.

"Fuck you, bitch!"

CHAPTER THREE

The next morning, I really, really didn't want to go shopping. Last night, after I found my third-cousin Derek at the police station and got a ride back in his squad car, I'd spent the next several hours crying in my room. While things like that had happened or nearly happened to me in the past, I was still shocked and hurt. Charles had seemed like such a nice man—normal, smart, gallant. Instead, he'd been hiding a monster inside. Every time I thought about his tongue in my mouth I shivered and gagged, and the scratches from his beard had left lasting marks on my chin and neck.

By the time the Rolls Royce appeared in front of our modest house the next morning, I'd managed to get only two hours of restless sleep, and my stomach was still in tight knots. I'd thought of calling and postponing, but as this was my first official duty as an employee of the Winters Corporation, I thought better of it. It wouldn't do to cancel on a woman like Amelia Winters at the last minute.

I watched George open the car door for her, and she got out, peering up and down our street with barely concealed disdain. The Bywater is a poorer neighborhood, though parts of it, like the rest of the less affluent parts of the city, were gentrifying. I doubted very much if she had ever set foot in the Bywater before, despite growing up in the city. She looked as out of place as humanly possible. Trying to save her from further sullying her Manolo Blahniks, I opened our front door and walked down our little set of stairs. She looked pleased to see me.

"Doctor Deveraux," she said. "Thank you for clearing your day for me today."

"Of course." I shook her hand. "It's not every day I get an escort to go shopping."

She squeezed my fingers before letting go. "I've made appointments throughout the morning and afternoon, and we have a reservation for lunch. Please let me know if you're tired at any point, and we can rearrange our schedule to include a break."

"Thank you, I will." We both got into the car and George closed the door after us. I glanced up at the window to the house to see my aunt watching us warily. I waved at her as we drove away, but her face looked grim.

"First up, of course, is your hair and makeup. You refrained from washing it this morning, I hope?"

I laughed and touched my dirty hair uncomfortably. "That's what you suggested, though I must admit I feel pretty scummy right now."

"Well, you don't look scummy," she said.

I went hot with embarrassment at her compliment and had to look out the window to hide my red face. We spent the next few minutes in, at least for me, an awkward silence. I wasn't sure what she meant by the comment or why she'd said it. As we drove, we watched the Bywater, the Marigny, and the Quarter go by outside the windows. Finally, nerving myself up, I looked over at her, wondering if she was embarrassed too. Her face remained blank, sealed, giving nothing away.

Sitting this close to her in the bright morning sunlight, I readjusted my estimate of her age. I had assumed, partly because of her great art empire, that she was my age or older, but I was starting to think I might be wrong and that she might be younger. Also, she was, if anything, lovelier than I'd remembered. Her face was a classic heart shape, with precise makeup framing her beautiful eyes and soft lips. Her thick, dark hair was arranged in lovely, old-fashioned finger waves along the side of her face, the rest of it set up on her head in a complicated French braid.

Her clothes, once again, seemed new but somehow dated in style, as if she'd gone back in time and brought them to the present.

They reminded me of clothes from film noir and flattered her slender, boyish figure. Indeed, her beauty was extremely intimidating, and that attribute, coupled with her extreme wealth, made me feel like a poor, ugly sidekick. I couldn't imagine becoming this woman's counterpart, no matter how much money she spent on my clothes.

She seemed to suddenly sense my eyes on her and looked over before I could glance away. I blushed, embarrassed to be seen staring at her. "I'm sorry. I was just thinking that everything I know about you I've read in newspapers and magazines."

She raised her eyebrows. "I'm sure we have plenty to learn about each other in the coming weeks, Doctor, and plenty of time to do it. You'll know me better than most people, and soon, I hope. I'd like for us to be…friendly, if possible."

We pulled up next to an exclusive salon on Magazine Street a few minutes later. After George opened the door and we climbed out, I saw that the sign had clearly said Closed on the salon's door a few seconds before someone opened it, the bells on the door chiming happily. A small, effete man stood there, motioning us in.

"Quickly, quickly!" he said, laughing. "I don't want anyone to see us! If they think I'm open, we'll have a mob on our hands. So nice to see you, Amelia, and to meet you, Doctor Deveraux. I'm Jean-Paul." He took my hand in his small, slim palm for a second and pulled me gently up the short flight of steps into the salon.

Once inside, he and Amelia kissed cheeks and then turned to me, openly appraising every inch of me. I felt hot under their eyes, but neither one seemed to notice my embarrassment. The stylist walked closer, examining my face from inches away, and I blushed harder, chuckling uncomfortably. He touched my dirty hair, running it through his fingers, and I felt as if I'd die from shame. While I didn't wash my hair every day, I certainly liked to have it clean if someone was going to be examining it so closely. For me it was like brushing your teeth before going to the dentist—common courtesy.

He stepped away from me and turned to Amelia. "I certainly have my work cut out with this one," he said, then turned back toward me with a laugh. "I don't mean to sound like I'm criticizing you, honey. You're actually lovely, and you have a wonderful complexion. So few people take care of their skin, and it's obvious you do. Your hair also has a lot of promise. I love the color and your natural highlights."

"But?" I said.

"Buuut," Jeal-Paul said, "the haircut is terrible, your eyebrows need work, and, from what I can tell, you don't know how to use makeup."

I felt a little miffed but didn't say anything.

Jean-Paul turned to Amelia. "May I have two hours?"

"Two hours! We have an appointment with Tiffany for noon. I wanted to have lunch first."

"Lunch will have to be on the go, I'm afraid," he said. "I need two hours minimum."

Amelia sighed and pulled out her smart phone, tapping a few buttons. "I'll try to reschedule with Tiffany for one then, though that will push everything else back too." She looked up at me, and I saw the ghost of a smile on her lips. "I'll be back for you. Try to enjoy yourself, no matter what this poof says or does."

Too nervous to respond, I nodded in agreement and watched her leave before turning back to Jean-Paul. He appraised me critically again for a long, awkward moment. His face suddenly brightened and he clapped his hands. "I know exactly what to do with you, my dear. I have a couple of calls to make, so go meet the girl in back, and she'll wash your hair while you wait."

I did as I was told.

After a nearly orgasmic shampoo and head massage from a teenage apprentice, I came back into the salon to find Jean-Paul and two young women waiting for me. Jean-Paul introduced them as Margaret and Lizbeth and explained that they were here to help with makeup and styling once he'd finished with my hair. They both approached and examined me with the same intrusiveness I'd experienced with Jean-Paul. I was beginning to become used to the scrutiny and managed to refrain from blushing.

"What are these scratches here?" Lizbeth asked, touching my chin lightly.

I jerked away before I could stop myself and then just stood there, looking into her startled eyes. I tried to apologize but found that I'd lost my voice. Tears suddenly pricked my eyes, and the next thing I knew I was crying and sobbing in front of three complete strangers. Soft hands led and directed me to one of the barber chairs, and I sat there, face in my hands, crying for several long minutes. Finally coming back to myself, I looked up at them, mortified beyond belief. They were, however, all looking at me with concern.

"What on earth happened, darling?" Jean-Paul asked quietly, rubbing my back.

Almost before I could think about it, I told them the whole story about Charles. It gushed out of me, my words almost tripping on themselves in their haste to get out of my mouth. As I finished, I almost bit my tongue in surprise. I hadn't meant to tell anyone, ever, let alone three strangers. I looked up at them, wiping my face. "I'm so sorry. I didn't mean to burden you with my drama."

Strangely, Margaret suddenly hugged me. "You don't have to apologize, honey. It was a traumatic experience. You can feel however you want about it. I'm so sorry it happened to you."

"That son of a bitch," Jean-Paul said, darkly. "He'll get what's coming to him—you mark my words."

I laughed and suddenly felt much better, far better than I thought I would about the experience. Jean-Paul took this as his cue to get started, and suddenly all three were on me—plucking, combing, straightening, and prodding. I spent the next two hours with the three of them in close quarters but felt as comfortable as if they were old friends.

Margaret was the makeup and skin artist, and after giving me some new lotions and scrubs, she soon showed me how to do different kinds of techniques on my eyes with the color palette she'd designed for my skin tone. Apparently, I was also going home with a brand-new makeup set custom-designed for me. It all felt a little bit silly, but I did like the way I looked with a couple of the dramatic shading patterns she showed me. It seemed a bit much, however, for the office, and I told her so.

"Oh, of course. These styles would really be for parties and dinners. I know you and Miss Winters will attend a lot of functions together. Let me show you some techniques for day-to-day wear next."

"I really don't wear a lot of makeup most of the time," I said, uncertain. "Just some lip gloss, usually."

"But Miss Winters will want you to," Margaret said, obviously surprised. "Isn't that what you're here for?"

I responded reluctantly. "I guess."

She seemed satisfied, then showed me several techniques for daily wear. I didn't exactly mind the way I looked, but it was certainly strange to see someone in the mirror that I barely recognized. My eyebrows, which I'd always regarded as live-and-let-live, were sculpted and arched, and my dark eyes stood out in startling contrast to my pale skin, the mascara and eyeliner making them pop. I also realized, because all this makeup took so long to put on, I would have to get up quite early every morning before work.

My hair was next, and, as Jean-Paul had finished cutting it, Lizbeth showed me several ways to style it. Some of the styles were far too elaborate to do myself, and I said so. "Well," she said, "for parties you can arrange an appointment with me or Jean-Paul. We always make room in our schedule for Miss Winters and her... friends."

"She's a very important client," Jean-Paul explained, throwing Lizbeth a dark look I couldn't decipher.

Lizbeth showed me some simpler styles for every day, and I practiced a few of them several times before everyone seemed satisfied with my technique. As they cleaned up, sweeping the loose wisps of my hair into a pile and putting their instruments away, I continued to stare at the stranger in the mirror, startled by my transformation. My usual mousy hair, now trimmed, was shiny and lighter, making it appear blonder than ever before. They had cut off the dry ends, and, though my hair was still quite long, had layered it along the edges of my face, highlighting my cheekbones. My eyes, what I'd always considered a muddy brown, stood out in darker contrast underneath my shaped eyebrows and the light makeup on my lashes. All of this had a surreal quality I couldn't get over. The contrast between my expensive makeup and hair and my casual clothes was ridiculous, and I grinned at myself, finally deciding that I actually liked what I saw.

The bells on the door chimed, and in the mirror I saw Amelia enter the salon, removing her sunglasses and stowing them. She blinked a few times to let her eyes adjust, then turned toward me as Jean-Peal spun the chair around. Her face lit up, and I stood, walking nearer so she could see me better.

"You look fantastic," she said earnestly, squeezing my hand. She turned to the others. "And of course, Jean-Paul, you've all done amazing work, as usual."

"Not at all, madam," he said. "When the canvas is as pretty as this one, the work is simple."

I shook his hand, then quickly hugged the two women. "Thank you."

"Don't forget. If you need something special for a party, we're only a phone call away," Lizbeth said.

Amelia and I went outside, and George raised his eyebrows when he saw me, obviously surprised. I laughed. "Am I that different, George?"

He looked sheepish and shook his head. "Still beautiful, just like before," he managed to say.

I laughed and climbed inside, Amelia sliding in just after me. She continued to look at me as we drove, and I blushed under her gaze, not sure whether she liked what she saw. Without saying a word or apologizing for her stare, she finally looked away.

"I hope you don't mind waiting for lunch," she finally said. "Tiffany couldn't reschedule for later, so we're going there now."

"To the mall?" I was confused.

Amelia laughed. "No. Later we're visiting Armani and some other stores, but no malls. Tiffany is my tailor."

"Ah." I was impressed despite everything I'd already seen. I'd never known anyone who used an actual tailor.

Chapter Four

Tiffany's workroom was in part of her house near the Garden District, which we reached after a few minutes' drive. Tiffany was strikingly tall and thin, and I was surprised to hear a French accent, considering her name. I greeted her in French, and she responded warmly and effusively, seeming happy to be able to speak her native tongue. Rather than leaving, Amelia sat down on one of the round chairs in the corner, and I realized she intended to stay. I felt my color rise after Tiffany asked me to strip down to my underwear, but Amelia was typing on her phone, completely wrapped up in whatever she was working on.

I did what I was told and stood on the little platform in the center of the room, clad only in my bra and panties as Tiffany walked around me, peering closely at my body. Once again, I felt like a piece of meat being graded, but I was beginning to get used to it. I glanced over to the corner again, but Amelia was still wrapped up in her work, not looking at me once. I let my shoulders relax a little and looked straight ahead.

Tiffany began measuring me, writing everything down in a little Moleskin notebook she kept in her pocket. At one point, she motioned for me to get down and then measured my head, which I didn't understand until she explained: it was for hats. I stayed, in the main, quiet throughout the experience, hoping this would be over as soon as possible. Finally, Tiffany told me I could put my clothes on again, which I did, quickly. Amelia never looked up while I was nearly naked, as far as I could tell, which was a relief. I certainly didn't need for her to know what I looked like in my underwear. After all, she was my boss.

"All set?" Amelia got to her feet and stretched.

"Yes, madam," Tiffany told her.

"Do you mind letting me know her European size, Tiffany? I want to call ahead to a couple of places so they can get some trials out for us."

Tiffany looked a little disgusted at the thought of off-the-rack clothing, but she glanced down at her notebook, did a quick calculation, and said, "She's a 34."

I was surprised. The last time I'd bought clothes in Paris, I'd been more like a 36 or 38. This explained why all the clothes I owned seemed to hang off me lately. I guess I'd lost more weight this summer than I thought.

Amelia looked momentarily upset for some reason, but the expression faded almost before I saw it. "That's what I thought." She looked me up and down. "Much too thin, really. Are you ready?"

"What do you mean? Don't I need to, I don't know, see some clothes or something?" I looked back and forth between Amelia and Tiffany.

They both laughed. "Tiffany will simply make your clothes, Chloé. We'll pick them up when she's done."

"Don't I get any say in the matter?"

"No. You don't." She shook her head but looked a little apologetic. "Now let's go get something to eat. I don't know about you, but I'm starving."

The rest of the afternoon passed in a blur. After a simple lunch of salads and sandwiches, we toured all the exclusive shops in town, Amelia choosing nearly everything and asking for very little input from me. I could, however, occasionally veto things, which I did repeatedly in the shoe stores. I refused to wear some of the ridiculously tall high heels she chose, mainly on principle. She had to compromise and allowed me to get several pairs of lower heels and one pair of flats, which I adored. I'd stopped counting dollars rather quickly, blown away by the price tags. We were likely spending more today than my new annual salary. To assuage my concern, I decided early on if Miss Amelia Winters insisted that I wear this stuff, she could very well pay for it herself. After all, she obviously didn't mind spending it, and all I had do to was agree to go along with the spree.

Though most of the clothes we bought for work were off-the-rack, they were all much nicer than anything I'd ever owned. Amelia explained that these would have to do until Tiffany finished some of my tailored clothes, but I couldn't imagine having anything nicer. For colder weather, she chose thick tweeds, usually in matching jacket and skirts, and nice linens, thick cotton, and silks for the rest of the year. Everything was black, white, blue, gray, or dark, muted gem tones, which Amelia said flattered me, and I agreed. Our second-to-last stop was at Armani, where she chose two "starter" rental gowns for me: one for tomorrow and one for an upcoming event next Friday.

"Where are we going tomorrow?" I asked as we got back in the car. At this point, I was working hard to stifle yawns.

"We have reservations for dinner at seven thirty at Broussard's. We'll have a private area of the dining room where I can coach you on table settings and meal behavior before the party next Friday."

"So why do I need a gown if it's just the two of us?"

Amelia raised her eyebrows and shook her head but didn't answer beyond that.

Our last shop for the day surprised me, and Amelia laughed when she saw my expression. "You've never been to *C'est Magnifique?*" she asked, smirking. My face must have been as red as it felt, because she laughed again. "You can't wear what you have on now underneath all these lovely new clothes," she explained, patting my hand.

Oh, I thought. She was looking when we were at Tiffany's.

"Amelia—I mean, Miss Winters," I said, stuttering a little in embarrassment. "I'm not so sure I'm comfortable buying lingerie with you."

She laughed again. "What's to be uncomfortable about? We all wear it, right? It's just like shopping for anything else. Come on."

She climbed out of the car before I could stop her. Swallowing my mortification, I slid over and climbed out after her.

C'est Magnifique is a high-end, French lingerie store. It was, like all of the places we'd gone today, the kind of place where you didn't want to look at price tags. It was better just to buy things and leave when they cost this much money. I felt incredibly out of place the second we walked in, and just about everyone in there seemed to look over at us when we came through the door. An assistant dropped everything she was doing and flew across the room, apparently desperate to get our commission.

"Miss Winters," she said as she reached us, slightly out of breath. "So lovely to see you again. How are you?"

"I'm well, thank you. This is Doctor Clothilde Deveraux."

"Doctor Deveraux." The woman bowed slightly in my direction, then turned to Amelia. "This is your new...assistant?"

Amelia nodded. "Brand-new, yes. We're getting her all set up today."

"Well, you've come to the right place," the woman said. "My name is Jennifer, Doctor Deveraux, and I'll be assisting you today. Could either of you tell me the kind of clothes you'll be wearing with our lingerie?"

I shivered slightly with something like nerves as Amelia explained what I needed. As they talked, I looked around the shop as covertly as possible, curious about the kind of women that would shop here. Almost all of them were much older than me, and all of them looked wealthy. Only one man was in here, sitting hunched up in the back in one of the chairs by the dressing rooms, clearly trying to appear as small as possible. He had several bags at his feet, and I imagined his wife or girlfriend had put him through the courses today already.

Jennifer took us back to my changing room, but I froze when Amelia entered the little room and sat down on the stool in the corner. I stood fidgeting in the doorway until she looked up at me.

"What's the matter?"

"I can't do this with you in here," I said, blushing even darker.

"Oh!" She stood up. "I'm sorry. I didn't mean to make you uncomfortable. Please, try everything on in private. I didn't think." She inched around me, her arm brushing mine and making me jump. Just before I closed the door after her, she turned and said, "If you find anything you'd be willing to show me, I'd be happy to give you my opinion." She sat down next to the all-suffering husband, taking out her smart phone.

I closed the door and stood there for a while, breathing deeply to steady myself. What the hell was *that*? I looked into the mirror at my large, frightened eyes and almost laughed at myself. After all, what did it matter? She really did seem surprised at my reaction, and she probably just hadn't thought about how strange it would be for me to change my underwear in front of my boss. I reminded myself that she had been professional and courteous all day, and at no point had I felt like she was interested in me in any other way. I shook the tension out of my shoulders and then took off my clothes.

Everything was lovely, and when I found myself debating between a few of the bras, I was tempted to ask for Amelia's opinion. If Meghan was here I would ask her, I thought, so how is this different? I knew it was different on some unexamined, fundamental level but decided I would make the effort since Amelia had offered to help.

I pulled on one of the silk slips I'd chosen and called out, "Miss Winters?"

"Yes?" she said from outside.

"Would you mind giving me your opinion on something?"

"Of course not," she said, right outside the dressing room.

I opened the door for her and she came in. After I'd closed it behind her, she stood a few feet from me, looking me up and down. Then she made a twirling motion with her fingers and I turned around for her, slowly. My skin warmed under her gaze and I swallowed, trying to dispel my nervousness.

"It fits wonderfully," she finally said.

"That's what I thought. I just wasn't sure which ones to get. There are so many bras here, and I don't know what kinds I need."

She looked at me long and hard, staring at my chest, and I colored again, realizing I'd made a big mistake asking her to come in here. Finally she raised her head. "That style is perfect for most occasions, but you'll need different colors. You'll also need at least two or three strapless in different colors for the gowns."

"Thanks," I said quietly, unable to meet her eyes.

"How are the panties?" she asked.

I felt for a moment as if my face might catch on fire but managed to nod. "They fit like a glove."

"I wear the same kind," she explained, pulling down her skirt a little to show me the top of hers. They were indeed the same. "They're the best." Seeing my expression, she smiled and squeezed my bare arm. "I'll leave you to it, then. Don't forget to try on some of the sleepwear."

I wasn't sure she or anyone else would see me in sleepwear for any reason at work, but I didn't argue. I opened and closed the door for her and stood there gazing in the mirror for a long time. What the hell are you doing? I asked myself.

After trying on one of the silk nightgowns, I decided I'd tried on enough clothes for the day and pulled on my jeans and T-shirt. I opened the door and showed Jennifer the pile I wanted before following Amelia over to the cash register.

Just as Jennifer finished ringing up and bagging our purchases, two women began to approach us, and I caught my breath at the sight of the stunning younger one. Her auburn hair fell in soft waves around her shoulders, framing a face out of classic films. Her body was sculpted, but curvy, with the kind of hourglass figure little girls dream of having someday. She was with an older, elegant woman of the ice-queen type, a cool, desperately thin blonde. Amelia froze as they approached.

"Dear Amelia," the older one said when they made eye contact. She air-kissed Amelia on both cheeks. "It's really been too long."

"Vivienne," Amelia managed to say, though she looked shaken.

"This is my new assistant, Beatrice," the older woman said, indicating the bombshell next to her.

"Charmed, I'm sure," the younger woman said, holding out a limp hand. I almost had to suppress a smile. The bombshell had a flaw: her voice was grating and nasal.

"And this is?" the woman asked, turning her sharp gaze at me. My face felt hot as she looked me up and down.

"Doctor Deveraux." Amelia's voice sounded pinched and tight with nerves.

Something about the way Amelia responded to this woman made me want to defend her. "Charmed, I'm sure," I said sarcastically, holding out my own limp hand.

The older woman touched my fingers with her icy hand and gave me what might pass as a smile, her eyes narrow and knowing. She then turned back to Amelia. "A new assistant so soon, dear? You're going through them like water lately. Soon there won't be any assistants left in the city."

"If you'll excuse us," Amelia said, flushing darkly. She turned and grabbed my arm, steering me around them as we made our way out the door.

Amelia was silent on the ride home, and as I contemplated what had just happened, my curiosity began to eat at me. I knew better than to ask about the woman in the store, but I still wondered what it all meant. What had that woman meant to imply by "assistant"? Could Aunt Kate and Meghan be right? Did Amelia usually sleep with her assistants? I glanced over at her again, thinking about her behavior today. While a few moments in the lingerie store had certainly *seemed* a little inappropriate, my own response had made it that way. If anything, Amelia had been more comfortable with my body than I was, treating the whole thing with her efficient, business-like persona. And anyway, I thought, it's not like she actually touched me. I blushed at the memory of her eyes on my breasts and decided to stop thinking about it.

When we finally pulled up in front of my house, I was wilting from exhaustion. I bid Amelia good night and poured myself out of the car, dragging my sad, tired body inside. Even if I'd had a full night's sleep, I would have been beat. My aunt was surprised when she saw me, and I realized after a moment that it was because of the makeup and hair. George came in and out of our front room several times, dropping off piles of boxes and bags before tipping his hat and excusing himself.

"What on *earth*?" Aunt Kate said, once she'd closed the door after him. She was staring around the room at all of the packages in disbelief.

"I don't know, Aunt Kate," I said, rubbing my tired eyes. "I don't get it either."

Chapter Five

I went to bed very early and got up very late. Between the incident with Charles and the whirlwind shopping trip, I felt worn out and depleted. As I rolled out of bed, I looked around the room at all the bags and boxes, stunned and a little pleased once again by Miss Winters's generosity. Is it generosity? I wondered, but shook the thought off. Regardless of her motives, which I very much doubted were as sinister as Aunt Kate and Meghan had predicted, I had enjoyed myself yesterday, and I'd enjoyed spending time with my new boss. That was all. If a natural opportunity presented itself to ask her about her old assistants, I would, but I wouldn't press her for an answer.

I took an extremely long shower, washing off two days' worth of grime and sweat, then dressed in my oldest pair of overalls and a T-shirt. I always paint in junky clothes, as I tend to forget what I'm doing when I paint and rest my paintbrushes on myself while I work. My studio was located in the highest part of the house, in what is called the camel's hump in a shotgun house like ours. It was sweltering up there, but it soon cooled down after I cranked the little window air-conditioning unit up as high as it would go.

I'd been painting for a long time when I heard a knock on the door at the bottom of the attic stairs. "Yes?" I called, snapping back into reality.

"It's me!" Meghan shouted from below. "Can I come up?"

I turned to my painting and pulled the drop cloth over it. "Sure. Enter at will."

She appeared a few seconds later, looking around the room curiously. Several of my older pieces were hanging on the walls, much to my embarrassment. I'd wanted to paint over them several years ago, but my aunt insisted on keeping them there "for posterity," as she called it. The paintings reminded me how far I'd progressed, but I didn't like seeing my own earlier mistakes. I did have, however, one newer piece I'd completed in Paris last year, a landscape. Meghan made a beeline directly to it.

"Wow! This is incredible!" she said.

"Don't exaggerate." I was proud of it.

She turned toward me, brow furrowed. "What are you talking about? This is really amazing. I've never seen anything like it."

"You'll forgive me if I don't believe you." I laughed. "After all, you told me *that* was the best thing you'd ever seen." I pointed at one of my oldest paintings.

Meghan rolled her eyes. "Forgive my sixteen-year-old tastes. I hadn't seen much of the world yet. And anyway, no matter what you think now, it's still good. Most people can only paint stick figures. You have a gift, you know. I wish you could see that."

I didn't respond and instead walked over and hugged her. "How are you?" I asked. "You're positively glowing today."

"I have every reason to be. Zach asked me to move in with him, and I said yes!" I hugged her again and we jumped up and down a few times, squealing.

"Wow! That's fantastic news! What made you decide to make the big leap?"

"We spend almost every night together anyway. After three months, I'm not sick of him and he's not sick of me. It seems like the right time to do it."

"So romantic." I rolled my eyes.

She pushed my shoulder playfully. "You know what I mean. The spark hasn't, you know, fizzled. I think he might be the real thing."

"I'm so happy for you, Meghan. I really am. We should celebrate."

"You're damn right!"

We found Aunt Kate on the phone downstairs, her face alight with mischief and happiness. It was obvious she was talking to Jim, her new boyfriend. Meghan winked at me knowingly, and we went back to the kitchen for some wine. I was surprised to see that it was already late afternoon. I'd gotten up at eleven, and somehow almost six hours had passed. Though I often lost myself in painting, it was rare that a whole day passed without my notice. I was, I realized, completely famished. I hadn't eaten since lunch yesterday.

I found a nice Prosecco in the fridge and popped the cork, pouring both of us a tall glassful. Aunt Kate joined us a few moments after this, and I got out another glass.

"Oooo, what are we celebrating?" she asked.

"I'm finally taking myself off the market." Meghan laughed.

"You're getting married?" Aunt Kate asked, her eyes lighting up even further.

Meghan laughed loudly. "No. We're just moving in together for now." She paused and said dramatically, "But who knows what time will bring?" Aunt Kate hugged her happily and Meghan filled her in on the details as I poured her a glass.

"To the future!" Aunt Kate said, holding her wine.

"To the future!" we responded, toasting and drinking.

"Soooo," Meghan said after a moment, winking at me. "When are we going to meet your new beau, Aunt Kate?"

"He's been in Florida this week, but he'll be back tomorrow. I was going to see if you could join us some night this week for dinner. You could bring your Zach with you."

"Well, I'll ask *my* Zach when he's free and get back to you," Meghan said. "Maybe Chloé will bring her Charles."

My face fell, and I turned away quickly. "That's not going to happen." I opened the fridge.

"Oh, no!" Meghan said. "Why not?"

"I'm just not interested in him." I shifted some things around on the shelves. My stomach turned fitfully, and I was suddenly no longer hungry. I stood there for a long time, trying to calm myself before turning back to them and closing the door. Both were looking at me critically.

"You have *got* to be kidding me," Meghan finally said. "Charles is friggin' man-candy. How could you pass him up?"

I blushed and looked away. I wasn't about to spoil the happy mood with any details. "Let's talk about it some other time, okay?" I asked, looking at Meghan, hard.

Meghan acted like she wanted to argue, but luckily, she seemed to sense something and, after glancing at Aunt Kate, she agreed. "Okay." She looked troubled for a moment longer and then appeared to remember something. "Oh, hey, that's right. How did the shopping go with Miss Winters yesterday?"

"It was fine," I answered, a little too quickly.

Meghan laughed. "What the hell does that mean?"

"Just that. It was fine. We went to a bunch of stores. We bought a lot of things. I got my hair cut."

"I can see that," Meghan said, sharing an incredulous look with my aunt. "What else?"

"What do you mean?" I asked, heat rising to my cheeks.

"You're being awfully cagey about it, girly," Aunt Kate said. "You were acting funny last night, too." She turned to Meghan. "You should see all the stuff she got. She could open her own boutique."

Both of them were staring at me, eyes wide with curiosity, and I finally laughed, breaking the tension. "I did get a lot of really nice things. In fact, I'm wearing an evening gown tonight. It's Armani but just a rental."

"Oooooo!" Meghan said. "Armani. Wow. So fancy."

"Fuck you," I said playfully, throwing the paper towels at her.

"I want to see you in it," Meghan said. "In fact, I want a damn fashion show, if you don't mind."

"Oh, gracious, so do I," Aunt Kate added, eyes glowing, "though it'd probably take all night to show us everything."

Embarrassed but pleased with their request, I finally agreed. Both of them clapped excitedly. "I'll show you a couple of my new work outfits, okay? Then I have to start getting ready for dinner."

"Where are you going?" Meghan asked.

I swallowed. "Broussard's," I finally admitted. Not only is Broussard's extremely expensive, but it is also known as a romantic restaurant for couples.

"Just the two of you?" Aunt Kate asked, sharing a look with Meghan.

"Yes," I said, exasperated. "Just the two of us. We have to talk about business."

They both looked uncertain, but I didn't want to argue with them and excused myself to my room.

I ended up trying on several outfits for them, finding that I enjoyed the attention more than I thought I would. Aunt Kate made popcorn, and they treated the experience like they were at a show, cheering loudly with each outfit. I also enjoyed the clothes even more now that I realized they were actually mine. As I changed from outfit to outfit, I decided to ignore my nagging thoughts about Amelia yesterday. I'm just nervous about the new job, I told myself. Nothing else.

Finally, it was time to get ready for dinner, and Meghan insisted on staying to watch me get ready. She sat on my bed, holding one of my old stuffed animals as I did my hair. I decided on one of the simple twists Lizbeth had shown me yesterday and was surprised to see that it was looking as I expected it to and staying in place.

"You're acting really strange about all of this," Meghan finally said.

I sighed. I'd known this conversation was coming for hours now. "No, I'm not."

"I don't get it. She buys you all this stuff and you don't have a problem with that? It doesn't strike you as strange?"

"Of course it does," I snapped. "But I don't know what I'm supposed to do about feeling *strange* about it. She's my boss. She insisted."

"Okaaay," Meghan said, shrugging, "if that's what you need to do to feel okay about it."

"Yes. It is," I said, hoping that was the end of it.

"But what happens if she—"

"Listen. I don't want to talk about her. She's nice, and yes, she bought me a shitload of clothes and I don't understand why. Rich people are weird. Can we just drop it?"

Meghan lifted her eyebrows and lowered them. "Sorry," she said quietly.

I sighed. "And I'm sorry I snapped at you. There are no ulterior motives here. She has a certain style, and she insists I share it since we'll be in public together. That's all."

"Okay. If you say so."

"I do say so. Now drop it."

We sat there in silence for a while as I applied my makeup, my hands shaking slightly with anger. I managed to cool down by the time I finished, and when I turned around, Meghan no longer looked upset.

"You look amazing," she said. "Where did you learn how to do that? I've never seen you wear makeup like that before."

"Just here and there," I said, not wanting to start another argument. "What time is it?"

"About seven fifteen," she said, glancing at her phone.

"Jeez, I'm cutting it close." I stood up. "Help me pick a pair of shoes, would you?"

"What are the choices?" Meghan said, getting up too.

"Those over there." I pointed to a pile of shoeboxes.

I flushed as Meghan examined all the shoes, gasping and looking incredulous with each revealed pair. "Are you fucking kidding me?" she asked.

"Come on, Meghan. I don't want to get into this with you again. Which ones should I wear?"

"These would look best, I guess," she said, handing me a box. "I can't believe you own heels, for God's sake."

"I know, too weird," I admitted. "Who would have thought?" I slipped on the shoes and stood there for a moment, letting Meghan take in the full effect. "How do I look?"

"Like the world's most expensive prostitute," she said. I picked up a pillow and threw it at her and we both laughed, my anger finally melting away. The truth was that it *was* weird, and I did feel very strange about all of this. I just wasn't sure what to do about it except go along with everything for now.

By the time we finally made our way into the living room, the Rolls was waiting for me outside. Meghan, Aunt Kate, and I looked out at it through the curtain and watched as George opened Amelia's door for her. I heard myself gasp when she stepped out. She looked absolutely gorgeous.

"Wow," Meghan said, "what a knockout." She looked at me curiously, as if trying to gauge my reaction.

Aunt Kate touched my arm and I turned to her, one eyebrow raised. "Please be careful," she told me.

"I don't know what you mean," I said, face flushing again.

"I think you know *exactly* what I mean," she said quietly.

Chapter Six

Amelia smiled warmly when I opened the door, and I saw George's eyebrows rise in surprise again. I winked at him and held out my hand to Amelia after I carefully walked down the stairs. While I'd worn heels once or twice in the past, I was by no means an expert and fairly certain I'd trip at least once tonight.

"You look incredible," she finally said, squeezing my hand in both of hers.

"Do I meet with your approval?" I tried to keep my tone light, as I wanted to let her know I was kidding, but the question ended up sounding earnest.

"Completely. I know it sounds terrible to say this, but when I saw your clothes during our interview the other day, I was afraid it would never work out."

"My appearance means that much to you?" I asked, sliding into the car.

Amelia climbed in after me and then nodded, somewhat sheepishly. "I'm afraid it does." Seeing my face, she looked embarrassed and began to explain. "In sales you're doing more than selling a product. You're also selling an image. At first contact, this image is actually more important than whatever you sell, because it creates a fantasy for the buyer: if I buy this thing they're selling, I can be like them." She paused, obviously trying to read my expression. "I've worked very hard to cultivate the Winters Corporation image, and my clients know what to expect."

She paused again. "Anyway, I'm sure you're tired of talking about clothes at this point, and that's not what tonight's about."

"What is it about?" I tried to keep the mounting impatience out of my voice. "You said something about table manners?"

"Yes. Fine dining requires that you follow a lot of rules. As we're attending a dinner on Friday together, I thought we should practice first tonight."

I sniffed and looked out the window, more than a little peeved. Who does she think she is? I asked myself. More to the point, who does she think I am? Does she think I've never eaten out before?

"I can tell you're becoming annoyed with me, Doctor," Amelia said, squeezing my hand again. "I simply want to see how you approach the table. Perhaps we don't even need the practice."

I turned to her and tried to make my expression calmer to reassure her. "I'm sorry—I'm being incredibly rude. You're taking me to one of the nicest restaurants in town, and I'm pouting like a child."

"An incredibly beautiful child." After this compliment she stared at me, almost boldly, as if waiting for a response.

My heart skipped a beat, and I tried to smile. "Thank you for saying that," I finally said, not meeting her eyes. My face was hot.

"It's completely true. You'll have clients eating out of your hand in no time," she almost whispered.

"That explains why you're so successful." I looked up at her, and her cheeks colored slightly.

We rode the rest of the way in silence, looking out our separate windows. My heart was racing, and I wasn't sure if was nerves or something else. What the hell has gotten into you? I asked myself. Were you actually flirting with her? I glanced over at her again and my stomach dropped a little. Flirting with her had never crossed my mind until it happened. Or at least that's what you want to tell yourself, I thought. The truth is, you were waiting all day yesterday for her to make a move. I realized that was entirely true, but I also wasn't sure what it meant. Except perhaps in jest a few times with friends, I'd never even considered flirting with a woman before. And what happens if she takes you up on it? I asked myself. The thought was too much to deal with, and I was happy when George finally pulled over next to the restaurant.

Broussard's is a New Orleans institution. Located in a seemingly incongruous place a block off the party capital of Bourbon Street, its elegance and fine food are world-renowned. When we entered, the dim lights cast a dreamy ambiance over everything, suggesting candlelight kisses and intimate privacy. The host knew Amelia, and without being asked he escorted us to a remote part of the dining room, far away from the rest of the tables. My chair was pulled out for me, and I sat down, the excitement of actually being here finally catching up to me. That's the thing about a lot of cities—when you live there, you often don't get to go to the very places that make them special. It was obvious from the start, however, that Amelia was a regular.

Almost before I'd had time to get settled, a sharply dressed young man appeared next to us, almost as if out of thin air. "Madam and mademoiselle," he said, bowing slightly.

"A bottle of Perrier-Jouët's 2004 Belle Epoque Rosé, please," Amelia told him. He nodded and dashed away, and she turned back to me. "It seems as if you've never been here," she observed.

"No, I haven't. My aunt would never have taken me here as a child, and I didn't exactly date the kind of guys who could afford this when I was in college."

"What kind of guys *did* you date?" she asked.

I swallowed a sip of my water and almost choked on it, more than a little uncomfortable with the question. Still, she'd suggested that we should become friendly, and friends shared things like this. Trying to sound breezy, I said, "Oh, you know, the scholarship kids like me. There was a distinct separation at Loyola between those that came from money and those that didn't." I took another sip of my water to avoid making eye contact. Still not looking directly at her, I steeled myself and asked, "What about you? Did you date a lot in college?"

"Not a lot. I may have had the opposite problem, Doctor, and still do. My name always precedes me, and it usually intimidates people." I could feel her eyes on me but couldn't meet them. "Do I intimidate you?" she asked quietly.

I looked up at her hastily and felt myself blush. "Of course!" I said before I could stop myself.

She laughed at my candor, and after a moment I joined her. The laughter helped me begin to relax with her, but I was grateful for an interruption when the waiter reappeared with the wine. Amelia went through the process of approving the bottle with a small sip poured in her glass. "It's delicious," she said, and the waiter filled our glasses before putting the rest of the bottle in a small bucket of ice.

She held her glass aloft and I did the same. "To the future," she said.

I almost laughed, hearing the echo of an earlier toast, but managed to respond, "To the future." The wine was tart and light, the bubbles kissing my palate. I closed my eyes, rolling the taste of it on my tongue and savoring it. When I opened them, Amelia was staring at me, her eyes dark with something I couldn't quite recognize.

"Do you like it?" she asked softly, swallowing.

"I love it."

"It's one of my favorites," she said, visibly relieved. "I actually asked the sommelier to carry it here when I discovered it in Paris a few years back."

I couldn't keep the surprise from my face. A few years ago, judging by her face, she would have been too young to drink. She raised her eyebrows. "You look surprised. You've never special-ordered a wine before?"

"No, I haven't, but it's not that," I said, embarrassed. "It's just, well, to put it simply, you barely look old enough to drink now."

She laughed loudly, throwing her head back in her amusement. I glanced around the room and saw several other tables look over at us curiously, but it was clear that she didn't care who looked at her.

"Just how old do you think I am, Doctor?"

"Twenty-two, twenty-three?" I suggested. In truth, she could pass for younger.

She laughed loudly again and for a long time, finally clutching her stomach and doubling over. I tried to smile at the other tables, embarrassed but strangely pleased by her reaction. Her laughter seemed, from the short time I'd known her, uncharacteristic.

She finally managed to calm down and wiped her eyes. "You kill me, Doctor," she said. "If I didn't know better, I would think you were flattering me on purpose."

"Why would I do that?"

"I don't know. Why would you?"

My stomach dropped again and I blushed under her shining gaze. Luckily, before I could say or do anything stupid, the waiter appeared again. Neither of us had a menu, but of course Amelia knew it by heart.

"We'll begin with two servings of the oysters and foie gras, followed by the strawberry salad. For our entrees, we'll both have the ostrich."

"Excellent choices, madam," he said, bowing again before walking away.

"I hope you don't mind the liberty, Doctor," she said. "You'll love the ostrich."

"I've never had it."

We spent the rest of the dinner enjoying some of the best food I'd ever eaten. She coached me briefly on the various different plates and silverware, but the "training" part of dinner was casual and unobtrusive, and really, I didn't mind it nearly as much as I thought I would. In fact, considering I would be eating in front of a large group soon, I began to feel grateful that she'd thought of practicing.

While I'd dined widely in Paris, my heart always stayed with the Southern flavors of my upbringing, and Broussard's was a nice mixture of two cultures, French and Creole. My family is French Creole, which meant that, though I'd never been to Broussard's, I could expect the food to resemble the foods Aunt Kate cooked at home. New Orleans always fashions itself as the daughter of France, and the restaurant also seemed to understand that concept. The dishes themselves were ostensibly French, but the seasonings came from the holy trinity of Creole cooking—onion, celery, and bell pepper. By the time they took away our last plates, I was pleasantly satiated and my head was spinning a little from the bottle of wine.

I'd noticed over the course of the dinner that she'd been drinking a glass of wine for every two of mine, but I didn't say anything as I enjoyed it so much. Now I started to think I should have watched myself a little more closely with the booze, as I began to feel a little silly and loud.

"Do you want dessert?" she asked.

"I don't think I could eat another bite," I said. "It was all so delicious. Thank you for bringing me here."

"It's my pleasure." She squeezed the top of my hand and left hers there for a long, extra moment. My face grew hot, but I didn't draw my own away. After a moment she released it.

"I'm going to order dessert anyway," she said. "You haven't lived until you've tried their crème brûlée."

"Really, I couldn't." I laughed. "I'd burst wide open."

"I like watching you eat," she said, smiling. "You enjoy it so much."

I didn't respond except to blush and look away from her. With the wine buzzing around in my head, I found it hard to react properly, and, even sober, I couldn't imagine a response that would fit. She called the waiter over and ordered the dessert, and we sipped on espresso as we waited.

"I'm going to be up all night now," I said, indicating the drink. "I really can't have caffeine at night anymore."

"So what will you do with yourself?" She leaned forward, her eyes soft, the lids slightly lowered. Her voice had a touch of huskiness. She seemed to be fishing for a specific answer, but all I could do was laugh.

"I'll probably paint," I said. "That's always what I do when I can't sleep."

"You paint?" She seemed surprised.

"A little," I said, cursing myself. Very few people knew about my pastime, and I hadn't been prepared to talk to her about that part of myself. I considered it a private activity.

"I'd love to see your work sometime," she said.

"It's terrible, really. That's why I moved on to art history in my masters. I knew I'd never make it as an artist."

"Somehow I doubt that," she said.

"What do you mean?"

"You're so modest that naturally I think you're probably very good."

I was once again relieved to see our waiter. He dropped off the dessert with two spoons and disappeared once again.

"Please try it," Amelia said, picking up her utensil.

I nodded, picked up mine, and cracked the top, digging out as much of each layer as I could. It was, of course, heavenly, and I barely suppressed a groan of pleasure. I opened my eyes to find Amelia staring at me again, and I smiled back at her, embarrassed.

"It's incredible," I said.

"I could tell." Her voice was quiet and her face serious.

I was uncomfortable, once again unsure how to respond. Despite my wine-muddled head, I could see that she was flirting with me.

Desperate to change the topic, I blurted out, "What time do you want me there tomorrow for work?"

She frowned slightly but said, "I'll have George pick you up at eight thirty. Is that all right?"

"You don't have to do that. I can get a ride from someone."

"I'll have a car for you to use soon, but until then, I insist."

The rest of the meal passed more comfortably. By the time she was dropping me off at my place, I'd almost convinced myself that I'd imagined anything beyond friendliness.

Almost.

CHAPTER SEVEN

*W*hen I brought in a pile of paperwork for Amelia, she stood next to her desk, her phone clamped against her shoulder. *She wore her little reading glasses and an uncharacteristically modern outfit with a loose silk blouse and pencil skirt. Her high heels were red, matching her garish lipstick. Overall, I was surprised by what I was seeing. She didn't look like the image she'd presented in the time I knew her. She caught sight of me and motioned me forward, still jabbering into the phone. I set the paperwork on her desk and she signed it as she talked.*

"No, I don't know," she barked into the phone, making me jump. "I tell you, I have no idea when that will go through." She listened for a while, flipping through the paperwork I'd brought and signing next to each of the little plastic arrows I'd put in the pile for her. "Goddamn it, Bill, if you ask me again, I'm going to fly up there and kick your ass!"

I had to turn away to keep from laughing, as the reality of her swearing was almost too funny to take. She was normally so prim and proper.

"Fine, fine. I'll call you later," she snapped, slamming down the phone.

She turned to me. "What is this?" she said, holding up a piece of paper from the pile. I tried to read it but found it indecipherable.

"I don't know," I said, confused.

"Why would you ask me to sign something if you don't know what it is? Don't you know how important I am?"

My stomach clenched with dread and I took a step back. "I'm so sorry, Amelia—"

"It's Miss Winters to you, bitch," she snarled.

Suddenly she grabbed my arm, pulling me roughly into her embrace. Her lips were on mine in a second, her tongue pushing hard into my mouth. I fought her briefly and then relaxed, kissing her back. Her hands rose to my hair, releasing it from the twist, and I felt my hair tumble down onto my shoulders. She pulled away from me, still looking angry.

"I like your hair down. I've told you that before," she whispered.

"You have?" I asked, confused and befuddled by the kiss.

"You know I have," she said, her lip curling in anger. She kissed me again, harder, pulling my hair painfully. I hissed in pain and felt her lips curl wickedly against mine.

"You want me to hurt you, don't you?" she whispered, her lips an inch from mine.

"Y-yes," I murmured, barely able to speak. My legs were trembling and my knees felt weak, and suddenly she was lifting me up onto her desk. My heels dropped off my feet, hitting the ground louder than they should. She quickly pushed my legs apart and slid her hands up my inner thighs. She encountered my underwear there and frowned at me.

"I told you never to wear these to work."

"But you bought them for me!" I was honestly confused.

Her face a wild mask of rage, she ripped the underwear off me. I yelped in pain.

"Quiet," she snarled. "Do you want Vanessa to hear you?"

"Who's Vanessa?"

She laughed. "As if you didn't know," she said, kneeling in front of me.

In a moment, I felt her teeth on my inner thigh, just above my skirt line. She bit me there on my leg, hard, and I screamed. She kissed the place she'd bitten and started licking and kissing her way slowly upward, her mouth setting my entire body on fire. I lay back, closing my eyes, waiting for her mouth to reach where I desperately wanted it to be.

"What's the racket in there?" someone said from outside the office, followed by knocking.

My eyes snapped open, and I found myself in my room at Aunt Kate's. After another knock on my door, Aunt Kate came into the room, looking around wildly. I flushed in deep embarrassment, pulling the covers up to my chin.

"Are you okay, Chloé?" she asked me, eyes concerned. "I heard a scream."

"It was just a dream, Aunt Kate. I'm sorry."

"Must have been a nightmare to make you scream like that," she said gently.

"Something like that." I still felt embarrassed. "I'll be down in a little while."

"Okay," she said and closed the door.

My sheets were drenched in sweat, and my body was flushed and hot with desire. I lay back on the bed, my mind a whirl of confusion. I'd never had a sex dream that detailed, let alone about someone I actually knew. What does it mean? I wondered. It was a long while before I was able to calm myself enough to get out of bed, and that was after I debated whether to take care of myself to calm down. I decided not. It was all too confusing.

❖

By the time I got to work, I thought I'd managed to suppress most of my embarrassment and confusion about the dream, but when I saw Amelia for the first time, I tensed with shame. She doesn't know what you dreamt about her, so calm the hell down, I told myself. That was an easy enough command, but it was hard to put into practice. I was jumpy and strange with her all morning, and I caught her looking at me a few times, seemingly puzzled by my behavior.

The work week passed quickly. I was busy every day from the moment I showed up until I left in the evening, which could be anytime between five and seven. George was still driving me both ways, to and from work, as there had been a delay on the arrival of the company car. My current project was to research the attendees at the dinner and reception we were attending tomorrow night and scope out potential new buyers. For this party, Amelia was covering possible sales to past clients.

In addition to the larger project, I was involved in plenty of day-to-day activities, like supervising the unloading of new shipments, monitoring the art restoration of two older paintings, and coordinating meetings with clients through Amelia's secretary, Janet. It was only Thursday, but I was already getting the hang of things, surprised to find that I loved every minute of my new job.

At four thirty, I knocked on Amelia's door, heart in my throat. I'd managed to avoid her for the most of the day, but I needed to ask her for a favor.

"Come in," she called. I opened the door and let myself in. She wore the reading glasses she'd worn in the dream, but her outfit was typical for her, a retro 1940s-style suit-dress. She looked up at me, clearly happy to be interrupted. "What can I do for you, Doctor?"

"I was wondering if I could leave a little early today," I asked. "My aunt is having a dinner party tonight, and I want to have time to get ready before it begins."

She seemed surprised. "Of course! You can leave whenever you need to, Doctor, early or not. I know we've been busy this week, but your usual hours shouldn't keep you here past five most days."

"Thanks." I turned to leave, memories of the dream making it far too awkward to be alone with her in her office.

"By the way," she said, "you've been doing great work this week. I really appreciate it. What do you think of it so far?"

I turned back, trying to look natural. "I love it."

She laughed. "You sound surprised."

I shrugged, somewhat embarrassed. "I guess I am. I didn't really know if I would be any good at it, but I think I might be. With time, I mean."

"You're already good at it, Doctor."

I excused myself, my heart racing in a now-familiar way. Just because you like her compliments doesn't mean you like her, I told myself. Dream or no dream.

❖

I arrived back at Aunt Kate's just before dinner. Her boyfriend Jim was due a little later. I'd met him briefly a couple of times this week, but this dinner was designed to help all of us get to know each other better.

Nothing like being the fifth wheel, I thought, unlocking the door. Zach and Meghan were already sitting in the living room, and Zach whistled when he saw me. He clutched his heart dramatically as if shot. "Wow! You look like a movie star, lady."

"You really do," Meghan said. Her face was grim, however, and I sensed that our conversation from Sunday was likely start right back where it had left off. This was part of the reason I'd avoided her all week.

"Thanks," I said, blushing. "I have to go change. I'll be right back down."

"I'll come with you," Meghan said, getting to her feet.

I sighed, accepting the inevitable. "Fine. You okay, Zach? Need a drink or anything?"

He shook his head. "I'm fine. Your aunt is making mint juleps."

Up in my room, Meghan watched me remove my fine clothes and replace them with my usual jeans and T-shirt. My face was still made up and my hair was still styled, but I'd begun to get used to seeing myself this way and decided to leave it as it was. I could feel tension and disapproval radiating off Meghan, but I let the awkward silence stretch on and on. I heard her sigh, loudly, and glanced over to see her shake her head.

"What?" I asked, not restraining my irritation.

She shook her head. "I don't like it."

"What?" I asked again.

"All of this." She waved at me up and down. "You've changed more in the last week than you have in the last ten years. Doesn't that bother you?"

"No," I snapped, "and I don't understand why it bothers you so much. You were so angry the other night when you told me that you're different than you used to be and I didn't believe you. Why can't I do the same thing?"

"Because I've been working on myself for years, Chloé. You did this practically overnight, and the changes weren't your idea."

I turned away quickly, angry, and sat down at my vanity again, touching up my makeup. I knew she was speaking the truth, but that didn't make it any easier to hear. "Maybe you're right, but that doesn't negate the fact that I like being different than I was before I started working there. And anyway, it's just clothes."

I saw Meghan get up from the bed and approach me from behind. Her expression was uncertain, and she clearly regretted her words. She met my eyes in the mirror and then hugged me from behind. "I'm sorry to give you such a hard time, hon. I'm just worried about you."

My anger returned full force and I stood up, shaking off her arms. "You shouldn't be. There's nothing to worry about. I have a new job and it requires a certain dress standard, a standard my boss paid for, I might add."

Meghan's eyes were sad. "That's the problem. It's too much, Chloé. There's something else happening here, and I think you know it." She looked at me for a long time and then shook her head again, slowly. "Look, I'm sorry. I know I'm too nosy—it's my tragic flaw. Just promise me you'll be careful, okay?"

Trying to quell my anger, I broke eye contact with her. "Are you ready?" I asked.

"Sure." I was relieved to hear that some of the tension had left her voice. "I'm sorry you're going to be all by yourself tonight. I know it's kind of awkward to be the only single person at a party."

"I don't mind. I'm used to it."

"Isn't there anyone you're interested in?"

Caught unaware, I felt my face flush red and turned away quickly, trying to hide my reaction. Meghan laughed. "If that's not a yes, I don't know what is."

Agitated, I found myself trembling a little. "I'm not interested in anyone. I just got back to town."

"Well then, what the hell?" She pulled on my arm, turning me to face her. I kept my eyes on the floor. "Jesus, Chloé, what's gotten into you? You used to tell me everything. Why are you hiding things from me? I tell you every little detail about every moment of my life."

I finally looked at her and was surprised to find that I felt like crying. She realized that I was on the brink of tears and hugged me, hard. She led me over to the bed and we sat on it together, her arm around my shoulders. "Christ, girl," she whispered. "What's happening?"

"Nothing," I said automatically, then blushed again. "I mean— it doesn't mean anything. Nothing's happening." She looked at me skeptically and I sighed, realizing she wasn't about to let it drop. I glanced over at my bedroom door, and lowered my voice. "I'll tell you, okay? But I don't want you to make a big deal out of it and you can't tell anyone. I mean it."

Meghan's eyes lit up with happy mischief, and she mimicked buttoning her lip.

Steeling myself, I took a deep breath and said, "I had a really vivid sex dream about someone last night."

Meghan laughed and rolled her eyes. "Is that all? I have sex dreams all the time."

I shook my head impatiently. "Well, I don't, and I've never had one so detailed, or about someone I know. It was very…graphic."

She thought for a moment, obviously making herself take me seriously. "Well, whoever it was, if it's bothering you this much, maybe you should do something about it. Ask him out or something."

I looked away. "I don't think so. I don't think…he…feels the same way." I blushed harder at my lie, but given the conversation we'd just had about my new boss, I wasn't about to open that can of worms.

Meghan was looking at me strangely, and for a moment I was worried she might ask me about Amelia, but she didn't. "Well, it's not Charles, is it? 'Cause he's called me a few times to get your number. I told him if you hadn't given it to him, it was none of my business."

I shook my head quickly.

"What happened with you guys, anyway? One minute you're ready to move in with him, and the next you don't want to see him again."

"I don't want to talk about it," I said quietly.

Meghan was quiet for a long time after this, and I felt her body freeze up with tension. "Did he hurt you?" she finally asked.

I didn't respond and kept staring at the floor. Meghan sprang to her feet and stood in front of me long enough that I was finally forced to look up at her. Her eyes were blazing with rage. "What the hell did he do?"

"It wasn't that bad," I said, trying to calm her down.

"That doesn't answer the question, Chloé. What did he do?"

I sighed, and a feeling of shame and fright swept through me again at the memory. "Can we not talk about this? I-I don't want to think about it anymore."

"Jesus, Chloé! He should go to jail!"

"It wasn't that bad," I said again, looking down. "He just groped me a little. I told him to stop and he wouldn't, and then I got away."

Meghan's face was a mask of anger and horror. "Jesus Christ! I'm going to kill him. I am literally going to kill him. And I'm going to kill his brother while I'm at it. He should have told me Charles was a fucking psychopath."

"Meghan, please don't do anything. It's over, okay? It's my choice, and I choose not to do anything about it."

"Goddamn it, Chloé," Meghan said, her anger now turning on me, "you're so fucking passive. It's no wonder you're still single." Realizing what she'd just said, she clapped a hand over her mouth, her eyes wide with horror.

I sighed and got to my feet. "This conversation is over," I said, the weariness of the day finally catching up to me.

"I'm so sorry, Chloé." She clutched my arm. "I don't know why I said that. I didn't mean it."

I sighed. "It's okay. You're probably right."

"That doesn't mean I should have said anything, especially after what you just told me. I'm really sorry. It wasn't your fault. He's the asshole, not you."

Suddenly bone weary, I decided to end the conversation. "Let's go join the others, okay? I need a drink."

I left Meghan with Zach in the living room and went directly to the kitchen without saying another thing to her. I knew I was being childish, but I was pretty sure at that moment that if I said anything to her we'd end up fighting all night. The dinner was meant to be a chance for all of us to get to know each other, especially the two new men in Aunt Kate and Meghan's lives, and I didn't want to ruin it for Aunt Kate. Still, I would have given anything just to leave and go hide somewhere for the evening rather than face another moment of Meghan's inquiring eyes.

The kitchen was a disaster—the usual state of things when my Aunt Kate cooks a big meal, or, well, anything. There was flour everywhere from the bread and roux, and the floor and counters were covered with a thin, tacky layer of various foodstuffs. Still, it smelled wonderful, as always, the air hot and heavily redolent of spices and baking bread.

My family is Creole going back several generations and, in our particular branch, almost entirely French. New Orleans was settled by the French and later the Spanish, and both groups were eventually referred to as "Creole," which simply means native-born. So, in the case of my ancestors, Creole refers to French men and women born in Louisiana. During the generations of the late nineteenth century and earlier, my ancestors grew up speaking only French at home and attended French-taught schools. This all changed in the early twentieth century, in part because of large immigration movements at the turn of the century that necessitated English-only schools. This meant that by the time my grandparents were growing up, it was unusual to speak only French at home. A phrase or two in French was common to most French Creole people today, but I was the first person in two generations in my family to be fluent in the language.

While the language might be lost, on the whole, to most Creole families in New Orleans (though it was spoken by some Creole people outside of the city), the food hadn't changed. Visitors to Louisiana generally conflate Creole and Cajun cooking, much to both groups' disgust. While there is a lot of crossover between

Creole and Cajun cuisine, the two are significantly different in a number of ways. During the eighteenth and nineteenth century, as the two cuisines developed, the Creoles, in general, had more money than the Cajuns, in part because they'd been there longer, and in part because, for a long while, some Creoles were part of the ruling class in New Orleans and Louisiana. This wealth meant that Creole cooking developed early on with more ingredients than the Cajuns could afford—things like butter and flour, and, most particularly, the tomato, which is traditionally not used in Cajun food.

If, like me, you grew up in a Creole home, you learned how to cook various Creole dishes, but these could vary from family to family quite significantly, in part because most Creole families have Spanish, Irish, Native American, and African-American branches now.

One thing common to many Creole family kitchens today is a bread recipe that has been passed down through the generations. We had one ancestor who was a baker, and we still make his bread, particularly his baguettes. My aunt bakes her bread fresh twice a week, and, even in France, I've never eaten its like. Her bread will ruin you for every other bread in the world.

Hearing me come in, Aunt Kate spun around to greet me, and I had to laugh at the sight of her. She was covered head to toe in flour and sauces, as if something somewhere in the kitchen had blown up on her. She'd neglected, as usual, to don an apron, so her clothes were, at best, filthy, but probably ruined.

"You're home!" she said, grinning. She walked toward me with open arms and I shied away, not wanting an afternoon of mess on my clothes. She looked down at herself and laughed. "Probably a good plan to stay away from me right now. How was your day?"

"It was fine."

I was still smarting from my conversation with Meghan, and my words didn't convince her. She looked at me critically for a moment and, without saying a thing, went directly to the liquor cabinet. She pulled out the Cognac and poured me a small glass. I took it from her and drained it in one go, shuddered slightly at its thick sweetness.

"Better?" she asked.

I nodded, my eyes watering a little from the liquor.

"Okay," she said. "If you want to talk about it, we can, but otherwise I won't bother you about it, whatever it is."

Grateful, I took her up on the offer and changed topics immediately. "When will Jim get here?"

"Any time now," she said, and I saw a flash of nervous energy go through her as she glanced up at the kitchen clock.

"Do you want to go get ready? I can finish up here."

Her face melted in gratitude, and this time, when she hugged me, I forgot how filthy she was and hugged her back, both of us squeezing the other fiercely. Pulling apart, we both looked down at my jeans and shirt, now with roughly half of Aunt Kate's mess squished into them.

"Well, at least you just got some new clothes," Aunt Kate said, and we both laughed.

CHAPTER EIGHT

My first official dinner party as Amelia Winters's assistant was held in the Federal Ballroom a block outside of the French Quarter. The event was ostensibly a charity ball for the Louisiana wetlands, but, like most $10,000 dinners, it also functioned as a means for the rich to rub elbows with each other and show off their new trophy wives. All of what would once have been known as the "blue bloods" were in attendance, along with a good selection of the newly rich, up-and-coming businessmen and women who wanted to be seen with old money. I saw a few people I recognized from politics and from society gossip columns, as well as the man rumored to be the head of the local mafia. If there's one thing that's true about the moneyed gentility in New Orleans, it's that everyone simply ignores the bad things about everyone else—at least to their face.

I was nothing but a bundle of nerves from the second we arrived, and I found myself rather quickly grabbing my third glass of champagne. Realizing that I'd be slurring my words if I kept up this pace, I made myself sip it, slowly, looking up from my glass to scan the room for the ten potential buyers I'd selected for tonight. I had some back-up possibilities, but the men I was looking for were the ones I knew we should approach first. I spotted one and touched Amelia's elbow, lifting my chin at him slightly. She looked away from the older gentleman she was talking to and nodded at me briefly.

"Phil, I hope you'll excuse me," she said.

He smiled at her. "Of course, dear. Just let me know about that figurine when you hear something."

"I will," she said. They kissed each other's cheeks and then she grabbed my elbow and walked us slowly toward the man I'd indicated.

"Tell me about him," she said quietly as we approached.

"His name is Brent Cameron. He's divorced. Fairly new to the city, but from the South—one of the Carolinas. He just bought a rather large share of a local marketing firm, and he owns a big part of the Upriver District development that's about to break ground in the Irish Channel."

Brent turned toward us as we approached, and his face lit up. "Well, aren't you ladies a sight for sore eyes," he said. "I was afraid nothing but old trolls were here tonight, but you've proven me wrong."

We both forced a laugh at his "witticism," and I stood by for the next few minutes, watching Amelia weave her magic. Since we'd arrived about an hour ago, she'd already managed to create ten potential sales. She was incredibly impressive.

"You know you're right," he said after listening to her for a while. "My new place does need a little something for the walls. I don't know about that modern shit, though. I'm more of an old-fashioned kind of guy myself. Portraits, landscapes—that's my bag."

"We deal in all kinds of artwork, Mister Cameron," Amelia said smoothly, unruffled by his vulgarity. "With new clients, we assess the location and then make suggestions based on your tastes."

"That sounds just fine, especially if it means getting one of you lovely ladies over to my place for dinner first."

We both forced another laugh. "Of course," Amelia said, smiling. "Whenever you're available."

Brent fished around in his pocket for a moment and withdrew his card, handing it to her. "That's my office line, but I've got my cell-phone number on the back for you, sweetie." He winked slyly. "Have your girl call my girl, and we'll set something up for next week."

"I'll look forward to it," Amelia said.

"Until then." He tipped an invisible hat before walking away. When he was out of earshot, Amelia turned toward me, looking genuinely pleased. "He was a perfect choice," she said. "Moneyed and stupid."

I laughed. "I don't know how you did that so smoothly. Five minutes and he was eating out of your hand."

"You'll get the hang of it." She patted my shoulder and then glanced at her watch. "I think dinner is about to start. I managed to get us a seat at the table closest to the mayor's table. Plenty of rich pickings for us to talk to while we eat."

"Us?" I asked, my heart in my throat.

She touched my shoulder again. "There's nothing to it. Get them talking about anything but artwork and then bring it up casually. Flatter them, flatter their wives and girlfriends, and then drop the hint."

"I'm not so sure—"

"Don't worry. You'll do just fine. Consider this a practice run. There's no pressure here tonight."

I was still uncertain as we made our way over to our table. Of the ten chairs, it appeared that the other eight were filled with couples, most of them in their fifties and sixties. All the men sat up a little straighter when we sat down, and I saw several of the women frown at me. So far, Amelia had been talking exclusively to men, so I wasn't quite sure how to even begin to speak with these women.

"That's a lovely shawl," I told the older woman seated next to me.

Some of the tension left her face. "Thank you. It was my mother's."

I continued to look at it. "I just love family heirlooms. They mean so much more than the things we buy."

"I agree completely." She looked surprised.

The rest of the conversation was actually far easier than I'd anticipated. Taking Amelia's advice, I kept the conversation to heirlooms for a couple of minutes before talking about a painting I'd inherited from my parents and then to the company I worked for. The woman recognized the name Winters and immediately asked her husband if she could make an appointment for a home consultation. He rolled his eyes but agreed, and my heart lifted in jubilation. While it was only a potential sale at this point, I was fairly certain that, after a visit, I would be able to get them to buy something. I saw Amelia wink at me as I put the woman's card in my purse, and I smiled back at her.

The dinner was surprisingly bland, given the cost, but I felt that I managed to comport myself fine, only hesitating between two forks for a couple of seconds before watching Amelia choose the right one. Dinner was followed by a silent auction. Amelia made a bid on a small painting that she won, and I could see that she was extremely pleased with her winnings.

Once we all stood up for the reception, she pulled me aside, shaking her head in disbelief.

"That painting is worth over four times what I paid for it," she whispered conspiratorially, her eyes merry. "Whatever numbskull decided to donate it doesn't know what he's doing. I just made back the cost of our dinners."

We made our way over toward the dance floor, Amelia looking around carefully for past clients. We stood there for a long while on the edge of the dancing, and I spied another potential new mark I'd researched this week. I touched her elbow again, and she turned toward me, her body and face inches from mine.

"See another target?" she asked quietly. Almost exactly my height, she was close enough that I could see the flecks of gray in her dark-blue eyes.

"Across the dance floor. He's standing next to that leggy blonde. His name is Peter Donaldson. He's Scottish. Rich. Shipping magnate. I think his girlfriend's name is Kelly, but she could be a new one."

Amelia looked back over at him, appearing devious. She turned back to me. "The only way over there is to dance our way to him."

I swallowed. "Dance?"

"It's rude to walk across a dance floor." She paused, and then, seeing my face, she added, "And it's bad luck." She raised an eyebrow at me to show that she was kidding.

"I'm not very good at dancing," I admitted, looking anywhere but at her.

"That's okay. I'll lead."

I looked around the room, panic rising. "Won't it be strange that, I mean, that you and I—"

She laughed. "People are used to seeing me dance with other women, Doctor. Don't worry about it."

I swallowed again and nodded, my heart racing. She held out her hand and pulled me into a twirl, and we were soon dancing our way around the small floor. She was an incredible dancer, as I knew she would be, and as we moved her hand rested on my bare back, exposed because of my dress. The touch of her fingers sent tingles up and down my spine, and I felt hot and dizzy at the same time. I was vaguely aware that people had stopped to watch us dance, but my attention was rooted to her and her hand.

She pulled me a step closer to her and put her mouth close to my ear, her voice barely above a whisper. "Have I told you how incredible you look tonight?"

I shook my head a little, too terrified to respond.

"Well, you do. You're the most stunning woman in the room."

"Hardly."

"Your modesty is very becoming, Doctor, but in this case it's misguided. You're beautiful."

The whirling motion of the dance and the heat spreading out from the hand on my back was beginning to make my head spin, but I couldn't wrench my eyes from hers.

"There's no one more attractive here than you, Miss Winters," I managed to say.

She threw her head back and laughed, then steered me around an older couple who glanced at us as we danced by them. "I love your flattery."

"It's the truth," I replied.

She laughed again. I was vaguely aware of a flash out of the corner of my eye but dismissed it, my eyes still rooted to hers. She moved her face toward mine, and for a moment I was certain she was about to kiss me. I held my breath, waiting.

"I think we've made our point," she said quietly. "On the next pass, I'm going to stop and lead us over to your Mister Donaldson."

I felt my face fall in disappointment and saw Amelia lift an eyebrow at me, but we were soon drawing apart as we hit the edge of the dance floor. Several men were watching us, openly interested. Amelia shook her hair back from her shoulders and looked over at me. "Ready?"

I could only nod.

As she schmoozed Mister Donaldson, I tried to center myself and calm down, but my body was a cascade of emotions and sensations, my head still spinning. My back still felt hot, as if her hand still touched it. I imagined I could look in the mirror and see the red outline of her handprint. My stomach clenched tight with something like panic, and my heart was pounding. My body was covered in a layer of cold, clammy sweat. Worst of all, however, were my racing thoughts. I kept chastising myself for overacting, but it was no good. I felt unmoored, confused, and distracted. I did, however, manage to nod in the appropriate places as Amelia made plans for another appointment with the potential new client. Once she'd stowed away his card, she grabbed my elbow and led me away from him and over to a small table.

She looked concerned. "Do you want to sit down? You look pale."

"Yes," I said, sitting heavily. When I looked up at her, she was frowning at me. I attempted a weak smile in response. "I'm sorry. I think all that wine is catching up with me. I don't feel too well."

Looking relieved, she sat down in the chair next to mine and squeezed one of my hands. "It's okay to be nervous the first time you do this. I should have realized."

"It's not your fault. It's mine. I kept drinking when I knew I should cut myself off. Nerves, I guess."

"This will all come naturally to you in time." She waved at the room.

I looked away. While it was true that I might eventually become more comfortable with these kinds of people and this kind of event, I doubted that I would ever get used to dancing with Amelia Winters. My body and mind were in complete turmoil.

"Why don't you let me take you home?" she offered.

A wave of panic swept through me. I certainly didn't want to blow an important dinner for her. "But it's so early!"

She shook her head. "It's fine. Please don't worry about it. In fact, it's better to leave these things a little early once in a while. Makes you seem less available."

Knowing that she was catering to my needs didn't help matters, but I agreed with her anyway. I needed to get home and soon. We stood up and approached the dance floor again, and Amelia laughed when she saw my face. "I think we can make an exception—let's just walk across the floor."

I sighed in relief and let her take my hand. In the back of my mind, I was aware that several people were watching us leave together, but dismissed it. Let them think what they want, I thought.

Amelia made a quick phone call to her driver, George, and we waited outside, the warm, fresh air reviving me slightly.

I saw someone approaching us, and when I glanced up, my stomach clenched in horror. It was Charles. He smiled widely as he came nearer, and I had to let him hug me, lightly.

"Hey, Chloé," he said. "I didn't know you were here. I was just out having a cigar. You're not leaving already, are you?"

"Yes," I said quietly, unsure how to react.

Amelia watched this exchange, her eyes intense and alive with curiosity. She saw my expression and frowned, as if sensing my tension. Turning to Charles, she held out a hand. "I haven't had the pleasure," she said smoothly.

"Oh gosh, where are my manners? I'm Charles King, a friend of Chloé's."

"Charmed," Amelia said, shaking his hand. "I'm Amelia Winters. Another *friend* of Chloé's." Her emphasis on the word friend made it clear that she understood, at least in part, that my relationship with him was more complicated than mere friendship.

He appeared surprised. "Really? I've done some work with your father. Of course I've heard all about you." Suddenly, as if remembering something, he looked back and forth between the two of us. "You came here together?" he asked after a long pause.

She gave my hand a quick squeeze. "Yes. Doctor Deveraux was my escort tonight."

I had to bite my tongue to keep from laughing at the expression on his face. He turned to me, eyebrows raised. "Really?"

I nodded, still trying not to laugh.

His brow creased, the information evidently filtering slowly into his mind. "So you guys are, like, together?" As if trying to clarify, he motioned with his cigar back and forth between us.

"Yes," Amelia said, taking my hand again. "We are. Now if you'll excuse us, our car is here. I want to get this one home before she keels over." She smiled at me wickedly and I managed to grin back at her.

Charles watched us, his mouth open, clearly in shock as we got into the Rolls. I could see him still staring at us stupidly as the car drove away. Turning to Amelia, I started laughing, and she soon joined me.

"Did you see his face?" I asked after a while, wiping tears from the corners of my eyes.

She was clearly pleased with herself. "I did indeed. What on earth was that about? Is he an ex-boyfriend?"

My mirth dried up almost immediately, and I looked away from her, out the window. "No," I said firmly. "I wouldn't date that man for all the money in the world."

When I was brave enough to look back at her, she was staring at me, her delicate eyebrows drawn in concern. I shook my head, and she said nothing, seeming to understand that I didn't want to talk about it.

When we pulled up in front of Aunt Kate's, I looked over at her again. "I'm sorry again that I wimped out so early tonight. Next time I'll take it easy on the booze."

"You did wonderfully, Doctor." She scooted toward me on the seat, and once again I braced myself for a kiss, my body warming in anticipation. Instead, she gave me a quick hug. "Good night."

"Good night," I managed, then fled from the car as if my life depended on it.

After briefly greeting my startled aunt, I went directly to my room, closing and locking the door before resting my forehead on it, my eyes squeezed shut. "What the hell is wrong with you?" I asked myself.

Wearily I removed my shoes and gown and stood for a long time looking at myself in the mirror. I was wearing the new bra and panties Amelia had chosen for me and had on a garter belt to hold up my stockings. Before tonight, I'd never worn garters.

Before tonight, I'd also never wanted a woman to kiss me. It was a night of firsts.

Glancing over at the door to make sure it was actually locked, I looked back at myself in the mirror and met my eyes. The garters made me feel wanton and sexy, despite being so old-fashioned and nearly obsolete. Tracing my finger down my stomach, I stopped just shy of the line of my panties. I slid one finger under the elastic band, not going farther than the top of the hairline despite the desperate fire burning between my legs. Pulling out my finger, I unhooked one garter and then the other, then slowly rolled down the stockings, watching myself the whole time. I stood back up. My cheeks were slightly pink. Stepping closer to the mirror, I gazed into my eyes and recognized the hungry expression I saw there. Going farther than this, I realized, would mean something, and I stared into my own eyes as if waiting for an answer.

I unhooked my bra in the front and let it drop to the floor, standing clad now only in my panties and the garter belt. My heart was pounding at this point, hard, and I met my eyes again, knowing what was coming. Sliding my hand slowly into my underwear, I felt my wetness coat my fingers and moaned before slapping my other hand over my mouth. Lock or no lock, my aunt would hear me if I was loud. I bit my tongue and moved my fingers farther down, finding my opening soaked and wanting. Beginning to feel desperate, I slammed my fingers inside myself, bending at the waist slightly to push back against my hand. Using my thumb, I massaged my clit in rhythm with the fingers sliding in and out of myself and felt an orgasm beginning to build up inside me. My insides clenched and rolled in anticipation, and in seconds the orgasm was cresting and crashing over my senses, my ears roaring and my vision clouded with pleasure. I was pulsing around the fingers inside me and had to nearly chew my tongue off to keep from screaming.

Sometime during my pleasure, I'd crumpled to the floor, and when the last ripples of the orgasm slowed, I rolled onto my back, staring up at the ceiling, my hand still underneath my underwear. I panted heavily and my tongue hurt from biting it.

Now what? I thought.

Chapter Nine

While I'd been working for only a week, I was grateful the next morning that it was the weekend. Shame washed through me at the thought of what I'd done last night, but I pushed it away. While I'd been raised to understand that touching yourself is natural and sometimes necessary, that didn't necessarily explain the reasons behind why I'd touched myself. In truth, I knew that if I was willing to think about it further, I'd been incredibly turned on—primarily because I'd been with Amelia. That morning in the shower, the water rushing down on me as I stood there, doing little, I tried to reconcile this truth with what I knew of myself, but I still struggled with it.

While I'd always found the female body attractive, before now it had always been in an abstract, artistic way. I preferred painting female models, for example, but most artists would say the same thing. Something about naked men, perhaps because of the extreme unfamiliarity with the male nude in our culture, made painting them less appealing and almost always embarrassing. Unquestionably, Amelia was beautiful. Anyone would be attracted to her, I told myself. Shaking myself out of my reverie, I finally managed to wash and then climbed out of the shower, pulling on my grubby painting clothes.

Aunt Kate and her boyfriend Jim were sharing breakfast in the kitchen, and both seemed a little sheepish when they saw me, drawing apart. I greeted them and grabbed the coffee pot.

"So how was the dinner?" Aunt Kate asked.

"Very strange," I said, sipping the coffee. Aunt Kate prepared it in the New Orleans style, with chicory and from a concentrate, and the chicory had a bitter, biting tang that I loved.

"How so?"

I blushed at the memory of dancing with Amelia and then quickly recovered. "I don't know, just all those rich people throwing their money around. It's weird, you know? All those clothes, all that decadence—I've never really been around it before."

"Can I fix you something to eat?"

"No thanks. Coffee's fine."

Aunt Kate sighed. "You really need to eat more, girly. You're wasting away."

I glanced down at myself and shrugged. While it was true I'd lost weight over the last few months, I couldn't understand what all the fuss was about. "I guess."

"Why don't you sit down and talk to Jim while I make you some eggs."

Knowing it would make her happy if I agreed, I sat down. While I waited, Jim and I shared a short, awkward exchange. He was a nice-enough man but, as Aunt Kate was clearly the talker in the relationship, not exactly a conversationalist. He owned his own construction company and was the company's general contract manager. I managed to get him to open up about a restoration project he and his team were working on in the Quarter, and I found myself warming up to him as we chatted. Aunt Kate cooked me Creole eggs, which, once I started eating, made me realize how hungry I'd been. As Jim and I ate and talked, I glanced over at Aunt Kate to see her smiling at us, obviously happy that we were getting along.

"Thank you so much for breakfast," I said after a while. "I guess I was hungrier than I knew."

She looked satisfied. "I thought so. What are you up to today? I take it from your outfit that you're going to waste this beautiful day up in your studio?"

"It's not a waste, Aunt Kate. The light will be perfect for painting."

She laughed and I excused myself, climbing up to the studio.

❖

I spent most of the rest of the weekend painting, happy to have free time and, for the first time in ages, able to use my time painting guilt-free. It'd been a long time since I'd been able to devote myself to painting for long, uninterrupted hours, and now that I was working again, I didn't have to watch every brushstroke or tube of paint. While I'd initially returned to working on my newest painting, at some point on Saturday afternoon, the memory of my first visit to the warehouse and the sensation I'd had as I looked at the beautiful mural hidden in the back inspired me. Knowing that the feeling was trying to tell me something, move me in some way, I put my half-finished landscape aside and started a new painting.

It absorbed me so wholly, I barely slept or ate all weekend. I was even tempted to cancel dinner with Meghan on Sunday night, but given the tension between us lately, I knew it wouldn't be a good idea. I wanted my best friend back. What's more, I'd started to feel a little guilty about how I'd behaved toward her. She and Aunt Kate were sort of right. Something was happening with Amelia, but I didn't know what it meant.

Meghan lived in a funky shotgun house about three blocks from my aunt's. Every inch of it held one of her many "treasures," the quantity of which bordered on hoarding. She had knickknacks and tchotchkes lying on every surface, in every corner of her house. While there were apparently themes to her junk, I could never detect them. She also made collages from the various bric-a-brac she found in the Bywater, which were occasionally interesting if, to my taste, cluttered. She'd lived here so long, it was hard to picture her moving out, but that was apparently the plan since Zach's place was bigger.

Meghan wanted us to have a girls' night, so Zach had made himself scarce. She opened the door in her sports bra, and I laughed at the sight of her.

"The damn air-conditioning's out," she explained as I came in. The room was sweltering and smelled distinctly like B.O. I made a face and she laughed. "I'm sorry. I can put deodorant on till the pigs come home, but there's not a lot I can do about it when it's this hot out."

"Maybe we should go out." I wrinkled my nose with distaste, waving my hand in front of my face dramatically

She sighed. "I guess so. I didn't want to spend any money, but I can't really have guests over when it's like this. I was thinking about going over to Zach's after dinner. It's so friggin' hot here, I can't sleep."

"Do you want to postpone?" I asked, trying to sound casual.

Her brow furrowed and she frowned, deeply. "No. Do you?"

"No." I shrugged. "Just an idea."

Meghan wasn't buying it. "Why are you avoiding me lately? We used to see each other or at least call each other every day. You've been back almost two weeks now, and I've seen and heard from you exactly four times."

I sighed, feeling angry again. "All we've been doing lately is arguing, Meghan. I don't know what to say. It's not exactly pleasant to be around someone who's constantly questioning your motives and getting pissed off."

"I'm not!" Meghan said angrily, and then we both laughed. The laughter helped the tension and we hugged each other, relieved to be returning to normal. "I'm sorry, Chloé. I didn't mean to be such a bitch. You know I'm only worried about you, right? But you're a big girl. You can do whatever you want."

Suddenly, Meghan grabbed my arm and pulled me over to the couch. "I guess this is probably the worst time to show you this, but I'm going to do it anyway."

She'd spread the newspaper on the coffee table by the couch, and when I saw the page she'd left open, my knees gave way and I sat down, heavily. There was a half-page photo of me and Amelia dancing at the dinner last Friday night. We were staring into one another's eyes, and Amelia's hand was incredibly close to my ass as she pulled me into a twirl. I looked both happy and excited, and, though the shot was in black-and-white, it was clear my cheeks were flushed. The caption beneath the photograph said, "Miss Winters Bags Another Blonde."

"Crap," I said quietly.

Meghan nodded. "You're damn right, crap."

"Do you think Aunt Kate saw this?" I asked weakly.

"What exactly is there to see here?" Meghan countered, her eyes mischievous. "You're dancing with a beautiful woman. You look thrilled, and she looks like she wants to eat you for lunch."

I stared at the photo again, examining Amelia's face. It was true. Even if one were being incredibly forgiving, Amelia's expression seemed hungry, predatory.

"It's probably just the lighting," I said lamely.

Meghan rolled her eyes. "You have *got* to be kidding me."

I was silent for a long time. To give myself some time to respond, I read the rest of the society column. Besides a report on several of the other attendees, the columnist reflected on Amelia Winters's new "dish," who, luckily, wasn't named. While the tone of the column was light and snide, the insinuation was still very clear.

"Look," I said, trying to keep my voice steady, "we danced for less than five minutes. That's all."

Meghan raised an eyebrow. "You're sure?"

I blushed darkly and looked away, remembering what had happened when I finally made it home. Meghan and I sat in silence for a long time until I was finally ready to meet her eyes again.

She looked amused. "You're blushing like a spring flower, girly. Something you want to tell me?"

I shook my head quickly, surprised to find my eyes fill with tears. "No. I mean, I don't know."

"What does that mean? And why are you crying?" She scooted closer to me and pulled me toward her, one arm over my shoulders.

"I don't know what's going on," I said, wiping at my face, furious and scared at the same time.

"Do you have feelings for her?" Meghan asked after a long time.

"No. I mean, sort of. I think she's attractive…"

Meghan pulled back from me, staring. "Attractive?"

"Don't you? I mean, she's objectively gorgeous. Even you said so."

Meghan shrugged. "She's very pretty, if you like that flat, androgynous type. I'm more a curvy-girl fan myself." She laughed at my surprised expression. "I mean come on—Christina Hendricks is the sexiest woman alive."

After a long pause and carefully weighing her words, she asked, "Are you thinking about doing something about this attraction?"

I shook my head quickly. "No. I couldn't. She's my boss, for one. And I'm not, I mean, I've never even thought about that with a woman…I wouldn't know what I was…No."

Meghan raised her eyebrows but wisely didn't reply. My protest sounded weak even to me. We were quiet for a long time again before she said, "She was the person in your sex dream the other night, right?"

I laughed and pushed at her playfully. "Fuck you," I said, wiping away my remaining tears.

Meghan stood up, stretching. "I'm going to say one more thing about this, Chloé, and then I promise I won't say anything else about her unless you bring her up."

"Fine." I was trying not to get angry again.

"I don't care if you sleep with men, women, or two or three of both. The only thing I'm worried about is you. This woman is a predator, Chloé. She has a reputation. I don't want you to get hurt. That's all. Would you think about it before you decide to do anything? Please?"

I nodded. "I will."

"Now how about I get a shirt on and we get the hell out of this place? I could use a drink."

I wrinkled my nose again. "Take a shower first, would you? You smell like shit."

Chapter Ten

On the following Wednesday, Amelia decided to take me along to Brent Cameron's home visit to show me the ropes. Brent, the rich real-estate developer I'd suggested approaching at the ball the other night, had been thrilled to have us over and "Get some shit on my walls," as he put it. He planned to have us over for some "Fancy chow," for dinner, made, he told us, by his gourmet chef. Amelia and I had been in near-hysterics of laughter after she phoned him and told me about their conversation. I could tell she expected to take him to the cleaners.

All day Tuesday, I spent time researching him, his family, and his interests, hoping to have fodder for flattery for a two- to three-hour consultation. Except for the fact that he was ridiculously rich, I'd known men like Brent all my life, and I felt fairly confident I wouldn't make an ass out of myself. That didn't, however, negate the fact that this could potentially become my first sale. I also helped Amelia create a binder of potential artwork in a variety of styles for him to look at, all of which carefully avoided describing cost. We would make suggestions, but ultimately, she reminded me, he would choose what "shit" he wanted.

As we rode over to his house that evening, both of us dressed to the nines, Amelia exuded her usual calm confidence. "You're going to be great," she told me, patting my knee and sending tingles running up and down my spine.

"I hope so," I said, my mouth dry.

"Remember—these first few outings are practice runs. If we can sell even one thing, you'll be doing incredibly well. Most of my previous assistants have taken longer just to get the first potential client lined up."

I was at this point dying of curiosity about her past assistants. I'd wanted to bring them up for a while now, but it seemed, somehow, intrusive and unprofessional. What could possibly motivate me, her new assistant, to ask about the old ones? I didn't have any excuse except curiosity. Still, I decided to take a chance. "Oh?" I asked. "How long did it usually take them to make a sale?"

She didn't take the bait and said only, "Much longer."

Brent's house was as ostentatious and ridiculous on the outside as I expected. Squatting like a toad among swans, its hyper-modern architecture stood out among the delicate Victorians in his neighborhood. All glass, angles, and stucco, it screamed new money and poor taste.

Ignoring his doorman, Brent pushed past him to open our car door for us, helping us both climb out of the Rolls. Once we were standing beside him, he whistled, long and low. "My goodness! Aren't you two the prettiest things I ever saw?"

Amelia gave him a phony smile. "Thank you, Mister Cameron."

"Call me Brent," he said, turning to me. He took my hand and kissed the back of it, his eyes alive with mischief. "It's an honor." He wiggled his eyebrows at me.

Taking my cue from Amelia, I took his behavior in stride. "You flatter me, Mister Cameron."

"It's Brent, really. I hate that formal 'Mister' crap." He gestured toward the door. "Shall we, ladies?"

We followed him into a large, cathedral-like entry room. Light from the setting sun filtered in through the many windows, and the effect made the inside of his home far nicer than I'd expected from its ugly outer shell. The room, however, was nearly empty except for some incredibly uncomfortable-looking furniture scattered in strange arrangements around the room. He didn't have a single picture or decoration anywhere. Even the floor was a solid, cold marble without a carpet to be seen. The whole place had the feel of an empty, clean warehouse.

"As you can see, I need some help," Brent said, chuckling slightly. "I used to have a bunch of crap for the walls and the tables, but my ex-wife took it all. Luckily that's all her blood-sucking lawyer got out of me, which means I can buy some new stuff. Stuff I like. She always liked all that modern shit. You know, like a big canvas with squares on it, crap like that. That's just not my thing."

We both agreed, but I felt a little overwhelmed. Given the modern layout and setup of the house and furniture, it would be difficult to find a style of artwork to suit his house that wasn't modern. Amelia, however, seemed once again to take all of this in stride.

"I'm certain we can accommodate whatever style you favor, Brent. From the looks of it, we do, as you say, have a lot to work with. But before we get down to business, I think you promised us dinner?"

"Of course!" he said. "How rude of me, ladies. I always say pleasure before business, myself."

Dinner was, as expected, over the top. The chef had prepared a feast that, if not exactly "gourmet," was sumptuous and rich. It clearly catered to Brent's tastes, which ran toward heavy meats and creamy sauces. I attempted to eat as much as I could, but it was tough going. I prefer light and simple food most of the time. Amelia, however, made enjoying the meal look effortless, polishing off plate after plate of the decadent dishes.

When the dessert trays were finally removed, Brent sat back in his chair, gazing at her with obvious pleasure. "I always love to see a woman enjoy a good meal. Judging by your size, you don't even look like you could eat a salad." Amelia continued sipping her cocktail and didn't reply. "This one on the other hand," he waved at me, "ate like a bird. Big surprise."

Before I could apologize, he held up his hands. "I'm only joking, Chloé. I don't take offense. I know you ladies like to keep your figures."

I nodded dumbly, feeling like I'd let Amelia down, but she winked at me from across the table. Seeing the look between us, Brent laughed. "Hey, that reminds me. I saw the two of y'all dancing the other night. Does that mean you're like together-together?"

I flushed and Amelia laughed. "I don't know if that's a topic for a business dinner, Brent," she said.

Brent held up his hands, "Hey, don't worry about me. I know I seem like a redneck, but I thought it was sexy as hell. After you two left, the whole place was talking about you. I think most of the men, and a lot of the women, were more than a little turned on by the show. I don't mind saying that not a few of us were pretty disappointed when you left, either. The two prettiest women went home together. Now if that doesn't say something about the state of the world, I don't know what does."

Seeing my face he laughed again. "Hell, I got a brother who's a cocksucker back in Raleigh, where I grew up. I get it. And like I said, you two are fucking hot together."

Luckily, after that, he dropped the subject, but I struggled the rest of the cocktail round to get my blood pressure back under control. As we toured the large, empty rooms of his house, he and Amelia chatting about politics, sports, and occasionally art, I forced myself not to run screaming from the house. Amelia, obviously sensing my turmoil, took command, making sure that Brent didn't see how upset I was. My mind was in complete tumult. His insinuation hadn't insulted me—after all, given Amelia's apparent past, everyone apparently assumed we were together. What bothered me more was the idea that we were somehow together for his pleasure, not our own. My recognition of this fact, and what it suggested about my feelings for Amelia, bothered me. Not able to quite understand entirely what this realization meant, I felt my stomach lurching from the rich food and my escalating distress. Once or twice, I almost had to excuse myself to the bathroom to be sick, but managed to avoid doing that, just barely.

After what seemed like an endless tour (a tour, I might add, that included his massive car collection), the three of us finally sat down to coffee in his empty living room. I was relieved to get off my shaking legs.

"What are your first thoughts, Doctor?" Amelia suddenly asked, turning to me.

Taken aback, I looked at her in surprise and she laughed. "We've seen the whole place now," she prompted me, "and Brent has told us about his tastes. What do you think we can offer him?"

Remarkably, I barely hesitated. While I'd been scarcely listening the entire time we'd walked around his place, something had apparently sunk in. Opening up the leather folder I'd prepared, I began to show him several options for the various rooms we'd seen, suggesting that each have a unified scheme either in color or style. I explained that while the folder was understandably limited in scope, each of the pieces I was showing him represented what I meant. He would, of course, have the final say in all the pieces before installation, but we could create a room centered around the painting or sculpture that I showed him from the folder. In addition, I suggested several rugs and tapestries that would help warm up some of the coldness in his house, each of which would correspond to the room in which it was placed.

When I'd finished, Brent laughed, shaking his head as if dazed. "You amaze me, Miss Chloé. All along, I was thinking Amelia would be the one to do the hard sell, but you come in here at the end like a falcon and sweep me away." He laughed again, looking back and forth between the two of us. "I love it. I love every single thing you just showed me." He nodded once, almost to himself. "Let's do it."

We all stood up and shook hands, the tension leaving my body almost as if it had never existed. My jubilance at the sale was something I'd rarely felt before. I was surprised by how happy it made me. When Brent turned to the bar to grab a bottle of champagne to celebrate, Amelia gave me a happy wink behind his back. I winked back, my happiness making me bolder than normal, and saw her eyebrows lift slightly in surprise.

"Now let's pop this bitch and toast our resident falcon here," Brent said, popping the cork. He poured three glasses and handed them around.

"To falcons!" he shouted happily.

"To falcons!" Amelia and I responded.

CHAPTER ELEVEN

The following weeks passed in a blur of activity. The New York trip was fast approaching, which meant preparing dossiers and art folders for past and potential clients, supervising the collection of artwork for transfer to Brent Cameron's house, monitoring its installation room by room, and schmoozing with him day after day. This last part, I found, was much easier without Amelia around. He rarely mentioned Amelia most of the time, and though he flirted with me constantly, I found I didn't mind, despite my complete disinterest in him. I find it easy to flirt with men I'm not interested in, especially when they're basically paying for my company. He, however, didn't seem to mind the farce—which even he must have recognized as one—and it didn't taint our business association, either. This was, perhaps, how he was used to treating women. At least he was courteous, if a tiny bit sleazy.

I also did my first solo house visit to the older couple I'd met at the charity dinner, complimenting, once again, the wife's family heirlooms and flattering her otherwise as much as possible on her taste and decorations. The flattery worked not only on her, but also on her husband, and, after another ridiculously rich dinner, I managed to sell far more artwork to them than I'd anticipated.

Returning to the Winterses' warehouse quite late that evening to start putting in their order, I was surprised to see that Amelia and her secretary Janet were still there. Janet looked haggard and worn. We'd all been putting in extra hours lately in preparation for

New York as well as the massive installation at Brent's house. Still, keeping the poor woman at the office this late seemed cruel.

"You're still here?" I asked.

She sighed. "Yes. And it doesn't look like I'll get out of here anytime soon. Miss Winters is in conniptions over New York. She doesn't think we're ready. I keep telling her that she always thinks that before a big trip, but she doesn't believe me. She has to make everyone else as miserable as she is, or she thinks we're not working hard enough." Janet sighed again. "Luckily we won't have another trip like this until Paris." She rolled her eyes. "You think *this* is bad, just wait until she gears up for a Paris trip."

I clucked my tongue and shook my head, trying to look as sympathetic as I could, but I was nervous about New York too. Up until now, except for some of my supervisory work in the warehouse, I had focused mostly on clients and clients alone, but in New York it would be clients *and* artwork. I would be responsible for helping to find new artists to promote, and the thought had terrified me from the moment Amelia asked me to start researching them.

"Well, I'll leave you to it—"

Amelia suddenly came out of her office. "Oh, thank God you're here, Doctor," she told me. "Would you mind coming in for a little while?" She turned to her secretary. "Janet, I'm so sorry. It's almost midnight. Go home and don't come in until ten tomorrow morning. I'm sorry I've been such a bitch. You know how I am when I have a trip coming up."

Janet didn't disagree. "Thank you, Miss Winters. Until then." She grabbed her purse and nearly ran for the door, obviously afraid of being called back.

I followed Amelia into her office, and she closed the door behind us. Her hair was mussed, her clothes were wrinkled, and her makeup was in desperate need of being either taken off or reapplied. She looked so entirely unlike her usual put-together self I was taken aback. In fact, her resemblance to my dream version of her made me flush with embarrassment at the memory, and I quickly turned away to hide my rising color. She closed her eyes and sighed, resting heavily against the door. After a moment she seemed to shake herself loose and made her way around to sit at the chair behind her desk. I sat down, still shaken.

"I wanted to take a moment before the whole New York thing to check in with you. You've been here for almost a month now."

"Really?" I was surprised. Somehow it seemed shorter.

"Really. It's amazing how quickly you've caught on. Every task I've given you, you've attacked it head-on and completed it with ease. You had some nervous moments at the beginning, but that's, of course, expected. You've done far better than I could have dreamed."

I felt awkward, unsure how to react to such praise. "Thank you."

"I should be thanking you," she said seriously. "I don't know how I would have gotten through the last month without you. As you can see I'm still overwhelmed even with you here."

I didn't know what to say.

"The Cameron sale is proceeding nicely. You did an amazing job not only in selecting Brent as a potential client, but in selling to him so magnificently. I genuinely believe you could get that man to buy anything at this point. How's the installation going?"

"Slowly, but well," I said. I explained the two rooms that we were working on.

"So that's what, two rooms out of how many so far?"

"Twenty," I said, laughing. "He's doing the whole place. He even asked me yesterday to help him pick out new furniture to match the artwork. I said I'd look into it."

Amelia sat up, eyes blazing. "One of my brothers is in the furniture business. I'll arrange a meeting with him after New York. You really are amazing."

I didn't respond.

"And how did tonight go?"

"Very well," I said, detailing the sales.

She seemed to take the news as my due. "As I said when I hired you, we need to start thinking about your commission now that you're making so many sales."

I laughed. "I don't think we're at that point yet, are we?"

"Do you have any idea how much money Brent Cameron is giving us right now, Doctor? Or how much more money he'll give us in the future? Not to mention this new sale of yours? Don't sell yourself short. You deserve every penny coming to you. I'll have Janet draw up a new contract to give you a general sales commission tomorrow—I think it's five percent—for everything you've been involved in, with a one-percent increase, let's say, every other month for the first year. You can also expect your sales to be reflected in your Christmas bonus."

My heart raced happily. Having received a couple of paychecks now, I already felt amply compensated for my hard work, but I certainly didn't intend to turn down a little extra money. Soon I'd be able to get my own place, which was all I'd wanted the job for anyway. In addition to wanting to be out on my own again, Aunt Kate and her boyfriend had begun to drop hints about moving in together, and I wanted to get out of there before that happened. Much as I liked the guy, it was too small a house for three of us.

Amelia was still looking at me, and I blushed again under her unwavering gaze. "What's that you're wearing?" she said suddenly.

I was so taken aback by the change in topic that I had to look down at myself to see what she was talking about. "Oh. Some of the clothes Tiffany made arrived yesterday. I was going to tell you about them, but we've been so busy."

"Stand up and let me look at you." Her expression was unreadable.

Obeying without thought, I stood up, turning around for her once, slowly. My face was red when I turned back to her. "What do you think?"

"It's marvelous," she said. "Now you see why I get almost everything tailored."

I nodded. I'd never had clothes that fit me so well. While the nice things we'd bought ready-made last month were flattering and stylish, it was remarkable having something that fit me and only me. The difference was apples and oranges.

"I'll send over some luggage for you for New York tomorrow," Amelia said after a moment. She looked down at her desk and started shuffling papers, her body language suggesting that she was anxious for some reason. "You have the schedule for New York, so you should have a good idea what you need to bring with us. I want you to take tomorrow off so you'll be packed before the flight Thursday. I don't want you to pack at the last minute. Remember to include two gowns for both of the dinners—Janet has rented them for you. The paparazzi are even more ridiculous in New York than they are here, so people will notice what we look like." She glanced back up at me, but her face appeared tense and drawn.

I wasn't about to argue with her. I'd actually been planning to take a half day off tomorrow to pack, so I welcomed the excuse. Still confused about her behavior, I felt a little strange just leaving and searched my mind for something to ease the mood.

Amelia reached across her desk, holding out one of her hands. Without thinking about it, I took it in mine and she squeezed my fingers.

"Thank you again, Doctor. I couldn't have done it without you this month."

My throat dry, I managed to say, "You're welcome."

The rest of the night and all the way home, my hand seemed to tingle from her touch.

Chapter Twelve

I usually find flying anything but pleasant. While I'm not afraid to fly, I do have a touch of claustrophobia that is exacerbated when I'm crammed next to a million people in a tight space. My European friends always mock what they call my American need for a "bubble," but in my case, it's absolutely true. Jammed in next to some gigantic man or, God help me, next to a chatty old lady that won't let me read and needs the bathroom every five minutes, flying anywhere always makes the thought of walking there more appealing most of the time. Further, forced to look for the best bargain anytime I went anywhere, I usually had to book flights with connections through someplace that simply extended the unpleasantness for more time than necessary.

It hadn't occurred to me that we wouldn't be flying in a commercial airplane. I'd anticipated, with great excitement, stretching out in first class and drinking as much free champagne as I could guzzle, but, as we approached Louis Armstrong International, we took a strange turn, away from the main concourses and terminal. I glanced over at Amelia to see if she noticed, but she was engrossed in her tablet, trying to cram information one last time before the trip. The Rolls drove up to a locked gate that opened electronically after a brief pause. We drove to a parking area near a separate runway that held several smaller airplanes, and my stomach dropped when I saw the Winters Corporation logo on the tail of a beautiful small jet.

"Ah," said Amelia, glancing up. "Here we are." She put her tablet away in her purse and waited as George came around to open her door.

Too stunned to say anything, after I got out of the car, I stood there dumbly and watched as several men appeared to carry our luggage to the plane for us, bustling around with great efficiency. Another group of men and women were inspecting the plane and moving around it out on the tarmac, taking notes and adjusting things as they went.

Amelia was now looking at her phone, tapping out texts. Mirrored sunglasses covered her eyes, and her hair was uncharacteristically down, falling in dark, loose curls around her shoulders. While we would have the evening in New York to get adjusted and relax before starting work tomorrow, she was dressed, as usual, as if she were going to be in a fashion shoot later. Her makeup was expertly applied, highlighting her high cheekbones and lips. Her cool beauty coupled with her clothes and sunglasses made her look very much the celebrity. I glanced around, expecting to spot the paparazzi she'd obviously dressed up for. Clad in my oldest yoga pants and a ratty, paint-spattered T-shirt, I felt like a bum she'd picked up on the side of the road.

"Ready?" she finally asked, looking up at me.

"I'm sorry I didn't dress up." I glanced down at myself and gestured at my clothes.

"Don't be silly. I told you that you had the day off today. You're allowed to dress as you want on your own time."

"Maybe I can change on the plane. I didn't think about it." I was still embarrassed. "Of course people might see us when we get there. I'm sorry. I always dress like this to fly. I didn't expect..."

She touched my arm lightly. "Really, it's fine. I'll have our driver in New York drop you off at your friend's house. No one will even see you."

She was probably just being nice. While I'd be staying in the same hotel as she was for the rest of the trip, I'd arranged to meet up with Lana, an old graduate-school friend of mine, and was staying with her and her partner tonight. We rarely got to see each other, and when I'd made plans with her, I hadn't thought it might not be appropriate to disappear on a business trip for an evening. At best, I was being rude leaving Amelia alone. At worst, I was being unprofessional. More than likely, I was being both rude and unprofessional. Still, it would be too awkward to cancel now and, as I hadn't seen Lana in months, disappointing for both Lana and me. Further, I couldn't tell if Amelia's breezy attitude about my night away was genuine or if she was disappointed in me. Her absorption in her phone was making her opinion about it hard to read.

The pilot approached us then and invited us to board the plane. I grabbed my little overnight bag and followed Amelia across the tarmac and up the walkway, still feeling like a grubby little sister next to her.

The inside of the plane was more spacious than I'd anticipated. The seats were all a creamy white leather, wide and inviting. There was a small eating nook in one area of the plane and, I noted, a miniscule bedroom next to the surprising large toilet and shower room. Already seated, tablet on her lap, Amelia looked up at me after I'd taken the tour.

"Do you like it?"

"My God! It's going to spoil me for regular flying for the rest of my life."

The pilot reappeared. "Please be seated and buckle in. We'll be departing in a couple of minutes."

Amelia was in a set of chairs that faced each other, and I took the one across from her. She continued to look at her tablet, and I took that as a sign to start working myself. I pulled out my new laptop and opened it, reviewing once again the various art shows that were happening this week. While I'd firmly decided on at least three shows to visit, I had room in my schedule for one more. I'd narrowed down my choices to about ten more shows that had potential, and after I logged onto the plane's wireless, I scrolled through the websites for the thousandth time that week. I was so engrossed in my search, I hardly noticed us taxiing and becoming airborne until the pilot announced that we were free to move about the cabin. I looked up, surprised to see Amelia watching me. She saw me see her stare and didn't look away. Not able to control the tumult of feelings her directness caused, I blushed under her gaze.

"You're a very focused person, Doctor," she said finally.

"It's a habit from grad school. If I get locked into what I'm doing, I'm not tempted to stop. Now I do it with almost everything."

"I wish I had that kind of discipline. I get distracted very easily. Especially by things I'd rather look at."

I felt my entire body flush and start sweating.

Seeing my face, she laughed. "I'm sorry, Doctor. I didn't mean to embarrass you."

"You didn't exactly embarrass me..."

"I've been meaning to talk to you about something." Her expression was serious. "You likely saw the society spread featuring us at the dinner a few weeks ago."

I nodded.

"And all of that talk at dinner with Brent when we were there also seemed to embarrass you a great deal. I hope it doesn't bother you to be...associated with me in that way. The gossip-mongers always seem to want to hook me up with any woman I'm seen with. My sister Emma was once the subject of their dirty talk about me until my lawyer sent the newspaper a clear statement about us. There will likely be more of the same during this trip. If it bothers you, please say so, and I can do the same thing as I did with Emma for you."

I hesitated, weighing my words carefully. "It doesn't really bother me, Miss Winters. I'm surprised by it, I guess, and a little embarrassed, but I wouldn't say it bothers me."

"I imagined you *would* be embarrassed," she said, looking a little defeated.

"What do you mean?" Her reaction surprised me.

She made eye contact with me. "To think that anyone would believe you would be with me in that way. I should be so lucky."

I looked away, not sure how to respond. I was quiet long enough that she apparently took my silence as assent, and when I looked back at her, she was staring out the window, her expression somewhat melancholy.

Before I could chicken out, I said, "Anyone would be lucky to be with *you*, Amelia." It was the first time I'd called her by her first name, and my heart raced with my daring. She looked back at me, obviously completely surprised, and then laughed. "I'm sorry. I'm being a petulant child. I wanted to hear you say something nice about me, and I basically forced you to. I shouldn't have brought it up."

Before I could retort, the co-pilot opened the door to the cockpit and walked back toward us. "Is there anything I can get for you ladies? Wine? A cocktail? We should be arriving at Teterboro in about two hours."

"Let's start this trip out right, James," Amelia said. "A bottle of the 2004 Belle Epoque, please."

He disappeared into the small galley kitchen, returning a few minutes later with two glasses and a bucket of ice. He set them down and returned a moment later with the champagne. He showed the label to Amelia and she gave her approval, flashing me a quick look to show her amusement with his formality. He popped the cork expertly, poured us two glasses, and excused himself.

"To a successful trip," Amelia said, holding up her glass. We clinked glasses, and I drank some of the very best champagne money can buy.

Chapter Thirteen

Lana seemed a little surprised to see me climb out of a limousine but didn't say anything about it. It'd been over a year since we last saw each other in Paris, and I was happy that she looked so much better than she had at the end of her degree. Her color was back, and she looked healthy and happy. A tall redhead, she had always been something of a fashion plate, and a year in New York hadn't changed that. We hugged for a long time, Lana exclaiming over my weight loss and long hair.

"Mostly it's long out of laziness," I said, following her inside past her doorman. "I kept meaning to get it cut, but you know how it is at the end of the PhD. Between the defense, graduation, and interning, I had no time at all."

"Well, it looks fantastic. I mean, you can pull off short hair, which is lucky for you, but I think this longer style looks amazing on you." Lana pushed the button for the elevator, and we stood there gazing at each other fondly as we waited.

"So how is MOMA?" I asked.

She sighed happily. "It's everything I've ever dreamed of. I mean, the money is shit. I think all museum money is shit, really, unless you're the director or something. It certainly wouldn't pay for my apartment if I didn't live with Jess. But the work is incredible. The art is incredible. Even the artists I've met have been incredible, for the most part. I keep saying the word, but basically everything is incredible. I couldn't be happier. If you have time this week, I'd happily take you on a private tour after hours."

Her apartment was far larger than any I'd ever seen in New York, with floor-to-ceiling windows all along the far edge of the room. The view of Columbus Circle and Central Park was impressive, and I stood there for a moment watching the traffic as Lana prepared coffee. Unlike my other friends in New York, who were lucky to have room for a pullout couch, Lana had a guest bedroom. The luxury of all of this was striking after our hovel-like, hole-in-the-wall apartments in Paris. The difference now was that Jess, Lana's partner, was a doctor, and between the two of them, they could afford a nice place. While I'd met Jess a few times while we were in graduate school, she had been interning and doing residency here in New York while Lana was in school in Paris, so the two had been forced to live separately the entire time Lana was studying there. Jess flew over as often as she could and vice versa, and the two of them generally hid from the world when she was visiting Paris. The stress of the degree and of being apart had taken a toll on Lana's health. By the time of her dissertation defense last year, she'd looked skeletal, she was drinking far more than was healthy for anyone, and she had a dry, rasping cough that wouldn't go away. Seeing her here in this beautiful place looking as good and healthy as she did now made me more hopeful about my own future.

Lana appeared a moment later with a French press and two mugs, setting them down on her coffee table. "Do you take cream or sugar? I feel like I used to know."

"Neither, thanks." I sat down across from her.

We sipped at the coffee quietly for a few moments before Lana said, "So tell me about this job. It's some kind of art business? Must be a pretty impressive one if you're jetting off to New York and riding around in limousines."

Since she was working in exactly the field we'd been trained in, I could sense her dismissal of the work, even, perhaps, her disapproval, and this didn't surprise me at all. I too had been somewhat dismissive of my job until I was actually doing it. I spent the next ten minutes explaining the work to her, doing my best to make it sound as impressive as it actually was. A born New Yorker, Lana, who was only vaguely familiar with the Winters Corporation, didn't understand what the name meant and implied in New Orleans, and despite my enthusiasm and excitement, I was doing nothing to change her mind.

"But you're basically in sales," she said finally, "and an errand girl."

"I mean, I guess technically, but it's more than that, too." I sounded unsure, even to myself.

She was still looking at me critically, but instead of getting angry, I found her disdain amusing. Seeing my expression she smiled at me. "I'm sorry. I don't mean to come off like such an ass. It's just..." She shrugged.

"I know, I know. It's not what I've trained for. I'm well aware of that. My Aunt Kate and everyone I know has basically made it clear that I'm wasting my talents."

"When you first told me about it in your e-mail last month, it sounded like you meant for this job to be a stop-gap until you could get on at a university down there. I hear you talking now, and it sounds more and more like you want to do this as a career."

I was surprised into silence and took a long time to reply. "I don't think I'd say that, but I do love it. I'm surprised at how much I love it, in fact. My boss..."

"Tell me about her," Lana said, watching me strangely. "You've mentioned her a few times. I take it she's big shit down there?"

I paused again, blushing as I thought about Amelia. While I desperately tried to think up a way to cover my embarrassment, I noticed Lana watching me, eyebrows raised. "Wait a minute," she said. She set her coffee down on the table and looked at me closely. "What's this? Do I detect something here? Is something going on between you two?"

"I don't know what you mean." I was looking anywhere but at her.

She laughed. "Sure you don't."

The blush on my face grew hotter and darker, and I had no immediate response to what she'd just said. The truth was, I'd been thinking about talking to Lana about Amelia since I'd had the idea of staying with her. Now as I thought of it, I realized what I'd been hiding even from myself: discussing Amelia was one of the main reasons I'd wanted to see Lana. I'd felt strange the last few weeks with no one to talk to about all of the feelings I was having. While Meghan was trying to be understanding, I still felt awkward bringing Amelia into conversation with her in part because of her clear antagonism toward Amelia. Lana didn't know Amelia, and she was the only lesbian I had even been close with. I knew she could help me figure things out. Still, that didn't make bringing up Amelia with her any easier. Now, put on the spot, I realized Amelia was the last thing I wanted to discuss.

As I tried to make myself broach the topic, I saw Lana's face split into a wide, knowing grin as she watched my struggle. She'd always read me better than almost anyone I knew, with or without words.

I started to sputter some excuse, too embarrassed now to say anything. However, before I could speak a single word, the door to the apartment opened and Lana's partner Jess came in, still dressed in her scrubs. An attending at Columbia Medical, she was in every way impressive and intimidating. Tall and muscular with a no-nonsense short haircut and a square, masculine face, she filled any room she entered with a strong sense of confidence and authority. Lana sprang to her feet and raced over to her, the two of them embracing and then kissing, deep and long. My face heated up again, and I looked away, trying to give them a moment of privacy as they briefly caught up.

"So nice to see you again, Chloé," Jess told me as she shook my hand. "You're looking well."

"We were just talking about her new boss," Lana said, grinning at me. I threw her a warning glare and she winked.

"That's right," Jess said. "Lana told me you were here on business. Some kind of art sales or something?"

"Something like that." I didn't want to explain myself again.

Jess looked sympathetic. "Well, I'm sorry you have to do that kind of work. I know it's hard to get a place in a museum or university in your field. I hope you're making a lot of money, at least."

Lana pushed at her playfully. "Don't put her on the spot, Jess." Turning to me, she asked, "Do you want to freshen up before we go out to eat? I know Jess needs a few minutes."

Glancing down at my ratty clothes, I excused myself and heard them murmur happily together as I closed the door to my bedroom behind me. Third wheel again, I thought to myself, a jolt of true envy spiking through my stomach.

❖

"I hope you don't mind," Lana said once we were seated at the restaurant.

I looked over at her and frowned, not following her drift. "What do you mean?"

She looked amused.

"She's being a vague little pest, like usual." Jess grabbed Lana's hand and squeezed it playfully. "She means because this is a lesbian restaurant."

I glanced around us, trying to appear casual. There were absolutely no men in the room, including the servers and hosts. To hide my nervous excitement at being surrounded by lesbians, I turned sarcastic. "Amazing that there could be enough of 'you people' in New York City to warrant your own restaurant." I put my fingers up in scare quotes as I said "you people" to indicate that I was, if feebly, joking.

Jess laughed and Lana stuck out her tongue.

"Of course I don't mind," I told Jess. "Why would I?"

"I took Chloé to places like this all over Paris," Lana explained.

"Without me?" Jess said, pretending to be jealous.

"Oh, you know me, baby," Lana said, her voice low and conspiratorial. "I still like to look even when I know I can't touch."

Jess blushed and looked down at her menu to cover up her embarrassment. This was apparently the way the two of them flirted in public.

"There's dancing upstairs," Lana added, turning back to me. "I thought maybe we could pop up there after we eat."

"That's not really fair to Chloé, is it?" Jess asked. "What will she do while we're dancing?"

"Oh, don't worry about her. I dragged her dancing with the ladies plenty of times in Paris. She claims to hate it, but I know she loves moving that tight little ass around as much as the next girl. And she's always getting hit on, no matter where we go. Men, women—Chloé reels them in like fishes."

"It's fine, really," I told Jess. "I want you guys to have a good time too."

Jess looked a little skeptical but let it drop. We spent the next few minutes catching up, Jess and I trying to get to know one another a little better. She and Lana met during their undergrad years at Yale, and Jess had grown up near there in Eastern Connecticut. She was, to my Southern eyes, the prototypical New England Yankee: stern, quiet, and reserved. If it weren't for her masculine haircut and her trim physique, she would have made the perfect WASP.

When Jess excused herself to the restroom, several women in the restaurant watched her move across the room, their eyes seeming to eat up every inch of her. I could, in theory, see Jess's appeal. Tall and commanding, she had a certain kind of presence and obvious physical strength that was attractive, but I was starting to recognize that my own taste in women was something softer. The idea that I had a type of woman was, in its own way, as much of an admission of my true feelings for Amelia as anything else, and I tried as hard as I could to ignore that idea for the time being.

"So tell me about this Amelia," Lana said, as if reading my mind. "It's obvious she's got you thinking things."

My initial defiance quickly died out when I met Lana's gaze. "I want to talk about it, Lana, but I just don't know how I feel."

"But you're attracted to her."

"Something like that." I paused to think. "The thing is, I don't think I could go further than that. I mean, I don't know if I'm, you know, *attracted* to her so much as I find her attractive. Does that make sense?"

Lana shook her head and I laughed.

"I know it sounds vague, but that's where I'm at right now. Being attracted to someone means something more than finding them interesting and appealing, or even good-looking. I like being around her. I think she's gorgeous. But doing more than that?" I shook my head. "I just don't know if I could."

Lana shrugged. "Why don't you try it and find out? You never know."

"You never know what?" Jess asked, sitting down.

I threw Lana a look, and she winked at me. "Nothing," Lana said. "Girl stuff."

Not wanting to talk about myself anymore, and while I'd heard the story a few times before, as we ate I goaded them into telling me the story of how they met and fell in love, feeling a sense of longing suffuse me like never before as they played off one another during the telling. Something of my feelings must have shown in my eyes as, once they'd finished the story, Jess laughed.

"I'm sorry," I said, trying to shrug off the sinking feeling in my stomach. "It just gives us singletons hope to hear that it can happen like that. Almost like magic. Pieces falling into place to bring two people together and all that."

They grabbed each other's hands and looked at each other happily. Lana turned to me. "We were going to tell you this later, but we have some big news."

"Oh?" I'd already expected something like this from the way they'd been mooning over each other all night.

"We haven't told anyone, so you're the first to know that we're engaged," Jess explained, her voice brimming with satisfaction.

We all stood up and embraced, and Lana shrieked happily as she showed off a ring I somehow hadn't noticed earlier. Other patrons clapped for them once it was clear what we were talking about, and the manager sent over a bottle of champagne. I toasted to their success and watched the two of them greet a few friends and acquaintances, sharing the news with them at the same time.

While I was happy for them, I couldn't seem to shake my almost overwhelming envy, something I recognized in myself with a deep sense of shame. Most of the time when I found out a couple was moving on to the next step, I was simply happy for them. This, however, felt different somehow, more poignantly personal.

I had, after all, known Lana for years, I told myself. It seemed like she would be going away for good now. In an effort to cover up my mounting dismay, I emptied my glass of champagne and took another one, drinking both as quickly as I could. If anything, though, the alcohol made my sense of defeat seem deeper, bleaker.

Lana and Jess invited three of their friends to join us at our table, and I found myself sitting next to Gia, a pretty Italian woman who was apparently unattached to the other two women who joined us. We all introduced ourselves, and Lana and Jess explained how the five of them knew each other. Throughout the story, I sensed Gia watching me. I looked over at her a couple of times only to find her still staring at me. The wine was beginning to help me loosen up, and I finally met her gaze dead-on, boldly challenging her to look away first. When she didn't, I saw one corner of her mouth lift up in a slight smirk, as if she were daring me to make the first move.

I decided to take the bait, but I wanted to appear casual at the same time. I moved closer to her so it would be harder for the others to hear us. "Is something wrong with my face? Do I have cranberry on me or something?"

"On the contrary. Your face is perfect. Perhaps one of the most beautiful I've ever seen." Her trilling, purring accent lifted her words beautifully, musically.

Despite being emboldened by wine, I found the flattery a bit much for me and felt myself color to the roots of my hair. Gia laughed, moving back a little. "I'm sorry. I've been told I come on too strong. It's the Italian in me. But I do, as they say, tell it like it is."

I tried to come up with a response, but my head was a little too foggy from the wine. Gia moved even closer than before, her lips almost on my ear. "Would you like to get out of here?" she whispered.

Taken aback, I almost jumped back, staring at her in shock.

Gia laughed aloud. "I mean, do you want to go upstairs? For dancing?" She made a little gesture with her fingers to represent legs moving.

Nodding dumbly, I got to my feet, picking up my purse and jacket.

"Where are you two headed?" Lana asked, her expression knowing and roguish.

Gia grabbed my hand. "I'm taking the good doctor here for a spin."

The way she used my title reminded me suddenly of Amelia, and a stab of guilt pierced my muffled, slightly intoxicated brain. I was, however, drunk enough to try to ignore it and let myself be pulled away. Gia grinned in happy triumph as I moved closer to her, clasping her hand.

Jess looked completely floored to see us leave together, but Lana laughed, throwing her head back. "We'll be up there in a little while. Have fun, you two."

It was all I could do to keep up with the smaller woman as she pulled me behind her and up the two flights of stairs to the dance floor. We checked my bag and coat and walked into a dark room throbbing with pulsing bass. Gia pulled me into the center of the floor that, at this early hour, was still relatively uncrowded. Putting her hands on my lower back, she pulled me in close, rocking my hips into hers. I let her lead me and started to relax into her body a little as time passed. Somewhat shorter than I, she looked up at me, the room far too loud for talking, which was probably good as I would likely have been slurring my words. When I'd stood up I'd realized how drunk I'd allowed myself to get. The liquor helped in other ways, however, and the longer we danced, the more I enjoyed the sensation of her body against mine.

I closed my eyes for a while, letting her rock me slowly around the room, her hands growing a little bolder now and again, tracing up and down my back and finally groping my ass. I sighed into her hair, a slow heat building between my legs. Opening my eyes to look at her, I saw that Lana, Jess, and their friends had joined us on the dance floor, and Lana and Jess were watching us, clearly amused. I rolled my eyes at them and then looked back at Gia, a little dazed.

She stopped rocking us. Then, standing on her toes to get close to my ear, she said, just loud enough for me to hear, "I meant what I asked earlier. Do you want to get out of here with me? My apartment isn't far."

Too stunned to reply, I stood there, gaping at her long enough that she laughed. "I think you want to, Chloé, but perhaps we should take another spin around the room first while you decide?"

Before I could reply, I caught a quick movement out of the corner of my eye and, turning my head toward it, thought I caught the tail end of someone I recognized leaving the room. Puzzled, I stepped out of Gia's arms, trying to piece my drunken thoughts together in a semblance of order. Who could it be? I wondered, my brain fuzzy. A few seconds passed between the memory of the person I'd just glimpsed and recognition. My stomach dropped and a cascading sense of terror suffused my every vein.

It was Amelia.

Not bothering to explain myself, I dashed from the room, actually running to catch up with her. At the top of the stairs, I could see her disappearing around the bend and started running again, nearly tripping down the second flight.

I caught up with her just outside the doors to the restaurant. She was hailing a taxi, but I managed to catch her attention before she succeeded in getting one. She turned toward me, clearly waiting for me to say something. I was panting from the run, and now that I'd caught her, I had nothing concrete to say. What had I planned to do? The answer was somehow missing from my brain. Instead, I just stared at her, the terror from my earlier recognition of her upstairs still palpably present and crushing.

"Doctor," she finally said, nodding curtly.

"Listen, Amelia—"

"I see you and your friend had some catching up to do." Her voice had a puzzlingly cold quality to it I couldn't pinpoint. She refused to meet my eyes.

"No, you see, we met up with some people here. And Gia, that is, the woman I was with upstairs, I mean, we're not..." I cursed myself for not being able to make myself clear.

Amelia turned her back to me and waved again at the passing cabs, this time with success. "It doesn't matter who she was, Doctor. Not to me. You're free, of course, to do what you please on your own time."

I finally recognized her tone as pained and disappointed. I could also tell that she meant anything but what she was saying, and before she climbed into the cab, I saw that her eyes were brimming with tears.

"Wait," I said desperately, grabbing the door before she closed it, "let me explain."

"There's no need," she said coldly. I heard her voice catch on a sob and then she continued. "I'll see you tomorrow morning."

Out of energy, I let the door close and stood there stiffly, despondent as she rode away. After a long time, I turned to find Gia, Lana, and Jess standing in the doorway to the restaurant. They'd obviously witnessed what had just transpired. Gia was livid and, after excusing herself to Lana and Jess, stormed off down the street. We watched her go, and I took the moment to try to calm myself. Unable to delay the inevitable any more, I finally walked closer to the Jess and Lana. Jess squeezed my shoulder, once, and then walked back inside, understanding that I needed time alone with my friend.

Once she was gone, I found Lana was looking at me sympathetically. "Your first lesbian drama." She patted my arm. "And it was classic. You had one woman in tears and another storming off. You're already a pro."

Laughing despite myself, I pushed at her arm. "Fuck you." Tears sprang to my eyes and, seeing them, she pulled me in close for a hug.

"So that's the famous Amelia Winters," she finally said.

"Yes." I wiped my eyes. "And I think I just blew it."

"You didn't blow it, Chloé. You were dancing with another woman. No big deal. If she's a grownup, she'll get over it. If anything, you just made something clear. She's obviously crazy about you." She paused and, looking me in the eyes, said, "And you made it obvious how you feel about her, at least to me. It's obvious that you care about her a lot."

I nodded, and my acceptance, the recognition of my true feelings, crashed over me in a panicky wave. Suddenly I was sobbing, and Lana led me over to a bus stop bench and held my shoulders as I cried.

After I'd settled down a little, Lana and I sat on the bench and she continued to rub my back. I was holding a soggy, snot-soaked tissue in my hands, twisting it nervously. I desperately wanted to talk with Lana about my feelings for Amelia, but I didn't know how to begin. I also felt like saying it out loud would make it real, like there would be no coming back from any announcement I made.

As if sensing my dilemma, Lana said, "Did I ever tell you about Tracy Parker?"

I shook my head, still staring at my disgusting tissue.

"Tracy Parker was my first major crush. I mean, I had crushes like all kids on my teachers and TV stars, but Tracy was the real deal. I couldn't think about anything else. Just seeing her would make my heart race, and I'd get these cold flop sweats, you know?"

I squeezed her hands in mine, still unable to speak.

"I couldn't sleep, I could barely eat. I was a mess." She paused for a moment, and, glancing at her, I saw the ghost of a sad smile on her face.

"Anyway," she continued, "I started leaving her little gifts taped to her locker. You know—kid's stuff. A velvet rose. A chocolate bar. A really bad poem."

"How old were you?"

"Sixth grade." She paused again, and I saw something like pain pass across her face. "Anyway, to no one's surprise but my own, I eventually creeped her out. I got sent to the principal's office and my mom was called in to talk with me and the school therapist."

"What did your mom say?"

"She was quiet the whole time. We both were. The therapist did all the talking. He told her that it was just a phase, that a lot of girls go through a little lesbian thing when they hit puberty, and not to worry about it. I'd be fine and grow up normal. He also told us that I needed to understand that it wasn't right to try and force myself on anyone else, and he suggested that I started seeing a therapist outside of school to help straighten me out."

"Asshole."

She agreed, and I could tell from her expression that the experience still hurt her.

"Did your mom talk to you afterward?"

She turned toward me, and I saw that her eyes were glimmering with tears. "You're damn right she did. The moment we were outside of the school, I could tell that she was livid with rage. I'd never seen her so upset. At first I thought she was mad at me, but when we finally got on the subway to go home, she gave me this big hug and told me not to listen to him. She said that my feelings were natural and real and not a phase, and that she'd support me no matter who I decided I wanted to fall in love with."

My own eyes were stinging now, and I waited for her to go on.

"It's important, you see, to have someone that has your back when you're coming out. I mean, I've known a lot of people, men and women, who had to do it on their own, and it was the pits. But you're not alone, okay? You can tell me anything, ask me anything. Or not—it's up to you. But I'm here for you, okay?"

We embraced, and I started sobbing again, so grateful and relieved that one person, at least, knew my secret. We stayed there for a long time, long after the bars released their patrons, and long after the traffic had nearly died out. Jess joined us after a while, carrying my purse and jacket. She sat down without a word, quietly listening to me and Lana talk and talk about Amelia.

Finally worn out, I went with Lana and Jess back to their place, where I fell into a restless, anxious sleep plagued with nightmares that kept me up for hours.

Chapter Fourteen

Makeup can only do so much for a person after a night like that, but I did my best to cover the damage I'd done. It did nothing, of course, for my hangover, but my headache and achiness felt a little like penance after the mess I'd made of everything. Jess and Lana exclaimed over my work clothes, Jess asking details about my tailor, obviously interested in the idea of hiring one. None of us mentioned the bags under my eyes or their cause, and we made plans to meet on my next free day, Sunday, for brunch.

When Amelia's driver called from downstairs, I rode the elevator with mounting trepidation. I couldn't think of an easy way to recover from a scene like we'd had, and I was very much afraid that the awkwardness would be too much to overcome. I didn't want to get another job, especially when this one had turned out to be so enjoyable and lucrative. Moreover, I felt terrible about what I'd done. I chided myself for the thousandth time that morning. This was precisely why you shouldn't get involved with someone from work, I thought. Steeling myself to face the problem head-on, I decided that when I saw Amelia, I would simply broach the subject without beating around the bush. While I wasn't ready to admit my feelings to her yet, we needed to talk about what was happening between us or my position with the company would become untenable.

Her face, when the driver opened the door for me, put all these plans to rest. She was drawn and pale—paler even than she usually was, which is saying something. Her sunglasses were on despite the darkness of the car's interior, and her whole body seemed to be drawn in on itself, closed off. She'd chosen the seat in the limo that faces the front of the cab and had drawn into the farthest corner from any other seat in the car, legs folded around themselves twice, pretzel-fashion. She looked up at me quickly in recognition of my presence and then returned to looking at her tablet, effectively silencing me for the entire trip.

We were doing our first reconnaissance missions today before the big dinner tonight. We'd scheduled meetings with two up-and-coming artists Amelia was interested in meeting, one of whom I'd actually studied in graduate school. We would be evaluating them together and deciding whether to distribute either one or both. While more and more artists have agents, Amelia believed agents weren't always best at getting distributors for an artist's work, in addition to the fact that artists made more money if they dealt directly with the seller. Further, if an artist we talked to this week insisted on going through his or her agent, we could simply contact the agent if we were interested in selling their work.

Tomorrow, on Saturday afternoon, we were attending a Sotheby's auction that promised to be one of the art world's highlights of the year. In fact, our trip here was primarily designed and planned so Amelia could attend this auction.

Two evening functions were planned as well for tonight and tomorrow. Tonight's was a charity dinner, a little like the one we'd attended in New Orleans, and tomorrow's was an artist's opening reception. Amelia had made a dinner reservation for Saturday near the warehouse in Brooklyn where the reception was taking place and had been very hush-hush about it, looking mysterious every time I asked her for details. I'd been excited to have dinner alone with her, knowing that most of our other evenings were booked with other people and events, but now, after the scene last night, the idea of being alone with her terrified me.

The first gallery we visited was a typical Manhattan affair, with stark-white walls and floor and minimal décor beyond the paintings. The saleswomen were those narrow, pinched women you expect in a place like that, dressed in solid black with high, tight hairdos, both of them probably models or actresses when they weren't here. Their looks mirrored their attitude, which was cold and aloof. They gave us the cold shoulder and only briefly greeted us as we walked around. Only when the artist, Pierre Gasteau, appeared, all smiles and handshakes, did they seem to understand that we were worth noticing. After that it was all ass-kisses. Pierre treated us to lunch at the 21 Club, a first visit for me and a genuine pleasure except for the company. His arrogance and machismo disgusted me, and neither of us was able to say much of anything as he gushed about himself and his work at effusive length.

The next gallery was more to my taste, with students working the floor and an eclectic, bohemian style of décor. The room had the quality of a workshop, with the artist and the some of the students actually working on pieces in the back of the room. The artist, Audrey Pieuon, was also French, and I was more familiar with her artwork than Pierre's, having studied her work in school. Audrey taught at the School of Visual Arts in the fine arts department and obviously employed her students at her gallery. While her work was now widely recognized and occasionally on view at various modern art museums around the world, she had yet to achieve the kind of acclaim that gave her celebrity status, and it showed in her behavior with us. She was far friendlier with us than Pierre had been, whose kindness had been phony and grasping. Audrey was also familiar with the Winters Corporation and asked both of us questions about the other artists we distributed and the restoration work we did.

"Is this your new piece?" I managed to ask when we were standing near it in the workshop. I hadn't expected to be starstruck but found myself almost tongue-tied the moment she appeared. Amelia had thrown me a couple of strange looks at my silence, so I was making an effort to get over it.

"Yes, and it's giving me migraines," she said, frowning at the piece. Audrey was primarily famous for her glass and mosaic work, and some critics had gone so far as to call her the next Louis Comfort Tiffany. Compared to most of her work, which was usually quite small—often small enough to hold in your hands—the scale of the new piece was impressive, stretching nearly twelve feet square. She had begun only one corner of the piece, the colors of the glass shards she used in her work sparkling with the light. A ladder stood next to it, and she climbed up, pointing at various areas and explaining what it would look like when it was done.

"I have lived away from France for almost a decade now, yet I always go back there in my artwork. They say an artist puts her identity in her work, so I guess France is mine."

She excused herself to help some of her student employees, which gave Amelia and me a chance to take a closer look at the work throughout the gallery. Amelia walked away from me, ostensibly to be alone with her thoughts, but it was clear that she simply didn't want to be around me. Sighing, I turned toward the centerpiece of the gallery, a large vase composed of various colors of glass punctuated by metal fragments throughout. Coming closer, I could see that the metal was actually French franc coins, which had been out of circulation since the currency reform in Europe. The piece was titled *Lost Singularity*.

We left after having a cup of lovely French coffee prepared by our hostess, and by then we were running a little late. The charity dinner started at seven, and now we were locked in rush-hour traffic. I'd been expecting to talk about what we'd seen today after both galleries, but Amelia was still not talking to me. She kept her eyes firmly rooted to her tablet. I had nothing with me to work on, so I sat there in quiet frustration as we slowly squeezed our way through from the Village to midtown Manhattan. Staring out the darkened windows, I watched as the teeming masses rushed home on the sidewalks, thousands expelled from the office buildings around us. The silence in the car was made more poignant by the contrast to the busyness outside, and I felt the crushing weight of my situation all the more clearly for having nothing else to think about. When we finally pulled up to the Peninsula, our hotel, my nerves were completely shattered. Overtired and anxious, the thought of making nice at a dinner party all evening was almost more than I could bear.

Amelia had reserved a suite connected to a second room for me. The suite and my room were the very definition of elegance and luxury, with lush bedding, enormous bathrooms, and elegant décor. Our rooms were connected by a door, and I was very happy to close it behind me as I excused myself to get ready. I was so relieved to be alone I almost started crying. There were flowers on the desk in my room and a small bottle of wine, which I quickly opened, pouring most of it into a tall glass. I had exactly thirty-five minutes to make myself presentable and human again, and I figured the wine would help.

My luggage had been set up in the walk-in closet, the gowns I'd brought hung up. I found a small note on one of the gowns.

I think this one would be most suitable for tonight, don't you agree?
—Amelia

Her audacity was galling, and the note, coupled with her ridiculous childishness all day, turned my day-long depression to near-blinding rage. Spitefully, I grabbed the other gown and took it with me into the bathroom. For the next twenty minutes I slammed around as I got ready. My anger energized me, and I spent the entire time attempting to make myself look completely and utterly unattainable. Rather than be hurt by her childishness, I decided to fight her ice with my own fire.

When I came into her suite, Amelia was standing with her back to the room, staring out the window. Even from behind she was breathtaking, and once again my plans for how to behave toward her took a nosedive. Hearing me, she turned, and for the first time today I saw beneath the coldness to the deep hurt underneath, but only for a second. Her eyes hardened quickly, making me doubt what I'd seen.

"I see you chose the other dress," she said.

"Yes," I answered simply, trying to mimic her cold tone. "It's more comfortable."

She didn't reply, and I followed her out of our rooms and downstairs to our waiting car. Despite having hurried, we were still running late, and I could feel her mounting tension as the car eased itself through evening traffic. The event was held at the Edison

Ballroom, and as we pulled up to get in line behind the cars in front of us, I could see a red carpet in front and the flash of cameras.

Two cars away from the head of the line, Amelia suddenly turned toward me. "Listen. Can we put this…misunderstanding behind us for the evening? We have a lot of work to do tonight, and it will go more smoothly if we can look like we like each other."

"I do like you, Amelia—"

"I know. I know you do, and I'm sorry for how I've behaved today. I've been very foolish."

"You haven't been foolish at all. I'm the one who acted like an idiot yesterday. I'm sorry. I really am."

"So am I." Her face was still drawn and wary, and she seemed reluctant to say the wrong thing. "Let's put it behind us."

I had just enough time to nod my reply when the door was opened for us, the flash of cameras blinding me as we climbed out. Amelia looked cool and collected, and I heard a press liaison tell one of the scribbling journalists who she was. No one knew my name yet, so Amelia provided it, making me realize that I would no longer be her anonymous "blonde" after tonight. Placing her hand on the small of my back, she led me through the flashing entryway and into the luxurious interior of one of the most exclusive ballrooms in the city. Attendants took our coats, issuing us a small coin for retrieval, and we got in line to wait for our table assignment.

As we waited, Amelia linked her arm with mine and drew closer. "You look wonderful this evening," she whispered. "I meant to say so earlier."

"Even in the wrong dress?" I whispered back, trying to sound coy.

She responded with a wide grin, and I was relieved to see that some of her earlier coldness was beginning to thaw. She seemed genuinely excited to be here, and I decided to join in her fun. Twice today I'd been overjoyed to experience a part of New York life with which I was completely unfamiliar, and the opportunity simply to be in this building was a treat. I had to stop myself from gaping once we finally entered the ballroom proper. This was old, moneyed New York at its finest.

A smaller contingent of press had been invited inside, and they discreetly took photos of the two of us. Word had already made it inside who I was, and I was surprised to hear my name carefully spelled out between journalists as we walked by. A small dance floor had been set up near the stage, on which a big-band orchestra was already playing softly. Our table was once again near the mayor's, and I wasn't surprised to see a contingent of his bodyguards nearby.

Just as we were about to sit down, someone called out from across the room. "Amelia! Amelia darling!"

We turned to find an older woman approaching us, followed by an entourage of much-younger men. She and Amelia kissed cheeks, and the older woman grabbed her by the shoulders, looking her up and down.

"My heavens, Amelia, where on earth do you get such wonderful clothes? I'm going to have to fire my designer, I really am." Suddenly spotting me, she arched an eyebrow and said, her voice teasing, "And who, my dear, is this?"

"May I introduce Dr. Clothilde Deveraux," Amelia said, pulling me closer. She left her hand around my waist, sending shivers up my back. "Doctor, this is a very old friend of the family, Daphne Waters."

"I'm charmed," Daphne said, touching my fingers lightly with hers. Looking at Amelia, she said, "Where on earth do you find them, my girl?"

Amelia blushed at this and we shared a quick, embarrassed glance, but she recovered quickly, turning the conversation to other topics. She and Daphne walked together over to the bar, leaving me to make small talk with the young men Daphne had left behind. They were all clearly younger than I was, and it was tough going until I found a shared interest in Europe with the very striking-looking David. He told me his mother was British and his father Italian and that he visited both countries as often as possible. With his dark, wavy hair and slight five-o'clock shadow, he was the very picture of manly beauty in his beautiful silk suit. He warmed up to me quickly when we started talking about Florence, where his father grew up, and I let him fill the awkward pause as we waited for our hosts to return with our drinks, nodding in agreement with everything he said.

Soon, Amelia handed me a glass of champagne, and Daphne returned with a waiter and a tray of drinks for her followers, all of them effusive in their thanks.

"I won't keep you two lovebirds apart any longer," Daphne said after a few more minutes of chatting. "I know how tiresome it can be to talk to someone when you only have eyes for one another." This time I couldn't help but blush, and Daphne chortled at my response. Drawing close to me, she whispered, loud enough for everyone to hear, "You keep your eye on Amelia, dear heart. She's a real lady-killer." Laughing again, she winked at me and led her men back across the room to their table. They trailed after her like baby quail.

Amelia breathed a sigh of relief and turned toward me, her eyes merry with amusement. "I am sorry." She was trying not to laugh. "She's an old letch, and like all letches, she thinks everyone else is one too. My father would be appalled to see her here with her posse like this in public. She replaces them all every few months, by the way. God knows where she finds them. I'm sure they adore the money she dumps on them. Probably almost worth whatever they have to do to get it. My father will get a real laugh when I tell him about her next weekend." She paused, glancing at me furtively. "That reminds me: my parents are having their anniversary party next Saturday. I was wondering…well, you see, I hate going to parties at their house alone. All of my siblings are married or attached, which means I end up sitting by myself most of the time, or with some old aunt no one cares about. It would be nice to have a friend there."

"I'd be delighted," I said.

"Thank you." She looked genuinely pleased, and I was happy to note that the feeling was mutual. Whatever had happened last night was starting to seem like it was behind us.

The food was, for once, excellent, and our tablemates were surprisingly easy to talk to. One of the young women opposite me had recently been involved in a film that was starting to get Oscar buzz, though if I remembered correctly from the preview, she had only a minor role in it. She had her own posse of admirers in the form of two dumb-looking, hulking men on either side of her, both of whom were completely quiet the whole dinner. Amelia worked on her while I once again directed my efforts to an older couple sitting next to me, both of whom looked incredibly uncomfortable here. Only when I'd been talking with the woman for five minutes did I realize that she was an author I very much admired. This explained why she seemed out of place here, as she'd likely been encouraged by her agent to make an appearance in light of her new book. She was rumored to be something of a recluse, refusing readings and paid appearances, but her work was well-respected in literary circles.

Forcing myself to avoid gushing, I praised her work long enough to flatter her before switching topics to literature in general, at which point her husband, a famous English professor at NYU, joined in. By the time dessert was served, I had an appointment to meet with them in their apartment later this week to discuss one of their favorite artists, whose work was notoriously hard to get. They eventually excused themselves to go dance, and I watched them for several long minutes, always envious of couples that grew old together. I suddenly felt a tap on my shoulder and looked up to see David standing next to my chair.

"I wonder if I might have this dance, Doctor," he said, bowing slightly.

Too surprised to protest, I took his proffered hand and let him lead me to the floor. He led me into an easy, slow foxtrot after showing me a couple of beginner's steps. Once or twice I glanced over at Amelia, still seated at our table, but she seemed not to have noticed our departure or she was pointedly ignoring it. Daphne, however, was watching us closely, her eyes narrow slits of rage. I enjoyed her anger almost as much as I enjoyed dancing with David, who was a perfect gentleman throughout the dance. In fact, he was so entirely hands-off—as much as that was possible when dancing— that I began to suspect he was doing all of this on purpose to drive Daphne crazy. He could dance with me and make her angry, but his body language seemed to say that was as far as he was willing to go. It was a relief, actually, as it meant I could simply enjoy being with him without wondering about his motives. We danced through "In the Mood" and "Cry Me a River" before I claimed fatigue, and he kissed my hand before rejoining his mistress.

Amelia's eyes flickered my way as I sat back down, but her expression was unreadable. I waited as she arranged to meet with the starlet at her hotel in a couple of days to discuss artwork more fully. Once they'd exchanged numbers, Amelia excused herself, standing up and extending a hand to me.

"Would you come with me, Doctor?" she asked. Her eyes looked cold, angry. I mutely followed her, and she led us back toward the bathrooms.

In the ladies, we found a small sitting room that was blissfully empty at the moment, and, after the door closed behind us, she turned toward me, eyes blazing.

"Are you trying to drive me crazy?"

I was so completely surprised by her question, I could only sputter, "W-what do you mean?"

She had tears in her eyes now, and her face was the very picture of desolation. "You probably, no, you *must* understand by now how I feel about you. I don't expect you to feel the same way about me, but do you have to flaunt your indifference?"

I flushed all over and walked closer to her. "Amelia, I—"

"No, don't." She nearly jumped away. "Don't come near me and don't say anything." She covered her eyes with one hand. "I can't believe I'm acting this way. You have me completely in knots."

"Amelia, let me explain—"

"There's nothing to explain." She removed her hand. She was crying now, the tears making a wreck of her makeup. "The only thing I see, *know*, is that you'd rather dance with anyone but me." Sobbing now, she staggered over to the couch, sitting down on it heavily and covering her eyes with both hands. Completely flummoxed, I stood there, stunned, unsure what I should do.

"Please leave me," she said between sobs. "I'll be all right in a minute, but I need to be alone right now."

Ignoring her, I walked over and sat down on the couch next to her, putting my arms around her shoulders. She resisted for a moment and then turned, pulling me into an embrace and sobbing into my shoulder. I rubbed her back as she cried, making shushing noises once in a while. Her body eventually stopped hitching against me, but we stayed like that, holding each other for a long time. Finally, she pulled back, but she was unable to meet my eyes. She riffled through her purse for a moment before pulling out a tissue and her compact, wiping at her eyes and nose while she looked in the mirror.

"God, what a fuckup I am, Chloé," she said finally, putting them back in her purse. She met my eyes briefly and then looked away again, clearly embarrassed. "You must think I'm a complete ass."

"I don't." Throughout the crying, I'd been pushing myself to say something, anything, to convey what I felt for her, but the thought of actually admitting it to her was too overwhelming. To admit it would be to make it once and for all real. I took her hands in mine. They were soft and small, and holding them sent a thrill through me. "Really. I don't," I repeated, meeting her eyes.

She tried to laugh. "Let's blame my behavior on lack of sleep, shall we? I didn't sleep at all last night."

"I didn't either. After you left in the taxi, I was just one big bundle of nerves. I tossed and turned all night."

She rolled her eyes. "I'm quite the drama queen, I guess, spreading drama everywhere I go."

I shook my head. "You're not." Steeling myself again, I went a little further. "I would rather have been dancing with you. Last night and tonight. Only you."

Her eyes met mine in surprise, and I could see her mind weighing my words for sympathy or truth. "Do you mean that?" she finally whispered, her voice low and hoarse.

Before I could chicken out I nodded, and the reaction was stunning. Her face lit up from inside, and all the stress and worry that'd plagued it all day seemed to vanish in an instant. A smile spread across her features in slowly escalating stages of pure joy. She squeezed my hands in hers and then moved forward a little, looking at me with sudden shy trepidation. I met her smile and bent forward a little myself. Millimeters from kissing, so close I could smell her delicate perfume, I saw the door to the sitting room suddenly open, and we sprang apart.

It was Daphne, and she laughed when she saw us. "I see the two of you can't keep your hands off each other. Don't mind me!" She disappeared into a stall.

"Let's get out of here," Amelia said to me, her eyes desperate.

Heading to the entrance and getting our coats was like walking the gauntlet. Several times people that Amelia knew or friends of people she knew who wanted to talk to her interrupted us. Throughout the ordeal, which lasted well over an hour, my body was alive with jangling, cacophonous nerves that radiated throughout my whole nervous system. Amelia presented her usual, seemingly effortless geniality to everyone we came across, but I had to force myself not to scream at them to get out of our way. Her hand, however, which was firmly on my back across the entire ballroom, conveyed an entirely different emotion. I could feel it shaking and hot against the fabric of my dress, and sometimes it traveled slightly lower on my body than was, perhaps, polite in public. At one point, when her fingers brushed the top of my ass, I nearly screamed with impatience at the woman we were talking to. I was gripping Amelia's arm, and I gave it a particularly harsh squeeze when her fingers brushed so low. She threw me a wicked look that nearly made my legs melt. My vision darkened and my panties grew damp from my overpowering need. My hands were shaking too much to put my coat on, so I simply draped it over my arms to hide them underneath. Our limo took an eternity to reach us, both of us standing a couple of feet apart as we waited.

Safely inside the limousine, and almost before I knew what was happening, I found myself in Amelia's arms. She wrapped me in a passionate embrace, pulling me close, hard. When she kissed me, the kiss was warm, soft, and gentle. Her mouth was soft—softer than any man's. Her lips were full on mine, and, after a moment, I felt her tongue part my lips and enter. I moaned into her, my body alive with barely contained fire. My moan seemed to encourage her, and our tongues caressed. I strained my body against hers, and she tightened her arms around me. Desperate need flooded me, and I grew wet with desire. I wanted those soft, beautiful hands to touch me, explore my body, and quench the growing fire burning inside me.

I tried to move my arms away from her neck and down to her chest, to her beautiful, pert breasts, but before I could, her hands began exploring my body. Her face moved away from mine and her lips found my neck. She kissed me there, and my pleasure soared to new heights. I sighed and moaned, and her hands slipped down to my ass again.

"Oh!" I sighed with pleasure, arching my back. She began sucking on my neck, cradling my head with one hand while the other made its way down my thigh. Her own body was flush with mine, her nipples hard and erect against my chest through the thin fabric of her gown. I longed to see her body, and, I realized in a moment of clarity, I longed to be naked with her too. The thought no longer fazed me. In fact, there was nothing I wanted more than for the two of us to be naked together with our desire.

I moved my head to indicate that I wanted her to kiss my lips, and she obliged me. Her mouth was sweet for a moment, and then she became rougher again. She darted her tongue into me, running her nails down my back before biting down on my lower lip. The pain was minimal, but the pleasure it sent through my body was instantaneous and powerful. I moaned with pure animal desire.

"Please," I managed to say between kisses, not even sure I knew what I was begging for her to do, but fully aware that I wanted to her to do it to me, whatever it was.

Pushing me back with her hands and mouth, Amelia took the top, settling me back and onto the seat and climbing over me. Her mouth broke from mine and moved back down to my neck. I gasped at the heat this action caused and clutched at her back, pulling her closer. Her hands lifted me from underneath, pulling at the zipper along my back to find my flushed and hot skin underneath. I hissed at the pleasure this contact caused, and she leered down at me before kissing me again. I arched into her body, my legs pinned beneath her, groaning in frustration.

"Take it off!" I pleaded, clawing at my dress with shaking hands.

She laughed and kissed me again. "We'll be at the hotel soon, darling. We can take it off in my room."

Waiting seemed intolerable, and I groaned out my frustration at her words. She laughed and started kissing me again, ripping up the bottom of skirt and settling her body between my legs. My body rose to meet her hips, and I ground into her in desperation.

"No cheating," she said into my mouth before giving me a kiss so fierce it was almost painful. "You have to wait."

"Just touch me," I pled again, my voice whiny and broken, "Please. Just a little. Please."

I felt her fingers then, lightly, on my knees. She sat up a little, holding herself up with her left arm, and traced the fingers of her right hand slowly, achingly slowly, up my thigh. I was trembling all over at this point, and watching her slow progress nearly made me scream in frustration. She stopped just shy of my underwear line and trailed her fingers back down my leg toward my knee again. I groaned and then grabbed her hand, pulling it between my legs, toward my center. She pulled it back and laughed at me again.

"There," I said with a boldness I hardly knew I had in me. "I want you there. Inside me."

She leaned down and kissed me again, slowly, softly. "All good things come to those who wait."

The car stopped then, and she moved away from me, giving me room to sit up. She had just enough time to pull up my zipper before the driver opened the door, but I was still blushing as we climbed out, unable to meet his eyes.

I was breathless as we crossed the lobby of our hotel, my legs shaking so badly I could hardly walk. I felt dazed, almost drunk with desire. Once again, we stood carefully apart as we waited for the elevator to arrive. The doors opened and we stepped inside. Once the doors closed behind us, Amelia shoved me into the back wall and crushed my mouth under hers. My desire, already raging, hungrier than I'd ever experienced, escalated further, and I jerked her into me, grabbing her ass as leverage.

The doors opened and we staggered out, Amelia clutching my hand, her color higher than I'd ever seen it. She too was trembling and had a difficult time getting the keycard out of her purse. We laughed to be so close to what we wanted, and I finally had to help her get the card in the lock. We nearly tumbled inside, our mouths attached again, both of us kicking off our heels and throwing our purses and coats on the floor.

"Oh God," I moaned as she unzipped my dress, almost tearing it off me. Grabbing me by the hips, she pushed me toward the bedroom, steering me backward as our mouths locked together. The back of my knees hit the edge of the bed and I fell on it, gasping with surprise. She stood there, looking down at me with almost angry, hungry eyes.

"Take off the rest," she said, indicating my lingerie. "I want to watch you."

Fingers shaking, I undid the clasp of my bra. Her eyes lit up at the sight of my freed breasts, but she remained silent, still looking at me with lust-darkened eyes. I took longer with my garter belt and hose, teasing her a little, and saw her eyes flash with anger and impatience. Finally, I was down to only my underwear.

"Let me," she said, stepping closer. Kneeling at the edge of the bed, she pulled them off slowly, laboring over their removal. When I was completely exposed, she gasped in pleasure, and her eyes, when she looked up at me, were deep and heated from within.

She pulled me to the edge of the bed, and then she had one of my nipples in her mouth, sucking it fiercely. I gasped and arched into her, throwing my head back in pleasure. She moved her mouth toward my other nipple, and I thrust it at her, pulling at the back of her head once she sucked it in. Her hair came loose from its tight French braid, and she took a moment to shake it free, pins flying into the bedroom. Finally finished, she returned her attentions to my nipples, which were now rock hard and painfully aroused. I felt her teeth lightly play with one of them and tensed, waiting and wanting her to bite down.

She continued to tease me until I groaned, "Please. Please," which was all I could manage. I felt her lips curve in amusement, and then she bit my nipple, making me whimper in desperation.

Her hands, all this time, had been resting on my knees, and she occasionally trailed them up and down the inside of my thighs, making my legs jump. Things were beginning to go from desperate to worse, my escalating desire starting to make me feel light-headed and weak. Almost as if sensing I could no longer wait, she moved her lips away from my nipples and started to kiss her way down my stomach. I froze, so desperate for what was coming I no longer knew how to react to what was happening. At the hairline below my belly button, she paused and looked up at me before kissing my inner thigh, making me shudder all over with pleasure. She thrust my legs apart, and then her mouth was on me.

The cascade of pleasure that washed through me made me groan loudly. Resting heavily on my arms, I threw my head back, rocking my hips into her mouth. Her tongue explored me, first lightly, then with rising pressure and heat, circling my clit and then dancing on it. The feeling of her tongue there made me jerk with electricity, and when her fingers, which had been resting lightly on my thighs, started moving, I thought I might scream. She traced her way slowly, by inches, toward my center until I finally felt what I so desperately needed. Her tongue and mouth still toying with my clit, flicking at it, circling it, sucking it in, she sank her fingers into me, and I took her fingers with my whole body as they moved inside. My hips responded of their own accord, lifting up so that her fingers could slip deeper inside. I shuddered with pleasure, but after just a thrust or two, she pulled them out again, and I moaned in frustration.

"Please!" I looked down and saw that she was grinning, triumphant with the power she had over my pleasure. Her joy and the teasing glint in her eyes made me hot with desire.

"I've waited so long for this, my darling." Her voice was low and husky. "I don't want it to be over so soon."

With a strength I wouldn't have thought she had, she managed to lift me momentarily and slid me farther onto the bed. She climbed onto the bed herself and lay atop me, kissing me again, long and deep on the mouth, then moving to my neck. My body arched into her, and I felt a single finger trail along my soaking-wet cleft. I gasped, and as her fingers came close to my clit, I thought I would finally come, but she pulled her fingers away again.

"You like that, my sweet?" she whispered against the skin of my neck.

"Yes. Yes!"

Her finger traced lazily up and down my slit, sometimes touching my clit, sometimes stopping just before she got to it. I thought I would explode with desire at any moment, but she never let me get there. She was in control the whole time, and that made me want her even more. Finally I felt her fingers slip inside me. She pushed and pulled at me from within, and in seconds she'd found the spot inside that began to push me over the edge. Noises were emerging from my mouth in a strange, wordless jumble, my mind beyond real language. I could feel my orgasm building as she massaged me inside and out, and when it finally crashed over me, my arms lost all their strength and I collapsed onto the bed behind me, thrashing against her mouth and fingers and screaming myself hoarse.

It was a long time before I had strength to even open my eyes. My body, after the final wave of ecstasy, had simply stopped functioning. I was completely and entirely spent. After a long, long time, and still feeling quite weak, I opened my eyes and realized tears were drying on my face. Sitting up and holding myself up on a shaky arm, I wiped at them distractedly, realizing they must have squeezed out of my eyes in pleasure. Amelia was still between my legs, resting her head on my thigh, and I stroked her hair. She seemed to come out of her own daze and looked up at me, her eyes veiled with something I couldn't read.

"Holy shit," I whispered, still stroking her hair. "I didn't know…I mean, I didn't realize it could be like that."

She smiled, finally, with what I realized was relief, and I was somewhat amused to understand that she had been worried about her performance. This despite all the screaming and yelling that'd just come out of my mouth. I motioned for her to move closer, and we both climbed up and onto the bed more fully, scooting over and onto the pillows. I was completely drained and, encased in her arms, felt a sudden desperate fatigue wash through me. She was stroking my hair now and, despite the fact that my nakedness felt a little strange against her dress, within her embrace felt like the most desirable place in the universe.

Chapter Fifteen

When I woke, bright light was already streaming through the window. My head still sleep-muddled, I propped myself up on one arm and looked around for a clock, finding nothing. The bed was also empty, but at some point Amelia must have pulled the blanket around us, as I was loosely covered with it. A silk bathrobe was lying on a chair nearby, and, glancing around shyly, I stood up and slipped into it, finding slippers under the chair. They were both a dark shade of pink—a color I would never choose for myself, but the feel of the robe on my naked skin was sensuous and slick.

Before I opened the door to the bedroom, I waited for a second, trying to gather my nerves. I'd slept with exactly ten people before this, most of them one-night stands, and never with a woman. I wasn't exactly experienced with the morning-after scenario, especially with someone I was beginning to care about. Somehow everything seemed more serious. I was decidedly frightened of saying or doing the wrong thing.

Taking a deep breath, I opened the door to find Amelia sitting at the small dining table, reading a newspaper. She looked up and smiled at me. Rather than making me less nervous, seeing her there in the morning sunlight made me instantly tongue-tied. Her gorgeous dark hair was down and framing her face, making her look even younger than usual. She was already showered and dressed, and she looked fresh and comfortable—not nervous like some people.

"Good morning," I finally managed, making my way to the other chair. I grabbed the coffee urn and poured myself a cup.

"Good morning. I won't ask how you slept, since you were out like a light all night."

Trying to sound casual, I said, "That's true. Something must have really tired me out."

We shared an amused look, and some of my nervousness dissipated. She suddenly grabbed one of my hands in hers, running her thumb up and down against the back of my hand.

"You're even prettier in the morning than I thought you'd be." Her eyes were hooded and dark.

I blushed and looked away. "I highly doubt that. My makeup's a mess, and my hair's completely screwed up."

She used her free hand to turn my face back toward hers, making me meet her eyes before letting go. "I never lie about a woman's looks, and I never flatter. You're gorgeous just as you are. And I love you in that color."

I blushed again and then looked away, too embarrassed to respond. While she'd used the word love in relation to my bathrobe, it hung in the air. I turned my attention to the coffee and sipped at it while I stared out the window. We passed the next couple of minutes in, for me, an awkward silence. Amelia continued to read part of the paper, which, I noted, was the Arts section. It had a large spread on the auction later today. I glanced over at the clock and gasped. It was almost noon.

"Jesus!" I jumped to my feet. "The auction's in two hours."

"There's no rush." Amelia looked surprised. "It's only a couple of blocks from here. Eat some breakfast and take your time."

"I can't eat now. It'll take me twenty minutes just to scrub off everything from last night."

Amelia frowned for a second and then agreed. "All right, get in the shower. You can use mine. I'll pick an outfit for you."

Not seeing any reason to argue, I made my way into her bathroom, which was nearly twice as big as the one in my room. The shower had an adjustable temperature dial, and I put it up as hot as it would go, scrubbing at my face to remove the caked-on makeup.

I'd brought a makeup remover into the shower and managed to get almost all of it off. When I stepped out of the shower, the mirrors were steamed up, and I opened the door without thinking about it to let some of the steam escape. Amelia was standing in the anteroom to the bathroom, and her eyes widened when she saw me standing there completely naked. Too surprised myself to do anything about it, I just stood there, letting her look.

Her eyes roamed up and down my body, her pupils dilating with pleasure. When our eyes met, it took about half a second before we leapt at each other, our mouths meeting with crushing pressure. She shoved me against the bathroom door, my head smacking painfully against the wood. I ignored the pain and sighed with pleasure as her mouth made its way down my neck again. Her hands were already on my body, one on my left breast, the other on my ass, both of them gripping me. I gasped, and suddenly she was biting my nipple, hard. I yelped and she looked up at me.

"Get on the bed. Now."

I made my way over to the bed and climbed back onto it. The sheets were still tangled from last night, and I kicked them out of the way as much as I could and rested against the pillows. Amelia was still standing where she'd been, her eyes blazing with desire. Slowly, still watching me, she unbuttoned her shirt and let it drop to the floor before slipping her skirt down and kicking it aside. Her lingerie was ivory and lace, gracing a body toned and sculpted to perfection. As she'd remained almost completely clothed during last night's escapade, this was the most I'd seen of her. She was enviably thin but lightly muscular, with surprisingly long legs for her height. Her breasts, still covered in her bra, were significantly smaller than mine, but still proportioned to her frame.

She stood there for a long moment, letting me gaze at her, and suddenly glanced around the room. Then she walked over to her dresser and pulled out a long silk scarf. Curious, I watched her turn back and approach me on the bed, a wicked grin on her face as she held up the scarf. Realizing what she wanted, I held my hands up above my head. She climbed onto the bed with me and then loosely bound my hands to the bed stand behind me.

Leaning close to my ear, she whispered, "You can get out of your binding whenever you want if you try hard enough. But you won't want to try." She kissed my earlobe, and I shuddered. I was getting wet again, my legs spreading apart as if on cue.

I swallowed, and then she was kissing me. Having my hands bound was infuriating but also wickedly hot, and desire crashed over me in rising waves of heat and desperation. She kissed my neck and breasts, lightly at first, then with a kind of hungry desire that seemed to match my own. My skin instantly heated in each place where her soft, sensuous lips touched me. Bound, I couldn't pull her closer or do much of anything, but I coiled my legs tightly around her, drawing her as close as I could. The touch of her skin against mine intoxicated me.

Evidently feeling my longing in the tense anxiety of my body, she looked up and met my eyes before sliding her hand down between my legs. She moved slowly, parting my lower lips with expert fingers and seemed somehow satisfied to find how wet and slick I already was. My back arched and I wrenched against my bindings. The feeling of my arms above my head was intoxicating, and I strained to move my legs farther apart.

"What a naughty girl you are!" said Amelia, her face betraying her own desire. "I like it."

Her thumb found my clit as she bent down to suck my nipples. She circled my clit slowly, and I gasped with desire, straining against my bondage.

"Oh, God, Amelia."

My head was muddled with desire, my skin inflamed, and I was growing wetter by the second. I let my head fall back and closed my eyes, luxuriating in the pleasure of the moment. I could sense her moving, and suddenly her mouth was no longer on my breasts but on my clit. I groaned with pleasure as her soft lips closed around it, her hot, wet tongue circling it just as her thumb had been a moment before. I arched against it, starting to feel the orgasm inside me building up, higher and higher, until I felt like a rubber band ready to snap with pleasure. Her tongue moved away from my clit, and I almost screamed with disappointment, but a moment later she started to lick deep into me, squeezing my ass. My pleasure began mounting yet again.

"Yes, yes. Oh, Amelia. I want you inside me."

"Your wish is my command."

She sat up and plunged her fingers into me. The sound that came from my throat was an inhuman mewling, and I closed my eyes, rising to meet her fingers. As her fingers moved in and out of me, her lips closed over one of my nipples, rolling it around on her tongue before biting it, hard. I yelped but didn't pull away, and she continued to suck on it, her lips and tongue gently kissing and licking me where she'd bitten. The combination of pain and the warmth of her slick tongue was pushing me near the edge again, and sensing this, I met her hand and fingers with rising speed. As if sensing that I was getting close again, Amelia withdrew her hand, and I groaned in frustration.

She pulled her mouth away from my breast and looked up at me, appearing almost angry. "Not so fast. It's better if you wait." I must have seemed disbelieving, and she chuckled before turning to my other breast, once again nipping me with her teeth before licking and sucking at it.

She alternated between my breasts, biting and licking, biting and licking, for seemingly hours. After an eternity of waiting and rising frustration, I was so close I began to think I might orgasm without her touching me again. She must have felt the tightening in my limbs, as she suddenly gave in, her fingers sliding inside me again. I screamed out my pleasure as the orgasm crashed over me. Throwing my head back, I felt it rock through my entire body in escalating waves of pleasure, the peak of my climax harder and higher than anything I'd ever experienced.

When it was done, I lay gasping, my eyes still squeezed shut—spent and wrecked, sore in a delicious, aching way. I finally opened my eyes, and Amelia lay beside me, watching my face, her fingers skimming up and down my leg. She kissed my lips before undoing the scarf. My wrists were red and chafed, despite the silk, and I rubbed at them absently. Seeing the redness, she took my wrists in her hands and kissed them, sending another shiver up my spine. She laughed at my expression of pleasure.

"Much as I would like to do this with you all day, Doctor, we really must get ready." She slid over to the edge of the bed and stood up, stretching her long limbs before walking over to her clothes. I watched her dress again, and when she had zipped her skirt, she glanced back over at me. "Really, we have to go soon."

"But what about…"

Her expression closed down for a moment, and then she smiled at me widely and, I think, somewhat falsely. "Later." She disappeared into the bathroom.

"You?" I finished my question in an empty room.

❖

The auction was a success for the Winters Corporation because of Amelia's ruthlessness and ability to outbid nearly everyone there. She lost out on two pieces she'd planned to buy but managed to acquire several others, including a piece not originally listed in the program. The whole process boggled my mind in terms of how much money was being bandied about, but I also enjoyed it. Sotheby's was, of course, the best, and just to be in the room was something of an achievement. Though I was entirely superfluous to the whole affair, I made notes in my tablet about our new inventory. This was pointless, as the Sotheby's people were clearly not in the habit of misplacing things that cost so much money, but I had to do something to look useful. Amelia had insisted that I accompany her for moral support, and I tried to enjoy it, worthy of the honor or not. We sat next to each other but were very careful not to touch there or on the walk between Sotheby's and the hotel. Touching would, we both seemed to know, lead immediately to something else, and we had work to do. This, however, led to its own kind of quiet desperation, and I spent most of the auction trying to ignore the volcanic heat between my legs. My passion must have reflected on my face, as I saw Amelia give me a sly glance once or twice, making me blush at my own lasciviousness.

We had a couple of hours between the auction and dinner for downtime, and we went to our separate rooms without discussing our reasons for keeping apart. It was obvious that if we wanted to leave at any time tonight, we had to stay apart for a while longer. Alone in my room, I debated calling Lana, but I felt suddenly strange talking about everything that had just happened. It all had the quality of a dream, and discussing it would, it seemed to me, sully it somehow. After all, I told myself, we were having brunch with her tomorrow, and I could tell her all about it in person. I made a quick call to my aunt and caught up on my e-mail before changing.

As I slipped into the other gown I'd brought, I realized that Amelia's suggestion about the choice of gowns yesterday had been correct. I cursed myself for my stubbornness. The gown I'd worn yesterday had been slightly less formal, more suitable to the reception tonight than yesterday's fancy dinner. With this gown, I looked overdressed. I decided to take all future advice about clothing from Amelia.

Standing there looking at myself, my hair and makeup as flawless and styled as I could make them on my own, I blushed at the memory of yesterday's gown being ripped from my body in our desperate haste for heat and contact. Running my hands up my body, I could feel the tender spots under my gown where Amelia had nibbled, bitten, or sucked a little too hard. In the shower, I'd been surprised by several small and not-so-small bruises all over my body, and I could sense them now, under my gown. An all-consuming heat swept through me at the thought of our next encounter, and I shuddered with suppressed anticipation. I removed my hands from my body, too tempted to do something with them to relieve the growing pressure between my legs.

When I walked into Amelia's suite, she was standing by the window again, looking out as she talked on the phone. Her dress and hair were stunning from behind, emphasizing her slight curves like an intimate embrace. She laughed warmly at the person on the line, and I wondered idly who she was talking to before I realized it must be one of her brothers or her sister, as she referred to "Dad" several times. She hadn't heard me enter the room, and when I slipped my arms around her from behind, she jumped slightly before resting back against me. I put my chin on her shoulder, gazing out at the city below us.

"I have to go, honey," she said on the phone. "I'll see you next weekend at Dad's thing, if not sooner." She paused for a moment, and I could hear a feminine voice saying her farewells before they both hung up.

"My sister Emma. She called to tell me that we were on TV last night."

"Oh?" I was genuinely surprised.

"Just in the background. That starlet we met at our table was being interviewed right as our car drew up behind her. I didn't even notice the cameras."

I kissed the side of her face and she turned, pulling me into her arms. She sank her face into my neck and kissed it, and I shivered all over. She laughed. "That was a mistake." She stepped back and away from me. "Sorry, but we have to leave in ten minutes."

"We could always skip dinner," I suggested, shrugging casually.

"I don't think so, young lady." She shook a finger at me. "I haven't seen you eat anything all day today."

I was surprised when I realized she was right. As if on cue, my stomach rumbled, and we both laughed. "That proves it. Dinner, reception, *then* bed."

I sighed, suddenly too hungry to disagree.

❖

The River Café in Brooklyn is breathtaking, the food excellent. I wolfed down a huge meal, complete with several kinds of bread and a large salad, my hunger a gnawing desperation by the time the entrees were set in front of us. Amelia watched me with obvious amusement, eating in her usual elegantly casual way. She ate in the continental style, I was surprised to note, something I'd adopted for myself while in Paris. I'd gotten enough grief about the way Americans shovel their food and switch hands that I'd finally managed to train myself to eat with the fork in my left hand.

Except for a few whispered sweet nothings, we sat through most of the dinner silently staring at each other, almost as if stunned. We held hands across our intimate little table, Amelia looking as dumbfounded as I felt. Something was happening here, I was beginning to realize, that had very little to do with sex. While I was still a bit shy of the idea of not only sleeping with a woman, but potentially *dating* one, I was already beginning to get used to it. It helped in this early stage that we were in New York, where two women holding hands didn't raise eyebrows in most places, but the idea of taking all of this—whatever it was—back to New Orleans with us still terrified me. I hadn't mentioned Amelia to my aunt on the phone except in reference to her idle questions about the trip and couldn't imagine coming clean about having a relationship with her. I tried to push the thought from my mind. I would wholly enjoy myself for the time being.

I suddenly remembered my ride down the elevator yesterday. I'd been dreading this dinner so much at the time that I'd been tempted to back out. Now here, alone with Amelia in one of the most beautiful spots in the city, I couldn't imagine being anywhere else.

"Penny for your thoughts?" she asked, running her thumbs along the back of my hand. The chafe marks on my wrists from the scarf had faded slightly, but she rubbed them gently. The waiter dropped off the check, efficient and unobtrusive. She had to take her hands away to retrieve her wallet, and mine immediately felt cold at the loss of contact.

"Just thinking about how fast things change," I replied. Amelia raised her eyebrows. "Yesterday morning, I was worried I might have to get a new job."

"And now?" she asked, taking my hands again.

"And now? I can't imagine it. I felt so terrible and now I'm so happy."

She smiled widely, eyes sparkling. "I'm happy too. I'm so glad things worked out."

I thought that was a coy way of putting it and laughed. Amelia winked. Glancing at her watch, she withdrew her hands again and signed the check, leaving a huge cash tip. We gathered our coats, and she called the car on her phone. The car was just down the block and arrived for us before we were even out the door. She reminded the driver of the address for the gallery, and we arrived a few minutes later.

Tara Michaels was a rising star in the New York art scene and, from the minimal amount of gossip I'd heard on this trip, something of an airhead. Her space was much bigger than it would have been in Manhattan—a large warehouse with exposed pipes and wood, likely an old textile factory. Besides the space itself, I noticed a distinct shift from the makeup of the crowds we'd been bumping elbows with the last few days in Manhattan. Here in Brooklyn everyone was younger, affecting poverty through expensive consignment clothes and, in the case of the men, unkempt beards. The room was a sea of flannel and skinny jeans, and my gown seemed even sillier than I'd already dreaded. I saw puzzled looks from everyone as we entered. I tried to quell my nervous anxiety by mimicking Amelia's cool indifference as we glided toward a group clustered around the artist. We stood on the outside of the circle for a while, listening to her talk about her work.

"I just think," she was saying, "that a woman is always more in touch with her creations? Her work? You know, because of, like, babies? Art is from, like, our bodies. It's primal, it's biological. We know what it means to, like, make things, not just kill them?" Tara apparently had the annoying city-girl habit of making everything she said sound like a question. She was young—perhaps twenty-three. Her hair was a tangle of greasy locks perched on her head and held in place by two fast-food chopsticks, her face free of makeup. Her clothes looked threadbare and worn, and overall she looked unkempt in that careful, studied way of her crowd, which took, perhaps, just as much time as someone who bathed and combed her hair regularly.

After a few minutes of listening to similar philosophizing, Amelia touched my elbow and we turned away. I met her eyes and could see the sparkle of humor in them. It was obvious that she, like I, was trying not to laugh. We walked around the large room, pausing at a few intriguing pieces and skipping some that looked derivative or too simple. I was especially appreciative of her sculptures, but Amelia seemed to be directing her interest at the paintings. We whispered about a few of them, trying to be as casual as possible, though we certainly couldn't blend in. After half an hour, I saw Tara approaching us, looking desperate.

"Are you from the Winters Corporation?" she asked when she was close to us. We nodded, and she sighed in relief. "I thought so. I'm so sorry about that earlier. I saw you come in, but I haven't had a chance to get away."

I was amused to note that the earlier, drawling stupidity and careful casualness had left her voice. Perhaps, like her clothes, it was all an act. "Please," she said, pointing to a small door at the far end of the room. "Let's get out of this crowd before they corner me again."

Her office was spotless and modern, with comfortable chairs and an espresso machine. I was once again surprised by this change in style and sat down next to Amelia on the couch.

"I think you had a chance to view most of the current collection?" Tara asked after she offered us coffee. She perched on the edge of her desk, looking extremely worried.

"Yes. I'm quite intrigued, Miss Michaels, with many of your pieces," Amelia said. "I have several clients who have indicated an interest in your work, and it's good to finally see some of it in person."

Tara looked relieved. "I'm glad to hear you say that. I just had to fire my agent, and I'm looking to expand into new markets. I have a secretary that can cover most of the details of shipping and payment and whatnot, and I think I have a current or mostly current catalogue of work around here somewhere." She stood up and began rifling through her desk drawers before pulling out a professional-looking printed portfolio. She handed this to me. "You'll find a DVD in there too that should be completely up-to-date with all of the work in the show here." Her dismissive behavior to me clearly showed me what she thought of assistants. She directed her attention back to Amelia without a second glance at me the rest of the time we were in her office. While her recognition of my position was correct, I hated feeling unimportant. She made eye contact with me briefly when we all shook hands to say good-bye, then gave me her secretary's office number.

Back in the car on the way to the hotel, I was still peeved and tried not to show it. Amelia, however, picked up on my emotions immediately. "I'm sorry she was such an arrogant pest. She shouldn't have treated you that way."

Realizing that I had been sulking, I laughed and shook myself out of my mood. "I'm sorry. I shouldn't be so sensitive. She's right. I am just the assistant."

Amelia agreed but looked troubled. Perhaps, like me, she was beginning to recognize the serious discrepancy between our positions.

Back in our room, I quickly forgot the stress and annoyance of the day in a rush of tearing clothes and kissing. But, as I lay in Amelia's arms as I dozed off, a new worry had begun to nag at me.

Amelia had still not let me touch her.

CHAPTER SIXTEEN

Brunch with Lana and Jess on Sunday was more embarrassing than I could have ever expected. Having rarely had boyfriends that I introduced to friends or family, let alone a girlfriend, I was unprepared for their unconcealed curiosity and teasing. I had thought that, without asking them, they would be on their best behavior, both courteous and respectful of Amelia and the fact that we had only just begun to date. I got a version of this behavior from Jess, but not Lana.

When we showed up, Lana and Jess's eyes grew about a million times bigger when they saw us holding hands. I hadn't wanted to make a big deal of bringing Amelia, so I hadn't told them that she was coming. This, of course, caused an immediately awkward situation, as they'd reserved a table for three, not four. This can be a major issue in the Village, where getting a table for brunch on Sunday morning at a popular place can be something like shopping on Black Friday. I started to panic, but, seeing my face, Amelia told me not to worry and then disappeared for a moment to the host's station. She came back and we were all moved to a bigger table. Lana and Jess were duly impressed, but Amelia, as usual, took it in stride. I can't imagine how much she had to bribe the host for us to get the bigger table, and I didn't ask.

The insinuations started almost immediately after we ordered drinks.

Lana leered directly at me and said, loud enough for both Amelia and Jess to hear, "So, what's Amelia like? Is she, you know, in charge of everything?" As if I didn't catch what she meant by this, she raised her eyebrows up and down several times to emphasize her point.

I stuttered a few times and Amelia grabbed my hand, squeezing it to reassure me. "We try to share our…work equally," Amelia said, meeting Lana's eyes. "I try not to think of myself as a boss, and I hope Chloé doesn't feel…pushed around too much."

I choked on my mimosa, and Amelia had to slap me on the back a couple of times to help me catch my breath. Her phone rang a moment later and she excused herself to go answer it outside.

"What are you doing?" I hissed at Lana. "You're embarrassing her."

"I think it's *you* I'm embarrassing, my dear. Amelia knows I'm joking."

I couldn't help but pout. I've never been good with teasing. I had no older siblings growing up to get me used to it. "Well it's not very nice. You've just met her. And you don't have to be such a letch."

She held up her hands in defeat. "Okay, okay, I'll stop talking about your sex life. Still, I have to say, now that I've seen her up close and in the daylight—wow. And that voice? It's so husky and breathy—*très sexy*. A little like what's-her-name, from that one movie." She looked over at Jess, as if what she'd said was enough of a clue.

For Jess, it was. "Emma Stone."

"Exactly—she sounds just like Emma Stone." Lana agreed. "What a catch, Chloé. And you say she's rich, too?"

I blushed and nodded, proud but not comfortable bragging about her yet, either.

"She's gorgeous," Jess said.

"You look like movie stars together," Lana added, "especially with your new clothes. You're both the fashion plate of the new lesbian chic."

We laughed just as Amelia rejoined us.

"Did I miss something?" she asked, looking around at all three of us.

"Nothing important." Lana grinned at me mischievously, as if we were hiding something from her.

"That's what I get for leaving the table, I guess," Amelia said, smiling.

It was one of the first times I'd heard her joke, and it took me by such a surprise that I choked, once again, on my mimosa.

❖

The rest of our time in New York consisted of a blur of activity, followed by decadent dinners and passionate nights. I'd tried to bring up my concerns about reciprocating, about wanting to explore her body, but Amelia dismissed the conversation without explanation, never allowing my hands to go farther than the outside of her lingerie, and even then, she deftly prevented me from exploring between her legs.

By Wednesday, I was becoming desperate. Since Monday, we'd been working on separate tasks during the day, and the time by myself had made the problem stand out in greater relief. I promised myself to bring it up during dinner, as she obviously wouldn't talk about it when we were in bed together. Then, just as I was finishing up with my client—the author from the dinner Friday night—I received a text message on my phone.

I'm sending you back early. Here is the information for your flight home. It's a commercial flight, I'm afraid, as I need the jet, but your ticket is first class and direct. I need someone in New Orleans to help sort out all of this new inventory and meet with some desperate clients down there. I know we had plans for tomorrow, and I'm sorry I'm not there in person to say good-bye. Your luggage will follow tomorrow.

I'm completely booked tonight, so let's talk tomorrow when you've had a chance to catch your breath.

The surprise change of plans took my breath away, and I stood on the front stoop of my client's brownstone, completely stunned for several long moments. Anger followed my surprise, and without thinking about it, I instantly called her. She didn't pick up. "Damn it!" I yelled, scaring a woman walking by with a stroller. I called out an apology, but she pushed her stroller away, quickly.

My anger lasted as far as the airport, and I continued to try to reach her on her phone and at the hotel. No response. By the time I boarded the plane, however, my anger had melted into a stony dread. I felt physically ill and gulped at my free champagne like a tonic. Why is she doing this? I wondered. Is she mad at me? Did I do something wrong? The various warnings I'd had from Meghan and my aunt echoed through my head as I flew farther away from New York and from her. Was she just using me? I had a hard time believing this, even in my mildly inebriated state, but the facts seemed to glare out at me. She'd dismissed me like a plaything she'd grown tired of.

By the time I reached my aunt's place it was almost midnight and, luckily, completely empty. I stumbled into my room and fell facedown on my bed, too exhausted to even cry.

❖

I was woken very early by a phone call from New York—a call made by a shipping organizer for one of the galleries, not by Amelia. The day passed in a blur of activity as I coordinated with him and with several other gallery owners and Sotheby's. Amelia's administrative assistant, Janet, acted with her usual super-efficiency, making my work much easier, but I still caught myself nearly breathless with anxiety throughout the day. The multi-line telephone in Amelia's office was ringing off the hook. Just when I'd finish one phone call, I'd be on the next. I had the calls forwarded to my cell so I could go over to the airport to supervise a delivery and was talking nonstop most of the day.

By seven that evening, I'd been working for well over twelve hours and was sagging with fatigue. Seeing me quite literally drooping, Janet laughed sympathetically. "You've been working harder than I have, Chloé, and that's saying something since I'm about ready to keel over. You should go home."

"But there's still so much to do!"

"It'll wait. Most of the delivery services are closed this time of day anyway. Just come back as early as you can tomorrow. I'll get George to drive you home."

Too tired to protest, I agreed, getting home quickly with the light traffic.

Meghan, Aunt Kate, and Jim were sitting in the living room when I walked in, and all three laughed when they saw me.

"You look like tired horseshit," Meghan said happily.

"Fuck you." I was too tired to be amused.

"Language, ladies!" Aunt Kate said facetiously.

I sat down heavily on an armchair, dropping my bag and keys on the floor. I rolled my head back and closed my eyes. "Holy crap. I've never been this tired in my life."

"Well, I hope you're well paid for all this dedication, missy," Aunt Kate said, clucking her tongue.

"I am. Very well, in fact."

"I just dropped by to wait, and me, Kate, and Jim got to talking," Meghan explained. "Never thought I'd have to wait so long."

Suddenly remembering, my eyes snapped open. "Oh shit. We were supposed to have dinner." Earlier in the day, Meghan had called right in the middle of three conference calls I was on, and I'd stupidly made plans to see her tonight. "You must think I'm a real ass."

"I don't have to think it. You are," Meghan said, though it was clear she was joking. "I knew when I talked to you earlier that you were distracted. I shouldn't have pushed you to make plans."

"Really, I am sorry."

"Well, you're here now," Aunt Kate said, "and knowing you, you probably didn't have anything all day but coffee."

She was right, and I nodded guiltily.

Aunt Kate sighed. "You go on and change, and Jim and I will go pick up some po' boys down at Dempsey's. If I call now, they'll have them ready when we get there."

Not bothering to comment, I pulled myself to my feet, Meghan trailing after me to my bedroom.

My luggage had arrived at some point during the day, and I felt another stab of betrayal. I'd left a few text messages on Amelia's phone and tried calling between work calls, but had no response. It'd been well over twenty-four hours since I'd heard from her, which, to me, could mean only one thing: she was dumping me. I still couldn't understand why she was doing this, however, and had a hard time rectifying the difference between the last time I'd seen her—blissful at breakfast yesterday—and this treatment. What happened? I wondered for the millionth time.

Hearing me sigh, Meghan said, "What's up?"

"Just tired." I didn't want to explain. I kicked off my shoes and pulled off my stockings. I was just about to unzip my skirt, but I paused. Something had shifted in my perception of things since I'd gotten together with Amelia, and despite all the time I'd known her, it now seemed strange to undress in front of Meghan. Still, it wouldn't help to make a big deal of it, so I tried to change as quickly as possible. Turning my back to her, I pretended to sort through my clothes so she wouldn't see me completely naked as I pulled off my shirt. I heard her gasp behind me and then she was whirling me around.

"Chloé, what the hell?"

Surprised, I looked down at myself before remembering the bruises. My breasts and stomach had several dark ones from bite marks, and my wrists were lightly bruised and chafed. I blushed at the memory of how they'd gotten there and tried to turn away.

Meghan yanked me around to face her. "Are you sick or something? What are all these marks?"

"No, I'm not sick." I wrenched my arm out of her grip and stepped away from her before moving across the room again.

"Then what the hell?"

"I don't want to talk about it right now." I tried to put as much warning in my voice as possible.

"Chloé, we *have* to talk about this. What happened to you?"

I didn't reply and managed to quickly pull on jeans and a T-shirt, covering most of the marks. I couldn't do anything for my wrists and touched them lightly, the echo of a thrill sweeping through me at the memory of Amelia tying me up. I grabbed a cardigan and, despite the heat in the house, pulled it on to cover my wrists.

When I turned around, Meghan was sitting on my bed, her face a mask of hurt and anger. She had tears in her eyes, and I quickly walked over to her and sat down next to her without saying anything. I took one of her hands in mine and rubbed it.

"Are you doing this to yourself?" Meghan asked between sobs. "Are you hurting yourself?"

I shook my head, tears filling my eyes in sympathy. I couldn't meet her gaze and kept my eyes rooted to our hands. After another long pause I glanced up at her and could see the tears now falling down her face.

"I feel like I hardly know who you are anymore," she finally said, shaking her head as if in disbelief. "You have all these secrets now. I don't understand why you won't tell me about this—how you got all these marks on your body. You aren't sick, and you aren't doing it to yourself..." I suddenly felt her body stiffen next to mine.

"Did Amelia do this to you?" she finally asked after a long pause.

Crying myself now, I didn't say anything, still looking at our hands.

Meghan wrenched her hand out of mine and stood up, pacing the floor in anger.

"Jesus Christ, Chloé!" she shouted. "How could you be so fucking stupid! Why would you ever let a woman like that hurt you like this?"

"She didn't hurt me," I said, quietly.

"What do you mean she didn't hurt you? You look like you've been beaten up, for Christ's sake. Is she beating you?"

I shook my head and kept my eyes on the floor. I heard her pause, and she was obviously staring at me, waiting for a response.

"Fine. You know what, Chloé? Fuck you. If you're not going to talk to me, you can just go fuck yourself."

She started to storm out of my room and I sprang to my feet, grabbing her arm. She spun toward me angrily, her eyes blazing with rage and hurt. I pulled her into a hug, and gradually the stiffness left her body. Finally, she hugged me back.

"Goddamn it, Chloé. What's happening?" she whispered.

"I'll tell you, okay?" I was still crying. "Can we sit down again?"

She agreed and we made our way back to my bed. We sat there for a long time as I screwed up my courage, trying to tamp down my own embarrassment and shame. This time she took my hands in hers, waiting patiently.

Finally I sighed and met her eyes. "It's a sex thing."

"What?" Meghan said, completely taken aback.

"It's a sex thing. I mean, the bruises. She likes to, you know."

"To what?" Meghan said, eyes blazing with fury.

"To bite," I said quietly.

"Those are bite marks?" She was nearly shouting.

"Most of them," I admitted. "Some of them are hickeys. Anyway, I bruise easily."

"Goddamn it! I'm going to fucking kill her!" Meghan leapt to her feet again. I pulled her back down and she sat heavily. "That bitch!" Her face was a mottled red.

"Meghan...I-I like it."

"You *what*?" she shouted again.

"I like it," I said, louder this time and meeting her eyes.

She looked completely incredulous, but after looking in my eyes for a while, she read the truth in what I was saying. "You like it," she repeated, brow furrowed in confusion.

"Yes. I do. At first it was just a little bit of tying up, you know. And then she started biting me." I couldn't suppress a shudder of pleasure at the memory. "It hurts but it's..." I looked up at her face, trying to make myself say it. "But it's a good hurt."

"Huh." Meghan still looked stunned.

"I've been asking her to do it since we started."

"Huh," Meghan said again, looking at me with a strange expression. We stared at each other for a long time, and I suddenly saw a glint of humor in her eyes. She tried to suppress it, but in a moment she was giggling, her eyes alive with merriment. "You kinky little minx. Who would have thought? Have you done this kind of thing before?"

I shook my head and then shrugged. "I haven't, you know, *acted* on it, I guess, but I've thought about it. I asked a boyfriend to tie me up once, but he wasn't really into it."

"Jesus." She was laughing again. "Why didn't you tell me about this before?"

I shrugged again, blushing. "I thought it would sound weird."

"You're damn right it sounds weird! You seem like the last person on earth that would be into that stuff, Chloé."

"What stuff?" I asked, genuinely confused.

"S & M. You know, bondage and pain and all that."

I blushed again, looking away. The truth was, while I'd always fantasized about being tied up, and possibly a little more than that, I'd never really thought about actually going through with it, and I'd certainly never researched it in any way. S & M was, to me, something foreign and threatening. I knew a lot of women, Meghan included, who watched porn of all kinds, but it had always just embarrassed me. For me, my fantasies had always been vague and uninformed. I'd never really thought to act on them.

"I don't know what I'm into. It just kind of happened. I mean, she's only tied me up once and bitten me a little. We haven't really, you know, done anything major." I shrugged, not really knowing what "major" would be.

Meghan's eyebrows rose, but she didn't comment. After a moment, she said, "Sooooo, what's she like in bed? Is she good?"

I blushed harder, not saying anything. I couldn't suppress a grin, however, and Meghan laughed. "Shit. She must be amazing." My face must have gotten even redder, as Meghan laughed again.

"So is it more than sex?" she asked.

I looked up at her, surprised to feel tears in my eyes again. "I'm not ready to talk about that yet, Meghan. Don't get mad at me—I just, I just don't know. I thought it was, but then…well, anyway, I don't know." I didn't know what was happening myself.

Until I discussed this problem with Amelia, it didn't seem fair to say anything about it to anyone else.

Meghan was clearly curious, but she managed to hold her tongue. We sat that way for a while longer, still holding hands.

Suddenly the front door opened down the hall and we heard Aunt Kate and Jim come back in, bags rattling.

We both got to our feet, and Meghan looked me up and down. "You might want to wash your face a little. You look like you've been crying or something."

I laughed and went into the bathroom before joining everyone in the living room. Aunt Kate looked concerned when she saw me, clearly recognizing that I'd been crying, but, because of Jim, she didn't say anything. I shrugged at her and tried to shake off my depression, but my fatigue was making it a hard go. My stomach was sour, too, and I picked at my food, not really eating. I kept glancing at my phone, hoping against hope that I'd at least get a text from Amelia, but it stayed silent. Meghan saw my nervousness and raised an eyebrow, but I shook my head. It was an hour later in New York, and soon it would be too late to expect a call.

Just as I was pushing away my uneaten sandwich, I heard a knock on the door. The four of us looked at each other, confused.

"Who on earth could that be?" Aunt Kate asked.

I got to my feet and opened the door, and there she was. Amelia was rumpled and tired-looking, with big bags under her eyes and smeary makeup, but she was the most beautiful thing I'd ever seen. Our eyes met, and the next second I was in her arms. We kissed, long and hard, and when we pulled apart, she had tears in her eyes.

"Chloé, I'm so sorry," she said, her voice catching.

"It's fine." I pulled her into an embrace again. "It's fine. You're here now."

She looked as if she was about to say more, and then I saw her eyes widen slightly as she looked behind me. I turned to see the others watching us. Aunt Kate's mouth was hanging open, a bit of unchewed food sitting on her tongue. Meghan looked as if she might start laughing at any second. She covered her mouth with a hand briefly to stifle her merriment and then turned to Aunt Kate.

"Maybe we should give them a minute, Kate," she said, patting her hand.

"B-but, but…"

Meghan got up and held out her hand, helping Aunt Kate to her feet. She threw us a quick grin and started leading her away.

"But," Aunt Kate said again, this time with less conviction. Jim raised his eyebrows at us and followed them into the kitchen, leaving us alone.

Amelia came into my living room, and we both sat down on the couch. It was surreal to see her there, amidst of my childhood memories. So far she hadn't crossed the threshold of my doorway, and now here she was, in our house, sitting on our couch.

"I want to explain," she said.

"You don't have to. You're here now." I was so relieved I was almost crying, and I didn't want to hear anything bad now.

"No. I need to. You didn't deserve to be treated like that. It wasn't fair and it wasn't right."

I didn't reply, keeping my eyes rooted on our grasped hands.

She sighed. "Yesterday, after you left the hotel, I heard from Daphne Waters—that older woman we met Friday? The one with all the young male escorts?"

I nodded.

"She invited me to an early lunch to meet a potential client, but she set me up. I showed up at the restaurant, only to run into Sara."

"Who's Sara?"

"My ex," Amelia said quietly.

My stomach seized with dread, but I remained quiet.

"She lives in New York now, but she keeps telling me she wants to move back here—and in with me. We never lived together, so I don't know why she thinks I'd want to live with her now, especially as I've been avoiding her since we broke up. She's been trying to talk to me for months. She calls me all the time, she fills my e-mail with messages, she sends me presents. I haven't been able to get through to her. No matter what I say, she won't stop pestering me. I've even been looking into getting a restraining order. I told her that yesterday." She paused, trying to gauge my reaction. "Chloé, it's been over for almost two years now. She isn't anything to me but a pest."

Some of the tension eased in my stomach and I finally met her eyes. "Why didn't you tell me this yesterday? Or even earlier today? I had no idea what was going on. I thought—"

She frowned and pulled me into another hug, kissing me. Then she sighed, looking more exhausted than I'd ever seen her. "I wanted to. In fact, I was going to tell you all about it this morning, but my purse was stolen. My phone and all my contact numbers were lost. I called the office a few times, hoping to reach you that way, but I kept hitting the phone tree and getting put on hold. I eventually decided that I would just head back and catch up with you in person."

"You tried to call?" Even more of the day's tension eased.

"If I could have remembered your phone number, I would have called you directly, but I couldn't. You can't know how upset I was all day. Then I had one delay after another at the airport. I would have been back hours ago, but some kind of weather system was causing delays, and we had to wait it out."

"So what happened with Sara?" I asked.

She sighed again. "We had lunch. Well, she had lunch and I kept trying to leave, but she insisted that I stay and hear her out. She saw us on TV, you see, and she wanted to tell me how you were bad for me. She's done some kind of research on you—"

"On *me*?" I was stunned.

"I told you, she's obsessed. Anyway, she thinks you have a checkered past or something, and I should leave you and come back to her."

I laughed at the idea of my "checkered past" of exactly ten partners, but didn't say anything.

"She's crazy. I really am going to have to get a restraining order." Amelia looked incredibly angry for a moment and then shook her head. "Anyway, when she mentioned you, I wanted to get you out of the city, fast. She's been…rude to some of my girlfriends before."

"Rude how?"

Amelia shook her head. "It doesn't matter. Anyway, my first thought was for your safety. I just never thought I wouldn't get a chance to explain it to you for so long. I'm so sorry."

I looked at her for a long time, my anger coming and going. I was so relieved to see her again and know that I hadn't been completely deluding myself about how she felt, that I was almost willing to just let it go. Almost.

"Can you tell me one more thing?" I asked.

"Anything."

"Where were you last night? I called the hotel and no one answered."

I was expecting to hear the worst, but then she laughed, and I suddenly knew everything would be okay. "Well, first, I was out ripping Daphne Waters a new one. It took me a while to track her down, but I managed to catch her at a dinner party with some fancy muckety-mucks on the Upper East Side. I caused a scene." She laughed and then shook her head again. "I threw things and threatened to sue her. By that point, I was so angry, it's lucky they called security instead of the police, or I might be sitting in jail."

I shook my head, unable to picture her anger. She was generally so calm and collected.

"When I got back to the hotel, I ended up sleeping in your room." She looked embarrassed. "I wanted to be near your things since I didn't have you there. I even used your pillow."

All the tension in my body relaxed, and I pulled her into an embrace. We stayed that way so long, so wrapped up in the other's presence, that I didn't hear the others come back into the room until Aunt Kate cleared her throat. We pulled apart, both of us looking at them sheepishly.

"If you don't mind, I think we'd like to finish our dinners now," Aunt Kate said.

"Of course!" Amelia sprang to her feet and looked around wildly. "I'm so sorry for my rudeness. I'll leave."

Kate waved her hands dismissively. "You don't have to go anywhere, girly. Sit back down. Chloé's sandwich is big enough for the two of you."

Meghan and I shared a glance, and I was relieved to know that she'd explained things to Aunt Kate. I'd been dreading telling her since Amelia and I had started sleeping together, and now the ice was finally broken. All I had to do was fill in the details when I talked to Aunt Kate about it later.

Watching Amelia Winters, decked out in her elegant suit and expensive shoes, eat half a po' boy was almost worth all the previous upset. She was polite but clearly nervous, and everyone was nervous with her.

Much to my dismay, Amelia excused herself after we finished eating and insisted that I take tomorrow off from work. We stood out on the stoop, the door safely shielding us from curious eyes.

"But there's so much work to do," I said just before I let out a loud yawn.

Amelia laughed. "Yes, but I can handle it from here. Anyway, I want you to be fresh as a daisy for Saturday."

In the hubbub in New York and the desperation of today, I'd completely forgotten about her parents' anniversary party, and my stomach suddenly knotted up with nerves.

"Does that mean I won't see you until Saturday?" I lowered my eyes flirtatiously, stepped a little closer, and ran my hands up and down the lapels of her jacket, leaning close to inhale the scent of her.

She pulled me into a long, deep kiss. "I can't wait that long," she whispered, voice jagged with desire. "Why don't you stay over at my place tomorrow night?"

"I won't be very fresh for the party if I'm with you all tomorrow night," I said, laughing, "but I'll be there."

"I'll send the car for you after I get home from work." She kissed me good-bye and I watched her drive away, my longing for her a deep pit in my center.

When I came back into the living room, all three of the others were waiting for me with barely suppressed curiosity. I laughed at their expressions.

"Can we save the twenty questions for another time?" I asked. "If I don't get to bed, I'll drop dead."

"Just one question, Chloé," my aunt said.

I sighed, dreading an argument.

"Is she good for you?"

I smiled. "She is, Aunt Kate. She really is."

Aunt Kate decided to take my word for it and, getting to her feet, came over and gave me a hug. "I'm so happy for you, dear. It's been a long time since I've seen you so happy."

"It's been a long time since I've been this happy."

Truthfully, I'd never been this happy before now.

CHAPTER SEVENTEEN

I slept very late the next day, and when I woke up, I lay in bed for another hour staring at the ceiling. I do most of my deep thinking, especially about emotional issues, while staring into space or painting. Amelia Winters was becoming an incredibly complex, emotional issue, and I needed to sort myself and my feelings. All week, I'd vacillated between near-crippling anxiety and near-overwhelming joy. The two extremes were far higher and lower than I was used to, and the whole thing had left me feeling like a boat adrift, like I had nothing concrete to hold on to.

The anxiety, I realized, sprang from many sources. The smallest part of this fear, I realized to my surprise, was the fact that she was a woman. While I'd never been with a woman before, it barely registered that some people might consider this a big deal. In certain circumstances in certain places, this might cause us problems, but they didn't worry me that much. I wasn't afraid of some hypothetical homophobia we might run into. In fact, being with her seemed to settle some long-suppressed curiosity, or perhaps longing, that I hadn't acknowledged before I slept with her. Seeing Lana in New York had also helped in this regard. Envisioning her relationship with Jess had satisfied me that it could work with a woman. They were one of the happiest couples I knew. It also helped to know that with Lana in my life, I had someone to talk with about coming out, any time, day or night. I hadn't taken her up on her offer since I got back to New Orleans, but just knowing that I could call her took a weight off my mind.

The biggest part of my fear and anxiety came from trying to understand how I felt about Amelia. It wasn't, I realized, as if these feelings came out of the blue the second we got together. I'd been drawn to her since the moment I saw her, and this attraction had grown during the weeks I'd worked with her. Finally being with her settled one part of this fear, but it didn't settle what came next.

I'd always hated to wait for uncertain outcomes. I could be extremely patient for almost anything if I knew what was coming, but waiting in uncertainty always did things to my head. For one thing, it had made me basically crazy all day yesterday. I'd had no reason to doubt how she felt about me, yet I'd been convinced that she intended to break up with me. I had, however, asked her the night before she sent me back to New Orleans to let me touch her more, a conversation that had obviously made her very uncomfortable. This, then, was another part of my anxiety about Amelia. We needed to talk about whatever made her so uncomfortable, and soon, or I'd drive myself nuts. I decided then and there that we'd talk before we had sex again, no matter what happened.

Decision made and feeling more settled and completely rested, I finally got out of bed around noon and ate a long, leisurely lunch in our tiny backyard, sitting by our fishpond. A loud frog in the pond was croaking out his desperation for a mate, but I always enjoy the sound of frogs. The birds were also going crazy, and once again, I recalled how lovely it was here in the autumn. Nearly anywhere else it would be too cold to sit outside, but here it was almost too warm in the sun. I read the newspaper—my go-to lazy-day activity—and ate an entire baguette with jam and cheese. Aunt Kate, a former schoolteacher, still helped out and subbed at a nearby elementary school a few days a week, so I had most of the afternoon entirely to myself, a luxury I'd missed. While I loved living here with her, and I liked being back in my old house, I was ready to be on my own again. I'd hated leaving New Orleans when I went away to school, but I'd enjoyed living on my own in Paris. I was, by nature, something of a solitary person, and missed having time alone. Between work and home, I was almost never by myself anymore. I decided to spend the afternoon looking for an apartment and finally made myself get up and take a shower.

I was still looking at real-estate ads when Aunt Kate got home. I'd called a few places listed online and finally decided that a realtor was probably my best option if I wanted a nicer place. I wasn't ready to buy anything, but some of the best rentals were listed only with agencies. I'd just finishing making several appointments to see places on Sunday when Aunt Kate burst into the living room in her usual bustle of noise and chaos. She waved at me when she saw I was on the phone before she collapsed on the couch. I hung up the phone and went over to give her a quick hug.

"Finally gonna get your own place?" she asked, having overheard me. "I'll be glad to be rid of you."

I smiled, knowing she would be happy to have me stay forever. "Yeah. I think it's about time. You know I love it here, Aunt Kate, but..."

She kissed my forehead. "You don't have to explain yourself to me, dear. I've loved having you here. I think if you wanted to stay here forever, we could make it work. But I know how it is. Before you were born, I had to live here for a while with your grandmother after college, and I nearly went crazy."

I agreed. "It's time."

"I hope you won't be too far away, hon. I'd still like to have dinner with you sometimes."

I gave her a quick, reassuring hug. "Of course, Aunt Kate. We'll plan it for at least once a week. I'm looking at some places here in the Bywater, in the Marigny, a couple in the Quarter, and two in Uptown."

"*Uptown?*" Aunt Kate was aghast. There was a distinct divide between people that lived Uptown and elsewhere in the city.

"Oh, come on, Aunt Kate, don't be such a snob."

She sniffed. "They're the snobs. Isolated, rich, *Americans.*" She said this last word as if she weren't herself an American. Uptown was the wealthiest part of the city and historically had been settled by Americans and the English, as opposed to the rest of the city, which was inhabited by French, Spanish, and African-Americans, primarily. Besides the class line, a certain amount of racial disparity existed between Uptown and the rest of the city as well. You could spend whole days Uptown and not see a single person of color—this in a city that was over 60% African-American. To people that lived in the rest of the city, Uptown was an exclusively white enclave of the super-rich as well as out-of-town, privileged students at the two private colleges up there. Hardly anyone went out there that didn't live there.

"I won't let it taint me, Aunt Kate. I promise." I gave her a hug. I couldn't admit *why* I was interested in moving there. It had never appealed to me before. Even when I went to school Uptown, I'd simply gone and come home, hanging out in neighborhood joints back in the Bywater and the Marigny. Still, I was tempted to move there now to be closer to Amelia, who had a house in the area. I didn't mention this to Aunt Kate, however, knowing how she would respond.

"Did you eat?" she asked.

"I ate the last baguette and most of the rest of the cheese."

"Good girl," she said, patting my leg. "What are your plans for the rest of the day?"

"I'll probably go upstairs and paint for a while." I paused and couldn't help but blush. "Amelia's picking me up later and…I'm staying with her tonight."

"I see." Her brow was furrowed, and I couldn't tell if it was with disapproval or not. At the very least, she was worried about my relationship with Amelia—that I knew, but I still didn't have a very good read on what she thought of the whole lesbian thing.

Not wanting to get into it with her, I excused myself to go paint, realizing as I climbed up to my artist's garret that I'd been longing to be alone with my new painting for days now. Within a few minutes I was lost in it, my worries slipping away to nothing as I worked.

The car arrived for me at seven. Not knowing how to dress for a casual evening with Amelia, I wore a combination of casual and work clothing—my nicest, darkest jeans and a sleeveless black blouse. She'd put so much emphasis on clothing the entire time I'd known her, I was actually a little intimidated by the thought of letting her down in some way with my appearance. I decided that, after this experiment, I would judge my choices based on the kind of things she wore when we were alone and not working. As the car approached her house, a chill of excitement swept through me. Not only would we be finally alone together, but I would also see inside her house for the first time. I'd only seen the outside, twice, when we'd stopped by there quickly for work.

Most of the Winterses' mansions were on Camp Street, including Amelia's. While there had been some change of hands over the years since the Winterses first moved to the area in the early nineteenth century, the primary house, now owned by Amelia's parents, had always remained in the family. Wealth among the descendants of the original Winters family had gone up and down over time, with mansions sold in down times and then bought again. Currently, as Amelia had explained, besides her parents and herself, two of her brothers and one uncle owned houses nearby.

Amelia's was a lovely shade of lavender, with a dark, tall, gated fence around the outside of the lawn, and a large front porch on the first and second floors. The hurricane shutters were a darker purple, as was some of the house trim. The car pulled through the gate and dropped me off before leaving again, and I nervously approached the front door. While I'd been in a few Garden District houses on tours over the years, this was by far the grandest I'd ever approached. I couldn't imagine what her parents' place would be like tomorrow.

Amelia opened the door before I had a chance to knock or ring the bell, and we stood there for a long time just staring at each other. She looked worn and tired and was still wearing her work clothes, but for all that, she was, as usual, stunning. She took two large steps and pulled me into an embrace, squeezing hard.

"God, I missed you," she said quietly.

Tears sprang to my eyes at this, and I blinked them away quickly. "Me too."

"I had a supper prepared for us." She indicated inside the house. "I also sent everyone home so we have the place to ourselves."

Of course she has servants, I realized, somehow still startled by the idea. The gulf between our stations in life constantly surprised me.

Her house was a marvel of design and taste, as expected. The furniture was a careful selection of art-deco and mid-century-modern design. The paintings were also in this style, primarily, each room seeming more like a museum showpiece than a place where someone actually lived. The dining room was stunning, with two places at the head and next to it lit by the warm light of a dim chandelier and two candles.

"Please sit," Amelia said, pulling out the chair at the head. "I'll go get the food."

I sat down, setting the napkin in my lap, and looked around the room with barely contained wonder. This room had apparently remained truest to its original time period, as the wallpaper was clearly original or re-created Victorian silk in dark-purple paisley. The table and chairs were high-backed Victorians as well, and the china and glasses were made of the heavy glass of that era.

Amelia wheeled in a small cart laden with dishes. She set one of these in front of me and dramatically pulled off the silver cover, revealing a masterpiece of cookery. She set one at her place and sat down next to me. We ate in silence for a while, and a strange, awkward tension seemed to prevail. I realized about halfway through my first dish that my hands were shaking, and I put my silverware down so I could regain control of myself.

"Is it not good?" Amelia asked.

"It's wonderful."

"It doesn't look like you think that." She looked concerned. "Don't worry—you won't insult me. My cook did everything."

"It's not the food."

"What's the matter?"

I gestured at the room, at the table. "I just feel…out of place. I'm sorry. I'm not used to all of this. Cooks. Servants. Big fancy houses. I feel like I stepped into an alternative universe."

"So it bothers you? My money?"

"I wouldn't say that," though it did, "just that…I don't know what I have to offer you that you don't already have. I'm just a lower-middle-class girl from the Bywater. I have nothing."

She took my hand. "You have everything I don't have, Chloé. Most of what I have was given to me. I've made a lot of my own money, but I couldn't have made any of it without help from my parents. Everything you have you earned. That's admirable." She kissed my hand. "And you're incredibly intelligent and adorable, too."

I blushed. Her eyes became serious again, and she suddenly stood up, helping me to my feet.

"What?" I was confused.

She pulled me into her arms and kissed me, hard. I kissed back, sliding my hands around her back, drawing her toward me. The heat between my legs was instant, scorching, and I was wet immediately. Amelia shoved me back onto the table and then swept the dishes off, most of them shattering on the floor. I yelped in surprise and then she was on top of me, climbing onto the table and covering my face and body with her mouth and hands. I wrapped my legs around her and arched up and in to her body, my need mounting with every kiss. Her lips were now on my neck, sending delicious shivers all over my body. Her lips were hot on me, igniting my desires further while her hands shucked off my shirt and unhooked my bra. That task accomplished, she yanked my shirt and then my bra off, tossing them off across the room before setting her mouth on my breasts. I sighed in relief, arching into her mouth, my nipples hard with desire. She bit down, and I moaned with pain and pleasure.

Taking this as permission to continue, she nibbled her way down my stomach, sometimes biting down harder, sometimes just sucking. My desire was beginning to feel almost painful, as the pulsing rhythm between my legs grew more insistent. I took one of her hands and put it there. She rubbed my sex briefly, but the material on my jeans was too thick. She stopped for a moment and yanked off my shoes, throwing them aside, then wrenched down my jeans. Consumed with the fire of my passion, I could hardly help her because I was so weak from desire. I watched in tense readiness as she ripped off my panties. She climbed back on top of me, sliding between my legs, and I rose to meet her again. I wrapped my legs around her back, and she began kissing, sucking, and biting my breasts and stomach again.

"Oh yes," I moaned as she pushed her knee against the throbbing between my legs. I moaned again and arched my back. She kissed me, her tongue pushing down into my mouth. I kissed back just as hard and could feel her body react to my aggressive kissing.

"You like it rough, don't you?" she asked, her voice hoarse, catching on each syllable. She was breathing hard, like I was, and all I could do was nod. Her mouth clamped onto mine again, and her tongue probed deeper as I felt her hand cup my sex for a moment before her palm rubbed against me.

Suddenly, her entire hand entered me, slamming in hard. I gasped for a second in surprise, then gritted my teeth and moved into the momentary pain, a pain that quickly subsided into heavenly relief as her fingers found the rhythm of my body. She sank in harder and farther than ever before, and suddenly it seemed as if I might explode with pleasure. The pain was there, but distant, adding a strange, burning heat underneath the pleasure, which made everything even better, more intense. Feeling my body stiffen in response to some place deep inside, she kept her fingers there, massaging the exact spot to make me come. I couldn't hold back any longer, and as I screamed in delight, she once again bit down on my breast, the simultaneous pain and pleasure overwhelming. I collapsed back into the table, shaking and quivering with the remains of the orgasm, unable to hold myself upright any longer.

We lay there on the table for a while, her head on my chest. I was stroking her hair, and her eyes were closed. Her expression was peaceful, calm. As my heart rate began to slow back to normal, I continued to watch her, tenderness welling up inside me as I looked at her. She held a piece of my hair in her left hand, twirling it through her fingers absent-mindedly. Her hair had come loose, and it cascaded down onto her shoulders in lazy dark waves.

A new passion began to build up in me, a crazy kind of desperate longing, and I sat up, propelling her back onto the table. She looked startled, and I used her surprise to my advantage, kissing her and climbing on top. She let me kiss her lips and neck, but when I started to explore underneath her shirt, her body stiffened. I decided to push through it, and let my hands climb up under her shirt to her breasts.

For a moment it seemed as if she might accept my explorations, but then she was elbowing and shoving at me, seemingly desperate to get away.

"No!" she said, sitting up and bringing me upright with her.

I was panting, still sitting on top of her, and I must have appeared completely dumbfounded. Our faces were only a couple of inches apart.

"What is it?" I asked, hurt. "Why won't you let me touch you?"

She couldn't meet my eyes, and her expression was dark, almost angry. I swung my legs free and slid up and off the table. I stood, naked, watching her just sit there, her arms crossed over her chest. She said nothing.

"Jesus Christ, Amelia! Say something!" I yelled.

"There's nothing to say." She met my eyes, her voice carefully casual.

"What do you mean there's nothing to say? Why can't I touch you? Why won't you let me? Are you afraid I won't be any good at it?"

Her expression changed to pained for a second, then the pain was gone, and that careful casualness was back almost before I'd seen the other look in her eyes. "It's nothing like that," she said, sliding over to the edge of the table. She slid off and stood next to me, taking my hands. "It has nothing to do with you."

I laughed, bitterly. "What the hell does that mean? *Of course* it has something to do with me. We've slept together I don't know how many times now, and you won't let me touch you. What am I *supposed* to think? It has *everything* to do with me."

She sighed and shook her head. She pulled me closer, trying to kiss me. I wrenched myself free and started picking up my clothes, pulling each piece on as fast as I could, so angry I barely knew what I was doing.

"Please don't be this way," she said, still standing there, just watching me dress.

"There isn't any other way to be, Amelia." My voice was shaking with rage. "You're trying to make it seem like it's not a big deal, but it *is*. Don't you understand?"

I pulled on my shirt and then looked over at her. Her face was still a mask of cool calm, which only infuriated me more. "Goddamn it, say something!"

"What do you want me to say?" she asked, hands out in defeat.

"I want a goddamn explanation." I almost stomped my foot.

"There's nothing to explain. I have limits, that's all," she said, her voice almost a whisper.

I jumped on this the moment it was out of her mouth. "What kind of limits? Why?"

She sighed, breaking eye contact with me. "It's not worth discussing."

I stood there for a long time, just staring at her. She was doing her best to look anywhere but at me, which only fueled my anger. Picking up my purse, I started making my way out of the room. Amelia, startled, was shaken out of her attitude and ran after me.

"Where are you going?" she said, grabbing my arm.

I yanked it free. "Anywhere but here with you," I spat, and ran out of the house.

CHAPTER EIGHTEEN

I barely slept. In fact, I hardly even tried to sleep, knowing I would just lie there tossing and turning all night. After rushing out of Amelia's house, I managed to flag down a cab on St. Charles and got home fairly quickly. Luckily, Aunt Kate was out when I got home, and I didn't reveal myself when I heard her come in a couple of hours later. The last thing I needed was to talk to her right now, let alone show her my defeat.

While I knew logically that I'd made the right decision to leave last night, that didn't help me feel any better. Further, I realized I could probably have handled the whole situation better. Storming out of there last night had been immature. Nevertheless, I hadn't seen many other options at the time. If she was unwilling to talk about things, I had nothing left to say. I didn't want to play games with her, and I didn't want to fight about it, but we had to discuss the elephant in the room before I would consider moving forward or, I was starting to realize, before I could consider staying in a relationship with her.

At three in the morning, after painting angrily for several hours, I'd actually picked up the phone to call Meghan. In the past, any time something major happened with a boyfriend of hers or mine, we would call the other with the implied knowledge that, night or day, the other was available. I'd stopped myself that night for a few reasons, namely that Zach was likely at her place, or she at his, and because I didn't even know where to begin to explain the problem. I didn't understand it myself. If I couldn't get anything out of Amelia,

I would never understand it. Further, saying something about it would, I knew, make it real. I wasn't sure if I was ready to face all the implications of what that reality might mean.

Next, I debated calling Lana, but something about doing that it seemed like a betrayal, in this case both of Amelia and of Meghan. Meghan was supposed to be my go-to friend for all things, and Lana was supposed to be my academic friend. If I called Lana, I'd be replacing Meghan, perhaps permanently, as my counselor. It was a silly way to think, and I knew that, but that didn't make it any easier to make the call. Further, I wasn't sure I wanted to talk about Amelia's problem with Lana. It seemed far too private and something like a personal failure on my part. While Lana and I were pretty close as friends, and getting closer lately, I couldn't picture talking to her about my sex life, at least not yet.

Around dawn I crept downstairs to make myself some coffee. The gray light coming in through the living room windows was hardly bright enough to help me navigate around the furniture, but I moved as slowly as possible, terrified of waking Aunt Kate. If she heard me, she would know something was wrong since I was home, and she'd want to talk about it. If I wasn't ready to discuss it with Meghan, I certainly wasn't ready to talk to Aunt Kate about it. She had made it clear that while she wouldn't necessarily protest my relationship with Amelia, she didn't, and possibly wouldn't, approve of it either. My current emotional state would simply add more wood to that fire.

I put some milk on the stove to heat and poured some of the coffee concentrate in a mug. Though I'd barely eaten anything last night, my stomach was so knotted up with anxiety I didn't even think of making myself any food. An idea occurred to me as I waited by the stove, and I rooted around in the cabinets until I found a small red tin behind the sugar canister. Inside, I found a desiccated pack of cigarettes. I'd quit smoking in my early twenties and had never been a heavy smoker even then, but when I quit, I hid some packs around the house for emergencies. This one had to be nearly five years old, and I knew the cigarette would taste god-awful, but I slipped one out anyway before searching for some matches.

I took my café au lait outside to the backyard, sat down on the little stairs by the door, and lit my first cigarette in years. I coughed and sputtered with the first few drags, the stale smoke tasting like burning hell, but I managed to push through and keep smoking. The morning was chillier than anything I'd felt since being back in Louisiana, and in my light pajamas, I shuddered. Winter was coming to New Orleans.

When I came back inside, Aunt Kate was sitting at the kitchen table with her own coffee. She sat in the chair facing the door, obviously waiting for me. I stood in the doorway for a moment and then sighed, realizing there was no way out of this. I sat down in the chair nearest to her and she took my hand.

"It must be bad if you're smoking again," she said quietly.

"I only had one," I said, rather stupidly.

She rolled her eyes. "Even one is too many, dear." She was quiet for a long while, just looking into my face, apparently trying to read my expression. "I heard you last night when I got home, and I heard you working and shuffling around all night and this morning. I understand that you didn't want to wake me up and didn't want to talk to me, and I guess I know that you don't want to talk now."

Tears sprang to my eyes.

She sighed. "You've been a wreck since you met that woman, Chloé. I think even you would admit that."

Blinking my tears away, I nodded, my voice caught in my throat.

"I just don't see that she's worth all this upset."

I started to protest, but she cut me off. "You're losing weight, you're barely sleeping, you're up at all hours, you're working like a fiend. Tell me: what are you getting out of this besides exhaustion and heartache?" Her eyes were pained and confused.

I didn't answer for a long time. I tried to see my behavior over the last few weeks from her perspective and couldn't find anything that justified how upset I'd been. While I felt very strongly about Amelia, it was already a difficult relationship, and we'd barely begun. The turmoil I'd felt before we got together had become worse, if anything, now that we were supposedly a couple. Her refusal to talk last night was starting to take on a greater weight in my mind. If we couldn't even talk about our sex life, how would we ever talk about other important things? Would she always just avoid discussions? Get upset? Try to distract me? These questions had been racing through my mind all night, and though I'd managed to push some of them away while I was painting, I'd simply suppressed them. They gnawed at my insides.

"I don't know what to do," I finally said.

Aunt Kate just looked at me again, her expression sympathetic but stern. She patted my hands and stood up. "You don't have to make any decisions right now, honey, but I want you to think about all of this turmoil seriously. I can see that you're trying to do that now, but I know you. You tend to find distractions to avoid facing serious things like this. Don't let yourself do that. Think long and hard and make a decision before you drive yourself crazy."

She made her way over to the refrigerator and pulled out the eggs. "Now you're going to eat breakfast before you do anything else. Agreed?"

I laughed, wiped away some of my tears, and then saluted her. "Yes, ma'am."

"Sunny side up or over easy?"

We'd just finished breakfast when the telephone rang. Both of us instinctively looked over at the clock, surprised by such an early call. The hour told me who it would be, so, steeling myself, I stood up. Aunt Kate's grim expression said a thousand wordless things, but she got up and left the room to give me some privacy.

"Hello, Amelia," I said when I answered.

There was a long pause. "I couldn't wait any longer," she said quietly. "I'm sorry for calling the house phone. I still don't know your cell number. I had to look this one up from your application."

I remained quiet, having decided I was through trying to get her to talk.

I heard her sigh with resignation. "Listen—I'm sorry about last night. I feel like I'm constantly apologizing to you for things, and that's not right either. You don't deserve this."

Her voice was clouded with tears, but I still didn't say anything.

"You should know. I know you should know. I was, I mean, I'm just afraid to talk to you about it. I thought maybe you would let it drop. Maybe I was hoping you would let it drop...I don't want you to think less of me."

"Any explanation would be better than none at this point," I said. I was trying to keep the rising anger out of my voice, but it was hard to stay calm.

She must have heard my anger, as her voice softened even further. "Let's get together. Right now, if you can. Or later this morning. We'll talk. I'll tell you everything."

I considered the proposal for a long time. While I was, I recognized, still quite angry with her, it didn't seem fair to dismiss her attempt to explain things now that she was willing to try.

"Let's meet for coffee," I said.

"Where?" The relief in her voice was palpable.

"Do you know CC's on Royal?"

"Yes."

"I'll walk over there. I'll be there in an hour."

"I could pick you up."

"I want to walk," I said firmly.

"Okay." She sounded resigned and defeated.

I took my time getting ready and didn't rush as I walked toward and through the Marigny into the Quarter. Moving quickly, I could reach the coffee shop in half an hour, but I decided to take it slowly and use the time to reflect on my feelings and plan a strategy for talking about them. Further, I took my time in part because I was afraid this would be the end of our relationship. While we'd hardly been dating for a week at this point, I was already mourning the end. Seeing her might mean breaking up with her, and I wanted to be ready for that possibility.

She was waiting at a table when I got there, and she rose a little when she spotted me. I waved her back down and went to get coffee, taking the opportunity to calm my racing heart. All of the things I'd planned to say seemed childish and stupid, but I knew the gist of what I'd come up with was still worth saying. I finally got my coffee and sat down across from her, as far away as the table would allow.

She was a wreck. Not only was her hair a snarl of tangles and her clothes wrinkled and misbuttoned, but she also had large, dark circles under her red-rimmed eyes. It was clear that she, like I, hadn't slept a wink and had also been crying. Still emotional, I kept my mouth closed, waiting to calm down before I said anything. She waited patiently for a long while, and then, to my astonishment, I saw tears welling in her eyes. Not able to help myself, I moved forward and grabbed her hands.

Evidently relieved, she kissed both of my hands and squeezed them tightly, almost painfully.

"I'm so sorry, Chloé. I'm such an asshole."

I didn't respond.

"I'm going to explain everything, but…it's hard for me. You get that, right?"

"I'm starting to realize that, yes. Considering that you let me walk out last night instead of telling me about whatever this is, I get that this is hard for you." I tried to keep the anger and hurt sarcasm out of my voice, but she flinched at my words.

"I guess I deserve that," she said, then sighed. She let go of my hands, wiping hers on her thighs nervously. She took a deep breath, released it, and then sat for a moment, looking at me.

"Okay," she said. "The short explanation is this: I don't like to be touched." She paused, shoulders slumped.

"So I gathered." I was annoyed. "What's the long explanation?"

"I don't exactly know why. In the past, I didn't mind it. I was never completely crazy about it, but I could go through with it. Over time, I liked it less and less, until finally, about two years ago, I just couldn't do it anymore. More than dislike, really, I started to hate it. It makes me incredibly uncomfortable to be touched in almost any way."

I was confused. "But you don't mind having sex? I mean, touching other women?"

"I love touching other women. I love touching you. I just...
don't want you to touch me."

"Did something happen to you? Is that why you feel this way?"

She hesitated. "No. There's no one thing. It just—it makes my
skin crawl, almost like I'm being tickled. It's not painful, it's not
pleasurable...it's just not pleasant to me at all." She paused, as if she
were going to say something more, but she didn't.

"So you don't like any part of you touched? Or is it just some
places?"

She writhed in her chair, obviously very uncomfortable with
the question. "That's not exactly it. I don't mind being touched some
places—my back, some parts of my legs, for example, but I also don't
really like it, either. I can put up with touching better there, I guess."

"So basically you'll *put up* with being touched in some places,
but not others."

She writhed uncomfortably again. "Basically."

"So all I can expect from you is for you to *put up* with me
wanting to touch you."

She sighed and then rubbed her face. "You're making this
about you, Chloé, when I've already told you it's about me. I'm the
one who's fucked up here."

"And I keep saying that it *is* about me. You're basically asking
me to ignore the fact that you're not interested in letting me be your
lover. That's about me no matter how you spin it."

She remained quiet, looking over at the courtyard at the other
tables. "Would it help to tell you that I hate that I'm this way? That
I wish I could be normal?"

After a moment, I agreed. "It does help, but it doesn't really
solve anything, either." I paused, looking into her eyes. They were
welling with tears again, and some of my resolve began to wane.

"When was the last time you tried?" I asked her, more gently.

"I've been trying since we got together. I've felt like trying for
you."

"What if we did things slowly?" I suggested. "Maybe I could,
say, touch somewhere you don't mind as much and then somewhere
you do?"

She sighed again and shrugged uncomfortably. "I'd be willing to try. I just don't want to get your hopes up, either. I might not be able to change, Chloé, and I need you to be okay with that."

Now that the problem was out in the open, I could consider it logically. Leaning back in my chair, I felt a crazy need for another cigarette and cursed myself for my morning's weakness. The cigarettes were, I knew, just a symptom of my anxiety, and if I didn't face what was happening, I wouldn't be able to make the right decision. Amelia sat there, her face mirroring the same anxiety I was feeling, and I finally realized that she was as nervous about all this as I was.

"Has this been a problem for you in the past?" I took her hand. "I mean, has this interfered with your relationships before?"

She shrugged. "Yes and no. Before this, my girlfriends have tried to touch me, to get intimate with me, but they haven't tried for long. None of them have asked me about it, if that's what you mean."

I raised my eyebrows, appalled. "So you've never told anyone about this before?"

"No." She shook her head firmly. "Never."

The sincerity of her answer made me realize that she was taking a major risk coming forward with this truth about herself, and the last remains of my anger drained away. Sitting there across from me, she looked vulnerable, miserable, and resigned to the worst. While the explanation she'd given for why she was this way didn't really measure up to the problem, I wasn't sure she even understood the problem herself. Now that she'd been honest with me—as honest as she was able to be at this point—I would be betraying her if I turned my back on her. She was, after all, willing to try, and considering everything, that was very likely a monumental sacrifice for her. I took both of her hands, and my act made her start crying again.

I kissed them both, then stood up and moved my chair closer to hers.

"I can try if you can," I said, embracing her.

She squeezed me back, and we stayed that way for a long time before moving apart again. I saw an older tourist couple openly staring at us and stared back at them until they looked away again, obviously embarrassed to be caught.

"We'll take things slowly, okay?" I said.

"Okay." She wiped her eyes. Even tear-soaked and exhausted, she was beautiful, and I kissed her, long and deep. "Thank you," she whispered.

I stood up, glancing over at the older couple, who were watching us again, open-mouthed, and helped Amelia stand up. "Let's go back to my place. I have to start getting ready if I'm going to look even halfway human."

"Get ready?" Amelia asked, seeming confused.

"We have to go to your parents' party soon, don't we?"

The relief and joy on her face almost helped me forget about all the anguish I'd experienced during the last twenty-four hours. Almost.

CHAPTER NINETEEN

I opened the front door with trepidation, but luckily Aunt Kate was gone when we got back to my place. She left a note to tell me that she and Jim were taking a walk in City Park and having lunch up there, and that I was welcome to join them. The quaintness of a handwritten note charmed me. Aunt Kate had owned a cell phone for years, and I'd recently convinced her to buy a smart phone, but she still didn't like to text. Half the time, she left the phone plugged into the wall in the kitchen. I showed Amelia the note.

"So we have the place to ourselves?" she asked, grinning slyly. She took a step closer and pulled me into her arms. The faint smell of citrus from her lotion was in my nose, and I nestled into her, inhaling deeply.

"Yeeeess, but that doesn't mean we can take advantage of it. We have places to go, people to see."

She nuzzled her face into my neck, sending shooting currents of electricity throughout me. My reservations began to wane, and I made myself back up and away from her, even walking a couple of steps away.

She laughed. "Can I at least watch you change?"

"Of course, but only if that's all you do. No touching!" I shook a finger at her, keeping my face stern.

She held up her hands in defeat. "Okay. No touching."

We walked back into the living room and into my bedroom, which, I was embarrassed to note, was a disaster area. I'd been in such a hurry the last few days I hadn't had time to straighten up. Clothes and half-empty suitcases were scattered everywhere, most of the surfaces covered with either underwear or dirty clothes. My bed was unmade, and boxes of shoes were spilling out of the closet.

"Well, this is embarrassing," I said.

"It's cute." She walked over to the bed, sat down, and looked at me as if waiting for something.

"I know what you're trying to do, missy, and I'll have none of that," I said, mock disapproval in my voice.

"Whatever do you mean?" She tried to look innocent.

"You can sit there, but you have to stay there." I surveyed the room. "So what do you think I should wear? How fancy will this be?"

"Not at all. It's a garden party, so a sundress or slacks and a nice shirt should be fine."

"What are you going to wear?"

"A sundress." She looked around the room at the various piles of clothes and pointed to one. "That lilac dress would work."

I pulled it out, holding it up to me. It was terribly wrinkled and I made a face. "It needs to be ironed."

"Do you have an ironing board?"

"Yes, in the laundry room behind the kitchen. There's a little closet in the wall just for it. It's an old house, and I guess they used to come standard. The iron's in there too."

She levered herself to her feet and walked over to take the dress from me. "I'll go iron this while you take a shower."

I handed her the dress and we stood there a long time, inches apart. The longer we looked at each other, the blacker her eyes seemed to grow. She was breathing heavily, and, seeing her excitement, I felt my heart rate pick up. She took a tentative step closer, and when I didn't protest, she moved even closer until we stood chest to chest, only the dress separating us. I was breathing quickly now, and, staring into her eyes, I realized the rest of my resolve had suddenly vanished. As if sensing my permission, Amelia dropped the dress and pulled me into her arms, kissing me deeply. I kissed her back even harder, as if I could kiss away the pain of the last few days. Her hands slipped under my shirt, and finding no resistance, she slipped it off over my head. My breathing was labored, and my desire was a wild, burning ache between my legs. She grabbed my hand and led me over to the bed, clearing off the dirty clothes and blankets before forcing me down onto it. I lay back, closing my eyes for a moment, then helped her slide off my pants and underwear.

She stood there in front of the bed, eyes blazing as she looked down at me. I sat up and drew her closer, hugging her around the middle and then unbuttoned her shirt. Her eyes grew hard for a moment, and she stiffened as my hands grazed her breasts, but she let me finish, and I slid it off her shoulders and threw it on the ground. We both undid her skirt, and she stepped out of it and her shoes before climbing onto the bed with me.

She leant on one hand next to me, tracing her fingers up and down my body and massaging my breasts. This went on for what seemed like eons. She was clearly teasing me, refusing to go further. My breathing was ragged and hitching, and I squirmed under her fingers.

"Amelia," I begged her, grabbing her hand. I tried to push it between my legs and she tugged it away, laughing.

"Not so fast," she whispered. She glanced around the room before scooting off my bed, then walked over to a pile of clothes. She picked out a pair of stockings, holding them up to show what she'd found. She came closer and I held my hands above my head. My tiny bed had a wooden headboard, and I prayed it would be strong enough for what it was about to endure. She tied my hands, seeming satisfied with my obedience, then glanced around the room again. She spotted what she wanted and returned a moment later with a scarf. This she tied around my eyes. She let me sit there, blindfolded, for a long, indescribably sensual moment. Desire welled up inside me, my skin growing hot, my sex getting wet. Then, finally, as if she'd been waiting until I couldn't stand it anymore, I felt her fingers again, lightly tracing up and down my calf. She kept them there for a long time, and I began to get impatient again as I grew more and more agitated with desire. I attempted to grab her arm with my legs, and she moved away.

"If you keep doing that, I'll have to tie up your legs, too," she said.

"Is that a promise?" I flushed with embarrassment at my own daring.

Amelia was on the bed in seconds, as if my boldness had broken her resolve. She kissed me, almost painfully, then settled her lips on my neck, biting and sucking hard. Her hands were on my breasts, squeezing painfully and twisting my nipples. I heard a strange, high-pitched sound and realized it was coming out of my own mouth.

"Amelia!" I begged again. "Please! I can't wait anymore."

She only chuckled and kept her lips and hands where they were. I wrapped my legs around her, trying to pull her closer so I could rub my furiously throbbing center on her, but she kept shoving me down and away from her.

"Not yet," she said, firmly. I let out a groan of frustration, and she laughed at me. She stopped kissing my neck and put her lips to my ear. "I want to make you come so hard you'll beg me to stop," she whispered.

The words nearly undid me. Had she touched me anywhere between my legs, no matter how briefly, I would have come almost instantly. Just her harsh ministrations to my breasts might make it happen anyway. The sensual blindfold, the stockings, and my limited movement added to the taboo. Evidently the fantasies I'd harbored about being tied up and blindfolded had been correct: this was exactly what I'd wanted her to do.

She moved her mouth down to one nipple and then the other, gripping my ass and massaging it as well. Her fingers were closer to my center than they'd been, but still too far away, and despite how wonderful her mouth felt on my breasts, I desperately wanted it somewhere else. Finally, as if sensing I couldn't wait anymore, she moved one of her hands between my legs. I rose to meet her fingers and she slammed into me, hard. I choked down a scream and threw my head back, using the momentum of my entire body to meet her fingers inside me. She used the pinky of the hand inside me to teasingly play with the outside of my ass, and I began to slip over the edge.

When I came, waves of tortuous pleasure rolled through me. I saw bright flashes of white behind my eyelids, pulsing in rhythm with the undulations of my body. I was too overwhelmed to even scream for several long moments, but as I began to crest, I screamed incoherently, rocking my head backward and forward in a desperate effort to make the pleasure last forever.

Finally, just as she'd predicted, I heard myself gasp out, "Stop, please stop."

Despite the blindfold, I could sense her triumph.

❖

In the afterglow of the best sex of my life, I took stock of what had happened. Amelia was cradled in my arms, her head on my shoulder, eyes closed in a light doze. While she hadn't taken off all her clothes, I was satisfied with how far she'd gone to please me. I knew I could try to get used to her situation. Moreover, she'd suggested that, however slim the hope, it might not be a permanent problem. She used to like being touched. Perhaps with time and patience, she could like it again. I decided to hold on to the hope that it would happen for us and keep trying. I would be gentle and loving, and maybe with time, things would change. I ran my hand up and down her arm, raising goose bumps, and she snuggled into me, sighing softly.

We might have stayed there all afternoon, but I made the mistake of glancing over at my alarm clock. I jerked upright. "Christ, Amelia, look at the time!"

She sat up lazily and looked over, her eyes widening. "Shit."

"We need to get moving."

She sighed and scooted over to the edge of the bed, helping me stand up. She reached down and then pulled on her clothes, buttoning her shirt reluctantly.

I pointed at the dress. "Iron that. I'll take a quick shower and do my hair and makeup."

"Yes ma'am," she said, snapping a salute. "Anyway, don't worry about being late too much." She bent down to pick up the dress. "It's just my family. You don't have to impress anyone."

I laughed and patted her arm. "You keep telling yourself that the next time you run into my Aunt Kate."

She nodded and raised her eyebrows, apparently recognizing the futility of her reassurances.

I showered quickly and raced back to my bedroom. After drying my hair as well as I could, I arranged it in a simple French twist. My makeup, like all of my clothes, was in complete disarray, and it took me longer than usual to find everything I needed. I was going for a clean look, but by the time I finished, I looked overly made up. I sighed and removed it all before reapplying, this time just darkening my lashes and putting on lipstick. I put a little concealer under my eyes to lighten up the dark circles and took a look at myself. While I still appeared overly tired and worn, I looked better than I had. Satisfied, I stood up and grabbed my bathrobe.

I walked out of my bedroom and called, "Amelia?"

I found her sitting at the kitchen table with Aunt Kate and Jim. Jim looked incredibly uncomfortable, and Aunt Kate and Amelia looked a little grim. They both glanced over at me when I came in, and I pulled the robe around me a little tighter in embarrassment.

"I thought you were going to be out all day," I said to Aunt Kate.

"The restaurant we planned to go to was packed, so we decided to head back. Amelia and I were just having a nice conversation."

Amelia got to her feet and handed me the dress. "Here you go." Her expression didn't reveal anything, but she widened her eyes at me slightly, a hint of panic there.

"I'll just go slip this on," I said, and hurried back to my room.

While I knew Aunt Kate wasn't likely to say anything overly critical, she could be very blunt. I could only imagine the kind of grilling Amelia was getting. I took one last look in the mirror, slipped on some ballet flats, and rejoined them as quickly as I could. Amelia almost jumped up when she saw me.

"Are you ready?" she asked, her voice nearly pleading.

"Yep. All set."

"I called the car since we're running a little behind. It should be here any minute."

"Well, have a nice afternoon, ladies," Aunt Kate said cheerfully.

"Thank you, Katherine," Amelia said. "You and Jim do the same."

"See you later, Aunt Kate." I grabbed Amelia's arm, and we walked to the front door to wait outside.

Once there, she breathed a long sigh of relief. Seeing my concerned expression, she laughed. "It wasn't that bad."

"That's good. I'm sorry you had to go through that. Did she say anything mean?"

She shook her head. "Nothing like that. It was more about how much she cares for you, how much she just wants you to be happy, and how upset she would be if someone hurt you. It was all very vague, but the implication was clear: if I hurt you, she'll hunt me down and strangle me."

I hugged her. "Don't worry about it. Once she understands how happy I am with you, she'll come around."

She nodded, but I could see her skepticism.

"Now you know why I'm so nervous about today."

Amelia laughed. "Don't be. No one will corner you like that. I promise."

"That's good," I said, but I was still incredibly anxious. I suddenly wished I'd thought to get a drink of something in the house to help me relax, but it was too late now.

The car pulled up a moment later, and we climbed inside before George could get out to open the door.

"We're in a terrible rush," Amelia told him.

"Yes, Miss Winters," George said, and we were moving seconds later.

"I need to go to my place first, George. We can walk over from there."

"Yes, ma'am."

She looked back at me. "I'm going to keep you close to me today, Chloé. Family functions make me a little nervous, too. I'm just so happy you agreed to come."

I laughed. "If *you're* this nervous, you can only imagine how I'll feel when we get there."

CHAPTER TWENTY

A s I'd predicted, the opulence of the Winterses' family mansion was beyond anything I'd ever seen outside of a movie. Straddling an entire city block, it was nearly four times the size of Amelia's sizable house. It had been kept its original white, and the large, columned front porch wrapped around the front and the side of the house. As this was the only mansion that had stayed in the family since it was built, it also served as the storehouse of the family's antiques and art. Tours for the public were held on Wednesdays in the spring and summer, and it was listed as a must-visit destination for tourists in guidebooks for the city. Now inside, I could see why. Several rooms on the ground floor had been kept in museum-quality condition, each looking like a window into the past. As we were led through the house to the back garden, I wondered what it had been like for Amelia and her family to grow up here. Nothing about the house, as far as I could see, suggested that anyone actually lived here. I saw no photographs, no televisions, nothing that gave away the real life of its inhabitants.

The garden was very crowded when we walked out. Several servers were walking around with champagne and hors d'oeuvres. Despite being early November, the weather was sweltering, and large ice sculptures had been set up around the yard with fans behind them to blow cool air into the crowds. A small jazz band was playing on a raised dais, the music quiet enough that people could talk over it. A tiny dance floor had been set up in front of the band, but so far it seemed that most people were too caught up in chatting with each other to use it. Almost all of the attendees wore typical Southern garden-party clothing, the men in either seersucker or white suits, the women universally in dresses. I was incredibly fortunate that Amelia had chosen my dress, as I would likely have worn slacks if I'd come on my own. I clutched Amelia's arm nervously, and she glanced over at me, the panic in her eyes mirroring what I felt.

Several people waved at Amelia when they spotted her, but the first to reach us was a pretty, younger woman, who clutched Amelia's arms like she was drowning. "Thank God you're here," she said, smiling with gritted teeth. "I was afraid you weren't coming, and Billy cancelled on me at the last minute. If I hear one more person ask about my boyfriend, I'll scream." She was a cute, petite blonde, much slighter and smaller than Amelia. I couldn't see any resemblance between them, but I assumed immediately that this was her sister.

Before Amelia could reply, an older, elegant woman, walking rapidly in our direction, called out, "Amelia! So glad you finally made an appearance." She held out her arms, and I moved aside so they could embrace. They did, somewhat awkwardly. She then held Amelia out at arm's length, looking at her critically. "You look terribly, honey. Have you been sleeping? You work too hard."

"You look lovely, too, Mother," Amelia said, then actually rolled her eyes.

Her mother was stunning. Her silver hair was cut in a chic style, and diamond studs sparkled on her ears. She wore a gorgeous, burgundy afternoon dress, which reminded me of the kind of dresses Amelia wore at work. The light lines around her dark-blue eyes only added to her striking beauty.

She turned to me, eyes piercing me with curiosity. "And who is this?"

"This is Dr. Clothilde Deveraux. We work together."

"Do you, now?" her mother asked. Her expression was hard to read, but it seemed somewhat dismissive. She held out her hand. "So pleased to meet you. And a doctor, no less." Here she gave Amelia what could be called a smile and raised her eyebrows before looking back at me. "What on earth do you do working for my daughter? Are there so many medical emergencies over there?"

I heard the younger woman next to us snort with laughter, and Amelia threw her a withering look.

"I'm not that kind of doctor," I said, shaking her hand. "I'm an art historian."

"Well, that makes more sense," she said. "So glad you girls could make it. I'll go tell your father you're here, dear." She bustled away, and I felt both Amelia and her sister relax again.

Amelia turned to me. "So that was my mother."

"And I'm her sister," the younger woman said, taking my hand. "Emma."

"Nice to meet you, Emma."

Emma turned to Amelia. "Why the hell are you so late? I've been here alone for hours."

"I can't help it if you're always early, Emma," Amelia said. "Anyway, we're not that late."

"Well, since Billy couldn't make it today, I've been here all alone for what seems like an eternity."

"Why didn't you hang out with Bobby?"

Emma snorted. "He's busy with the kids. As usual."

"Are Michael and Dean here?"

"Yeah." Emma looked around. "Bobby and all the kids are playing *boules* on the lawn, and Dean and Ingrid are talking to Dad, I think."

Amelia looked over at me, "Those are my brothers, if you didn't catch that. Ingrid's my sister-in-law."

I nodded.

Emma turned her bright eyes to me. "Ready to meet the rest of the family?"

Before I could reply, Emma took my arm, and we all started walking through the crowds. "Now don't be nervous. Only Mother and Ingrid are intimidating. Mother's not very nice to anyone's significant other, so don't take it personally. She and Ingrid are two of a kind, but they hate each other, so Ingrid will probably be nice to you."

"Why?" I asked, confused.

"Since Mother hates you already."

"She does not!" Amelia said, flushing red with embarrassment. Emma just rolled her eyes and then leaned closer to me. "Anyway, I'm so happy you're here. Ever since Amelia told me about you, I've been just dying with curiosity. I almost never get to meet Amelia's…friends."

"That's enough of that," Amelia said, eyes wide with alarm.

Emma laughed. "Anyway, she's never brought a girlfriend to Mom and Dad's before. That must mean you're something special. We're going to be good friends."

I looked over at Amelia to reassure her. She looked relieved but still somewhat on edge.

We soon reached a group of people, and Emma released me, which allowed Amelia to grab my hand. She clutched it nervously, and I squeezed back, surprised at her nervousness, but, considering what Emma had just told me, this situation was new for her too.

"There's my pumpkin!" the elder of four men said. He detached a little girl from his shoulders, set her down on the ground, and walked over to Amelia, pulling her into a deep hug. He pulled back and, like Amelia's mother, held her out at arm's length, examining her up and down. "You look so tired, honey. Are you okay?"

"I'm fine, Dad," she said. "I just got back from a trip to New York, so I'm a little worn out."

Her dad smiled widely. "Nothing a little R&R won't fix, then. And some champagne." He motioned toward a waiter, who brought over a tray of champagne flutes, and we all took a glass.

"Dad, I want you to meet Dr. Clothilde Deveraux. We work together."

He turned his gaze to me, and I met a pair of mischievous green eyes. I liked him immediately and knew I could count on this man and Emma as my allies for the day. He was tall and very solid, with wavy gray hair and a full, gray beard. Knowing that he must be in his sixties at least, I was surprised at how fit and healthy he looked. He didn't resemble Amelia in almost any way except perhaps for his smile, which was equally disarming. We shook hands.

"Ted Winters," he said. "So glad you could join us today."

"Thank you for having me, Mr. Winters." I blushed a little under his curious gaze.

"Call me Ted. Now let me introduce you to the rest of these dunces." He put an arm around my shoulders and steered me closer to the group nearby, all of whom were looking at me with open curiosity.

"Hey, everyone! This is Clothilde Deveraux, Amelia's guest. Clothilde, the one with all the munchkins crawling on him is my middle son, Robert," Ted said.

The younger man detached a couple of the children and stood up, holding out his hand. "It's Bobby," he said. We shook.

Ted continued. "This charming couple is my oldest, Dean, and his wife Ingrid." We all shook hands, and I could immediately see that Emma was right about Ingrid and Mrs. Winters's similarity.

"And this is my youngest son Michael and his girlfriend Jenna." The three of us shook hands, and then I was able to reattach myself to Amelia, clutching her hand nervously.

All of us stood there awkwardly for a moment before Emma broke the tension. "Say, Bobby. Where's Jackie?"

Bobby's face fell. "We broke up. She said that the kids were too much for her after all."

"Oh no!" Emma said, walking over to him. They took a couple of steps apart from the rest of the group, whispering together.

Amelia moved her mouth close to my ear and whispered, "Bobby's wife died a couple of years ago. He has three kids, so he's been having trouble getting serious girlfriends. It's too bad. We all liked Jackie, his last girlfriend, a lot."

I smiled, grateful for the context. There were, however, six children in the nearby vicinity. "Which ones are his?" I asked her.

"All of the girls." Amelia pointed at an older girl and two younger twins. The boys were darker and younger than the older girl, but looked older than the twins. "The boys are Dean and Ingrid's kids. Don't worry about any of the kids' names this time around. They'll probably ignore you at first." She winked at me, and I felt grateful for the excuse to concentrate on the adults.

"So Dean's your oldest brother?" I asked, trying to clarify the situation.

"Yes. It goes Dean, Bobby, Michael, then me, and finally Emma. We were all born almost exactly three years apart. My mother wanted to make birthdays easier so she could just do one big party every year. And I think she said she read somewhere that three years is the best gap between ages for siblings. She always plans everything to the minute. All of us except Emma have birthdays in the same week in January. Emma was, as they say, an accident, though of course she's Dad's favorite. She's five years younger than I am."

"It must have been hard to arrange that with the rest of you," I said, thinking about the logistics of planning the birth of four children so exactly.

Amelia nodded. "My mother gets my dad to do whatever she wants."

Ingrid and Dean walked over to us, and I could feel Amelia tensing up. Dean was a younger version of his father except for one feature—his eyes. Instead of the cheerful, mischievous green I'd seen on the older man, Dean's were the cold blue of his mother. His expression was blank and unfriendly, as was his wife's.

"We're so glad to meet one of Amelia's friends after all this time," Ingrid said, her voice surprisingly low.

"It's been so long," Dean said shortly and without warmth.

"So what exactly do you do together?" Ingrid asked.

I had to swallow hard to stop myself from spewing champagne out of my nose, but I managed to cover up my laughter with a cough. Amelia patted me on the back. I glanced up at Amelia in desperation. If I opened my mouth, I'd start laughing. Her eyes were likewise full of merriment, but I saw her gain control of herself.

"Amelia is my researcher, primarily. She also helps with home sales, shipping, things of that nature."

I cleared my throat, my amusement contained. "And what do you do?" I asked. I looked at both of them.

"I'm in the real-estate and oil business, like my father," Dean said.

"I'm in charity work," Ingrid said, looking, if possible, colder than before.

Amelia's brother Bobby suddenly appeared next to me and grabbed my arm. "Would y'all excuse us for a second?" he asked the others. "I need Clothilde here for something."

Confused, I excused myself and followed Bobby behind a nearby hedgerow. The hedge divided the lawn and garden from the patio. Several children were playing *boules* on the lawn, and others were racing around playing tag.

Bobby smiled at me. "It looked like Ingrid might bite your head off there for a second. Thought I'd step in and rescue you."

I laughed. "Thanks. I guess I said something to upset her."

"What did you say?"

"I just asked what she did for a living."

He grinned. "A woman like her thinks it's beneath a woman of her position to work," he explained. "On the other hand, she resents it that some women do work and probably envies them. I think she's afraid that women who work look down on her."

I was mortified. "Shit. Guess I really put my foot in it."

"Don't worry." Bobby patted my arm. "She hates everybody. You're not a part of this family until Ingrid Winters hates you, so you've taken the first step."

I chuckled, and we both turned and looked out at the lawn and the kids. I watched him spot his daughters playing on the swing set, and his eyes warmed at the sight of them. We both watched them for a while, and I took the opportunity to glance over at him a couple of times. He and Amelia bore a striking resemblance except for their eyes and hair. He had green eyes, and his hair was wavy and dark blond—probably like their father's had been when he was young. He was tall and muscular, and his cheerful disposition was instantly winning. All-in-all, I found him incredibly charming and, in a past life, would have likely wanted to get to know him personally. The thought of this personable man becoming a part of my life in a different way pleased me.

Michael and Jenna appeared around the corner of the hedge and strolled over to us. Michael was apparently the odd one out, as he didn't look like either of his parents or his other siblings. Lean and tall with nearly black, curly hair, he dressed in clothes more casual and worn-looking than the rest of his family. Seeing that I was attended to, Bobby excused himself to go play with his daughters on the swing set.

"Hello again," Michael said. "I'm the resident black sheep."

Jenna swatted his arm. "You are not!"

"Am too." He turned to me. "Both of my brothers and Amelia inherited the ability to make money. I'm only good at spending it."

Jenna rolled her eyes. "Anyway, we're just so happy you could come. Amelia never brings anyone to these things, and you look like a regular person." She blushed when she realized how this sounded. "I'm sorry—"

I laughed. "Don't worry about it. I pride myself on looking normal. That's how I get away with so much."

She was relieved at my joke, lame as it was.

"I'm a musician," Michael said, "and so is Jenna. We both play downtown. I'm drums, she's bass."

"Oh yeah? My best friend is in a band, too. Mostly bluegrass and folk."

"What's her name?" Jenna asked.

"Meghan Powers," I said.

They both looked startled and then laughed. "Really? How funny!" Jenna said.

"I just played a gig with her last week. I've known Meghan forever," Michael added.

"We've never met, but I've heard about her from Michael and a lot of our musician friends. She's really well known in our scene," Jenna added.

I found it very easy to talk to Michael and Jenna, and the three of us more or less hid from the rest of the party for the next half hour, chatting about the New Orleans music scene. Because I'd been living in Paris for the last four years, I didn't know it as well as I used to, but I managed to hold up my end of the conversation pretty well. Michael was extremely flirtatious, but in a way that was clearly nonthreatening, both to me and to his girlfriend. I found him likeable and approachable in a way that some members of his family were not, though Bobby and Emma seemed nice enough. Michael lived simply and cheaply downtown, and most of his references were to people and places I knew or was familiar with. Jenna grew up in Metairie, a suburb, and was, like me, unaccustomed to this kind of wealth.

We were so caught up in our conversation that I hardly noticed when the band stopped playing. It wasn't until Bobby and the children quickly walked by us that we followed them back to the other side of the yard. I spotted Amelia and walked over to her, and she almost sagged in relief.

"I couldn't find you," she whispered. She grabbed my hand and squeezed it painfully.

"That's 'cause I was hiding," I said, and winked.

Amelia's parents were up on the bandstand in front of a microphone. Ted spoke first.

"Welcome, welcome everyone! Thank you so much for coming. The weather is cooperating with us, unlike last year, so for once we'll be able to stay out here this afternoon." There were several chuckles at this. "This week marks our fortieth anniversary," here there was applause, "and we're thrilled that all of you could join us for our Ruby Wedding. Some of you out there—like Dan, and Georgia, and a few of you other old farts—were there at our original wedding forty years ago, and you've been with us ever since. I count myself lucky to have such long friendships in my life and such a gorgeous woman to share them with." There was more applause after this.

Mrs. Winters took the microphone from him and bowed slightly, as if it the applause was for her alone. "Thank you, thank you, all of you. As I look back on the last forty years, I feel so blessed to have met and known so many of you for so long. These years have brought me five wonderful children and a lifetime of happiness. I wouldn't do a thing differently."

"Except have me. She hates it when something is unexpected," Emma whispered next to me, and I threw her an amused look.

Mrs. Winters continued. "We will have a light buffet dinner in about an hour, but until then, please help yourselves to snacks and drinks. We'll try to catch all of you for a chat." She put the microphone back in its stand, and Ted helped her step down off the platform.

Amelia turned to me. "Are you enjoying yourself?"

"You basically disappeared!" Emma chimed in. "Where on earth did you hide?"

I laughed. "Michael, Bobby, Jenna, and I were over on the lawn chatting."

"Damn it! Why didn't I think of that?" Emma said, scowling.

"You got caught in Aunt Trudie's tentacles, Emma," Amelia said.

Emma scowled further. "She's always sucking me into her vortex at every family event. Half the time I think she's trying to set me up with her son. Like, hello, he's my cousin!"

We all laughed.

Emma's eyes suddenly widened at something behind me, and, turning, I saw a giant moose of a man walk outside from the house. He was easily close to seven feet tall, solid in the way of a construction worker or lumberjack. His hair and beard were a fiery red, and he was dressed in a light linen suit that looked as if it might burst off him at any moment. Emma squealed and ran at him, launching herself into his arms and wrapping her legs around his middle in an embrace. He kissed her and swung her around a couple of times before setting her down on the ground. The discrepancy between their sizes was amusing, but the man did his best to help Emma, almost crouching down as she spoke with him. They chatted for a couple of seconds, and then they were kissing again. This went on for quite a while, and several groups of people glanced over at them, obviously embarrassed by the public display of affection.

"I take it that's the boyfriend, Billy?" I asked.

Amelia nodded, clearly amused. "They're always like that. They've been together for so long now, you would think the honeymoon phase would fizzle out, but I guess not. I just know one of these days she's going to tell us she's pregnant. Or getting married. Probably in that order."

We watched them a moment longer before Amelia caught my eye, her eyes dancing with mischief. "What do you say we take advantage of the next hour and disappear for a bit? I could show you my childhood bedroom."

"Let's see it."

❖

The second floor of the house was clearly less formal than the ground floor, and I guessed that the family spent most of their time up here in these rooms, keeping the ground floor authentic to its original time period for tours. Without asking, I could guess that Mrs. Winters had influenced that decision, but up here was clearly family space. We passed several open doors, one a living room, one a cozy library, and then a couple of bedrooms before we reached Amelia's old room. It had obviously been kept as it was when she lived here, as a couple of band posters from a decade ago were thumbtacked to the walls next to some cheap art prints. Amelia sat down on the bed, watching me as I slowly took in the room. I picked up some of the framed photographs, amused at the young Amelia, then saw one of her and another, unknown girl. Amelia's arm was around her shoulders. They both looked to be about high-school age. I held it up and Amelia laughed.

"My first girlfriend," she explained. "Erin. We wanted to go to the prom together, but we weren't allowed to at our school. My mother was shocked that I even thought of taking a girl to prom."

"When did you come out?"

"I was seventeen. Once it got out, the school wanted to expel me—it's Catholic—but my father's money made that impossible."

I set the photo down and walked over to her bookcase. She had a wide assortment of novels—mostly romances, I was amused to note—mixed in with books of artwork. I slid out a large collection of Albrecht Dürer and held it up for her to see. "I love Dürer. I went to a show of his etchings in Berlin a couple of years ago."

"I actually own a Dürer now," she said, looking a little shamefaced about it, but also proud. "I'll show it to you the next time you stay over."

I put the book back and then walked over to her, sitting next to her on the bed.

"Have you had a lot of girls in here?" I was only half-joking. I didn't know a lot about her past girlfriends, as she'd been cagey about talking about them since the moment we met.

She laughed. "Only Erin. That's actually how my parents found out I was a lesbian. They caught us together."

I winced. "Ouch. Talk about embarrassing."

"One of the scariest moments of my life. I actually thought my dad would kill her. Or me. For about a week, my mother looked like she was going to have kittens." She thought for a moment and then shook her head. "It's funny now, but Christ, at the time..."

I kissed her, softly. "You don't have to worry about being caught now. Your parents are busy."

Amelia kissed me back and then pushed me gently onto my back.

❖

When we emerged from the house an hour later, the food was already out. Almost everyone was seated at one of the tables set up on the patio, so of course they noticed when we rejoined the party. I realized then that we should have taken a moment longer upstairs to compose ourselves a bit, as—if Amelia's wild hair was any indication—it was clear what we'd been doing. I saw, to my amusement, that Amelia's cheeks were slightly rosy with embarrassment, and when she noticed me looking at her, she squeezed my hand. We quickly walked over to the buffet table, and I realized that I was completely famished. Trying to give the crowd a moment to forget about us, I spent a long time carefully piling my plate as high as it would go, and Amelia laughed out loud when she saw my huge mountain of food.

"Come sit over here!" Emma called when we turned around. She'd saved two seats at her table for us. Besides her boyfriend, Michael and Jenna were also seated at her table, as were Bobby and his three girls. We sat down between Emma and the oldest of the nieces.

"You guys are insatiable," Emma said, leaning close to whisper to us.

Amelia swatted her playfully on the arm. "Oh, hush. I've seen the two of you at enough of these things to know you do exactly the same every chance you get. You're just sore you didn't think of it yourself."

Michael, affecting the haughty expression of authority, said, "Jenna and I would never *think* of desecrating such a sacred event."

Amelia laughed. "What about last Christmas?"

Michael and Jenna blushed scarlet and we all chuckled.

"What happened at Christmas?" I asked.

"You don't want to know," Amelia said. "Let's just say a certain older brother, a certain sister-in-law, and a certain mother were too indignant to eat dinner at the table that evening."

Everyone laughed again, and I suddenly realized I felt natural, almost completely like myself with her family. All of the dread from the last week, between worrying about Amelia and worrying about this party, suddenly seemed to have disappeared. While I was still on the fence about a couple members of her family—as they clearly were with me—I found Amelia's dad and everyone at this table warm, welcoming, and charming. I didn't know what I'd expected of her family, but it certainly wasn't this group of friendly people.

CHAPTER TWENTY-ONE

We danced for a while after dinner, and then I begged off, wanting to go home and rest for the evening. The week had been tumultuous, and, between traveling and working and worrying, I'd barely slept. Amelia had a hard time covering up her disappointment, as she'd wanted me to stay over, but I insisted on leaving. As a means of pacifying her, I'd agreed to let her come with me to see apartments the next day, though I'd originally planned to go alone with Meghan so we could catch up. I realized the error of double-booking when Meghan showed up bright and early the next morning.

"What do you mean Amelia's coming?" she asked, clearly miffed.

"Well, not to all of them," I said. "She's only going to look at the ones Uptown with me."

"So I'm not invited to see those?" Meghan asked, her eyes blazing with fury.

"Of course you are! It's just that Amelia will be there too."

"I thought we'd get to catch up today. I hardly ever see you anymore."

"And we will! We have all morning and part of the afternoon for just the two of us," I said. "Anyway, don't you think you should get to know her better?"

"I guess." Meghan was clearly disappointed, but seeing my face, she suddenly smiled. "I'm sorry. I'm acting like a child. Of course it's fine, and you're right. I don't even know the woman."

I gave her a quick hug. "Thanks, Meghan. I'm sorry. I should have just planned to meet her after."

Meghan shrugged, obviously still hurt, but her anger seemed to have dissipated. I had been avoiding her, and I'd felt like a complete ass about it for weeks now. While we hadn't talked too much, Lana had become my go-to guide to lesbianism and relationships since I left New York. We had been texting back and forth and having quick chats most nights. I knew this was unfair to Meghan—just because she was straight didn't mean that she had nothing to offer as far as relationship advice, but Meghan's barely concealed antagonism toward Amelia was off-putting. It was making me trust her less and less, even if she didn't deserve it. Still, I wanted to preserve our friendship if I could, and I did feel bad about ruining our plans. But there was nothing for it. Amelia was joining us and that's all there was to it.

I excused myself to get changed, and, after a quick breakfast, we both walked over to the first apartment, which was only a couple of blocks from my aunt's house. The first one was also close to my old haunts, but it was run-down. The landlord dismissed all of my concerns about the exposed, shoddy plumbing and crappy drywall, claiming that he would fix them before I moved in, but I knew better than that. Sometimes landlords in New Orleans will give you a discount on the rent to fix things yourself just to get out of paying for it themselves. Meghan had gotten herself into that situation before, and I knew this was a clue to avoid that landlord's properties. The next place we saw was nicer inside, but on a slightly rougher street. While a lot of the Bywater has gentrified since Hurricane Katrina, a few streets were still less desirable. I wasn't opposed to living on a street like this, but I also wasn't thrilled, as I often came home late at night. The outside of most of the houses in the block here was covered in peeling paint or graffiti, and trash and junk littered the gutters.

We saw two more similar places in the Bywater before going over to the Marigny. Here the problem was money, as the rents in this part of town were very high. I'd wanted to see what the fuss was all about, but, after looking at a couple of smaller apartments for almost double the cost of the larger places in the Bywater, I wasn't convinced it was worth it. We had lunch at a combination laundromat/grocery store/diner before seeing the two places I'd arranged to visit in the French Quarter. The Quarter apartments were the most expensive and had the further drawback of being too close to the tourist areas of town. The Quarter is beautiful and it's the city's pride and joy, but that doesn't necessarily mean it's a great place to live.

By the time we left the final Quarter apartment on Chartres, my hopes of finding a place that day were beginning to wane. While I'd been game to look at places Uptown, I suddenly knew I didn't really want to live up there. I'd always lived on the downriver side of Canal, and the idea of being so far from almost everyone I knew didn't really appeal to me. It would be nice to be closer to Amelia, but I wasn't necessarily ready to make that leap yet. In fact, as I'd thought about it more clearly, if I ever made the move Uptown, it would be to move in with her, and that was a while off yet. She'd hinted very obliquely yesterday that I should just wait a while before moving, as it would save the effort of moving again when we were ready to live together. Though Meghan and her boyfriend were already in the process of joining households, I'd never fancied myself as the type to make that choice lightly. It would take me more time to make that kind of commitment. Further, I was actually looking forward to having a place of my own and wanted it to be perfect for me.

I'd arranged to meet Amelia at CC's on Royal again so she could take us to the Uptown places, and as we walked over there, I thought about what kind of excuse I could make to avoid seeing any of them.

Meghan must have sensed my reluctance, as she said, "If you saw something you like, you don't have to look at the rest of the apartments you have lined up."

"It's not that—I don't think I could live in any of the places we've seen so far. It's just that I'm not really interested in living Uptown. I thought I'd be okay with it, but I don't really want to be that far away from Aunt Kate. Or you. Or all of this." I gestured around me. "It almost doesn't seem like New Orleans over there. That's why I never wanted to live there when I was in college."

"So don't bother looking! I'm beat anyway. You can always check the Bywater again next week. Maybe something new will turn up."

I shrugged. It was easy enough to make that decision now, but it would be hard to tell Amelia about it. She'd been very excited when I mentioned the Uptown apartments I was seeing.

She was waiting with a cup of coffee when we got there, and we hugged quickly before I got in line. Meghan, somewhat reluctantly, sat down with Amelia to wait for me to get our coffee, and I glanced over at them a few times as I waited. Luckily they seemed to be making nice, and when I sat down with our coffee, neither of them seemed too uncomfortable.

"Meghan was just telling me that she's in a band," Amelia said. "We both just realized that she knows my brother Michael."

"He's an excellent drummer," Meghan said. "I've heard good things about Jenna, too, but I haven't had a chance to play with her."

"She's wonderful," Amelia said. "She mainly plays with one band, but I think she does the occasional set with different people."

"Tell her I'm interested," Meghan said. "My bass player's moving to San Francisco soon, so we'll be looking to fill his shoes."

As they exchanged phone numbers and e-mail addresses, I breathed a sigh of relief. It was nice to know that the two could be pleasant to each other, even if it was, at this stage, only for my benefit. I felt very strongly about both of them and wouldn't want to have to choose between them. Maybe they could become friendly, if not friends, with time.

"So when's your next appointment?" Amelia asked me when they were finished.

"Not for over an hour yet. I thought the others would take longer, so we have some time to kill."

"I wonder if I could show you something," Amelia said, looking mischievous. "It's a place I know for rent that's not far from here— maybe a five-minute walk."

"In the Quarter?" Meghan asked.

"It's right on Esplanade," Amelia explained. Esplanade is the avenue that divides the Quarter from the Marigny, so it would be closer to my aunt's house than the places we'd just visited.

"I didn't see a listing for it," I said as we gathered our things.

"It's not listed in a lot of places," Amelia said. She wouldn't make eye contact with me. She seemed a little cagey, but I decided to play along with whatever she was hiding.

It wasn't as warm as it'd been at the party yesterday. A distinct chill in the air suggested that the famous warm New Orleans weather might be finally ready to take its two-month winter break. I'd worn a light jacket out of the house that morning and regretted not grabbing a heavier coat. Knowing that this time of year could occasionally bring snow or icy rain to Paris didn't help—I'd already readjusted to the Southern climate of my childhood.

We walked up Royal, and when we hit Esplanade, we crossed the street and turned right. Amelia stopped in front of a two-story Victorian house. I didn't see any signs out front to suggest that this was anything but a single-family home or that it was available for rent. Only by looking closely at the house could I see two entrances, one at the front and one on the side. We followed Amelia up the front steps, and she removed a set of keys from her pocket to unlock the front door.

"Why do you have keys?" I asked.

"I'll explain after you've looked around," she said, not making eye contact.

Meghan and I glanced at each other, shrugged, and started exploring. The ground floor was gorgeous, with dark wood floors. It had a small, lovely, old-fashioned kitchen with updated appliances and a tiny powder room near a small living room. I could already picture the loveseat I would place in the living room, and there was just enough room for a couple of bookcases and my reading chair. A steep staircase took us up to two small bedrooms, one at the front with tons of natural light and a smaller one in the back. In between the two bedrooms was a full bath that, I was amused to note, had, in addition to a toilet, a bidet.

When we went back downstairs, Amelia was standing by the large front window in the living room, and she turned as we approached.

"So what do you think?" she asked.

"It's incredible," I said.

Meghan agreed. "It's the nicest apartment we've seen all day."

Amelia nodded, clearly unsurprised. "My father owns it. He owns a lot of properties around the city. This one actually hasn't been listed yet. The tenants only moved out a couple of weeks ago, and he had to have some things fixed before renting it again."

That boded well for him as a landlord, but I wasn't convinced yet. "Do you know how much it is?"

Amelia shook her head. "I don't think my father would know, to tell you the truth. He runs all his rentals through his rental agency, which is where you would pay your rent. But if I tell him you're interested, he'll hold it for you and get you the price tomorrow when they're open. He might have an idea of how much it will be if I ask. Do you want me to?"

Meghan and I shared a look. The idea of renting from her father didn't bother me, particularly since I wouldn't have to deal with him directly. Places like this were rare, and it would be foolish not to try. Still, I didn't want to get my hopes up.

"I'm a little afraid I won't be able to afford it," I said.

"Well, let's ask anyway." Amelia pulled out her phone, and Meghan and I wandered back into the kitchen while she talked.

"This place is a dream," Meghan said, running her hand over the marble countertop.

"Right? That front room upstairs would be perfect for a studio."

She snorted. "Only you would put your studio in the nicest room in the house."

I ignored her dig. "The living room down here is a little small, but it's big enough to have a few people over. It's not like I ever throw big parties or anything."

"And the kitchen is just large enough for a little table, right over there," Meghan said, pointing.

"Totally. There isn't space for a big dining-room table, but if I had people over, we could sit around the coffee table, or I could get a folding table or something."

Amelia joined us and handed me a slip of paper. "That's the price he thinks it would be."

Meghan and I read the number, and she whistled. "Whew!" she said. "No wonder we never heard of this place. Luxury rental, I guess."

Heart sinking, I handed back the slip of paper. "That's way too much for me, Amelia."

"How much can you spend?" she asked.

I blushed, more than a little embarrassed to talk about money with her. "A little over half that."

Amelia looked startled and then crestfallen. "I'm so sorry! I didn't mean to show you something so far-fetched. That was stupid of me."

"Don't worry about it!" I gave her a quick hug. "It was nice to actually see inside one of these places. I've walked by the houses on this street a thousand times and have always wondered what they were like inside."

"It really is beautiful," Meghan said, likewise trying to reassure her.

"Let me make it up to you both for wasting our time." She was still looking a little upset. "Can I take you both to dinner later?"

"I have to work, I'm afraid," Meghan said.

"And I wanted to paint tonight," I added. "It is a work night, after all."

Amelia pulled me in for a kiss. "I think your boss would let you come in a little late tomorrow after all your hard work last week."

I kissed her back, and Meghan started making gagging noises. We laughed.

"If you two don't mind, I better head home now," Meghan said, clearly embarrassed to be around us. "I want a couple of hours to myself before I have to go to that noisy bar. Sundays are almost as busy as Saturdays lately." I knew she was making excuses to get away from us, or possibly just Amelia, but as she was already out the door before I thought to stop her, there was nothing I could do about it now.

After she was gone, Amelia turned to me, pulling me closer again. "What about you, my sweet? Are you sure I can't entice you to stay out?"

I shrugged. "I was planning to see some places Uptown, but I'm too tired. I could call and cancel, and then we would have all afternoon for ourselves."

"That sounds lovely," she said, and kissed me again.

Chapter Twenty-two

The next two weeks passed in a blur, and before I knew it, it was Thanksgiving weekend and I still hadn't found a suitable place to rent. Amelia gave everyone a half day on the Wednesday before the holiday, and we'd agreed to meet up to watch Meghan's band play later that evening. I'd been at my new job for two months, and it was starting to feel like I could stay in it for the long haul. While I wasn't ready to give up my dreams of working in academia, the thought of staying in my current position for a year or two was actually appealing. Between the variation in my day-to-day responsibilities and my constant contact with beautiful works of art, the job was challenging, interesting, and visually stimulating. The Cameron sale, as my project at Brent Cameron's was now called, was bringing in a lot of revenue for us and for Amelia's brother Bobby, who was now in charge of furnishing the house. Overall, I counted my time with the company so far as highly successful.

Thanksgiving had caused some debate between Amelia and me, chief of which was where to eat dinner. Aunt Kate always put on a full Creole spread, and as I hadn't been back in the States for Thanksgiving in several years, she was going all out. Amelia's brother Bobby, on the other hand, had invited me for traditional American fare, boasting about his cooking acumen, as he'd apparently attended a culinary school for lessons over the summer. We'd decided to try to attend both dinners, as there was simply no way of bowing out of either, and both Aunt Kate and Bobby had accommodated our request by putting the meals a few hours apart.

Still, the idea of eating two huge meals in one day was daunting, and I didn't relish the idea of how nervous I would be at both of them, for different reasons.

On Wednesday, when I got home from work, I immediately changed into my painting clothes. Between staying at Amelia's house every other night and collapsing from exhaustion on the others, I'd barely had time to paint at all lately. I tried to squeeze in an hour or two every week, but even that didn't always happen. Still, my new painting, the one inspired by the slave mural on the Winters Corporation building, had managed to hold my interest in a way few paintings had before. Usually if I put aside my work for too long, I couldn't get back into it. Every time I worked on this one, though, it was like I'd never stopped.

Aunt Kate had shouted something about going down to the docks for the seafood, but I was still surprised when I heard the doorbell ring several times until I remembered that no one was downstairs to answer it. Setting my brushes on the easel, I ran down and answered the door. Amelia was standing there, and she smiled when she saw my paint-spattered clothes. She carried a small overnight bag. Our dinner here tomorrow was going to be at noon, so we'd decided it would be easiest to have her stay over. It would be her first time here overnight, and we were both nervous about it.

"Finally," she said. "I thought I might have to break in."

"I'm sorry. I forgot Aunt Kate was gone. I should have left you a note."

"That's okay." She walked in and we kissed.

"Let me change and we can head out. I don't have time to do my hair or anything, but Mimi's isn't very fancy, so I don't mind if you don't."

"Why would I mind?" she asked, following me into my bedroom.

"You're just always so put-together." I indicated her clothes and hair. "Even in my nice stuff, I still feel like your poor cousin when I'm with you."

She laughed. "You look fantastic anytime. Even now." Her eyes darkened a little, and a flash of heat raced through me.

I took a wary step away from her. "None of that, lady, or we'll be even later than we are already."

She stepped closer to me. "Why, whatever do you mean, Doctor?"

I shivered a little, her tone turning me on more than was warranted from the words themselves. We'd been so busy this week getting ready for the break that we hadn't been together for a few days now, and my body seemed to want to remind me of this.

"We could wait…" I said, sounding, even to myself, uncertain.

"We could." She took another step closer. "Or we could be quick about it."

I drew her quickly into my arms. She yipped in surprise, and I used the momentary break in her defenses to top her, pushing her onto my bed. She stared up at me as I surveyed her beneath me, her eyes dancing with merriment at my unusual aggressiveness. I reached down and yanked off her shirt in one long movement and, once it lay in a crumpled pile behind me, found that she was panting slightly from excitement. The rise and fall of her chest was making me excited too, and I lay myself on top of her, maneuvering her back onto my bed with my mouth. She let this go on for a while, even to the point of letting my hands rest farther up on her stomach than she'd allowed before. Another inch or two, I realized, and I would be touching her bra. I could feel her desire thrumming beneath my fingers as she trembled under me and had a momentary feeling of hope that her desire might lead somewhere further.

Almost as if sensing my resolve to do something, she suddenly stiffened under my hands. Soon her hands were moving mine down and away, and she was flipping me onto my back. She shoved my legs apart and settled down between them, her actions seeming almost angry in their haste. She had my pants and underwear off a moment later, and she began licking and sucking at the wetness between my legs. I was already so turned on that I began bucking my hips against her soft, warm mouth after only a second or two. Still sucking on my clit, she slipped her fingers inside my wetness, quickly, hard. She curled them inside me and, frustrated by days apart from her as well as by her tantalizing desire moments before, no sooner had she moved her fingers inside me than I was slipping over the edge, calling out her name incoherently.

Cradled in her arms on my small bed moments later, I felt a fleeting sense of complete fulfillment before the nagging worry that had plagued the last three weeks marred my contentment. While she'd explained her problem to me, it was no less mysterious now than it had been when she told me about it. Her behavior showed me that she desired me, and the way her body responded made me believe that she liked touching me and being touched, to a degree. Nothing in her body language gave a clear impression that she didn't want me to do so until I tried, and I'd been trying.

She'd allowed me to touch some places, but others she didn't, and the line between them was still very vague. We needed to talk about it again, soon, but the idea of spoiling what we had now intimidated me. I didn't know how far I could go before she'd start drawing away from me again, and the memory of the last time we'd fought about it haunted me. What we had, even if it wasn't entirely what I wanted, was very good. But how could it be enough for her? That question troubled me and made it hard for me to accept the good parts of our relationship.

I finally made myself sit up and scoot out of her arms. She lay there, watching me dress, eyes still dark and hooded with desire. Just seeing her there, her shirt off, her hair in disarray, was almost enough to make me want to jump back into bed with her again, so I forced myself to look somewhere else as I finished. I ran a quick comb through my hair and wiped away my smeary eye makeup, and by the time I was ready, Amelia had put herself back into a semblance of order. Anyone studying her could see that something had ruffled her a little, but she looked, to an untrained eye, fairly put-together. She loosened her hair and then pulled it up into a bun again, securing it with a wooden black clip.

"Are you ready?" I asked.

"Yes." She sighed, looking back at the bed.

"If we leave now, we'll be just in time for the second set." I tried to keep the impatience out of my voice. Meghan was going to kill me.

Amelia sighed. "Fine, but let's drive. The car is out front."

"Okay." A fifteen-minute walk was certainly not something we needed to add to our lateness, and Amelia rarely drank enough to make driving a problem.

As we walked into the living room, Aunt Kate and Jim arrived, carrying bags of food.

"You girls off, then?" she asked.

"Yes," I said, "and we'll probably be very late. We'll try to keep it down when we get back." I blushed when I realized the sexual implications of this remark, though I hadn't meant it that way.

Aunt Kate's face was a barely contained mask of derision. While she told me she didn't mind me having Amelia over for the night, she clearly did mind. So far, despite the added weeks of relative peace between me and Amelia, Aunt Kate hadn't warmed up to Amelia at all.

"See you tomorrow then," I told her, giving her a quick hug.

Outside, a new black Mercedes coupe was sitting directly in front of the house, the dealer tags still on the bumper. This wasn't Amelia's car, but when she unlocked it, I assumed she'd simply traded hers in. The inside was a creamy white leather, and the ride over to Mimi's, despite the atrocious condition of the roads, was smooth and quiet. We managed to find a parking space about a block from the bar and quickly walked over, inside, and upstairs where Meghan's band was playing.

Zach waved from a small table that had been reserved for us, but the server looked annoyed at our lateness. We ordered drinks and turned to watch the band.

Meghan played with a lot of different kinds of bands and players, depending on the venue, but there was generally always a drummer, a guitar player, some horns, and a bass player, and Meghan sometimes played the banjo, fiddle, or accordion. In larger venues, more horns or strings were added, but Mimi's, like Meghan's band tonight, was pretty small. When I finally turned toward them, I was surprised to see Amelia's brother Michael playing the drums and his girlfriend Jenna on the bass. Amelia was unfazed, obviously prepared to see them. The band finished their song, and after the applause, Meghan called for a quick break. The three of them put down their instruments and walked over to us.

"Nice of you to finally join us," Meghan said, eyes narrow.

"I'm sorry," I said. "We were—"

"I know what you two were doing, girly," Meghan said, closing her eyes. She held up a hand. "I don't need the gory details."

Michael and Jenna laughed. "Were you surprised to see us?" he asked me.

"I was! But I'm so happy this worked out for you."

"They're both fantastic," Meghan said, most of her annoyance gone. "We've played together a couple of times now, and we're getting more requests to play gigs than I've ever had with anyone else."

"I'm so glad you set this up," Michael said, squeezing Amelia's hand. "We both really needed the work, and Meghan's awesome."

Meghan puffed up her chest. "You're damn right I am." She moved around the table, kissing Zach, and I watched the two of them with fondness. They looked great together, and Zach actually seemed like a pretty nice guy, even if he was very quiet. Meghan was loud enough for both of them, so they seemed to balance each other. For once, I thought Meghan had found a guy as nice as she thought he was. It was a pleasant change from the kind of losers she used to date.

Meghan glanced at her watch. "Okay, I guess we better get back to it. Drinks are on the house, but don't go too crazy or they won't invite us back." She paused. "Also, after this, you guys are coming to my new place for a nightcap. You haven't been over once since I moved in, so no excuses." She pointed at both of us to show us how serious she was, and I laughed.

"We were planning on it," I said.

"Wouldn't miss it for the world," Amelia said.

"Good." Meghan nodded firmly.

About halfway through the band's second set, I got up to go to the bathroom. The little, one-stall affair upstairs was occupied, so I went down to the larger restroom. When I came out of the stall, a thin, tall woman was standing by the sink, waiting. I tried to move to the side to give her room to go into the stall, but she kept standing there, staring at me.

"I'm sorry, excuse me," I said, indicating the sink behind her.

"You're not going anywhere," she said, eyes narrowed.

"What?"

"You're not going anywhere until I talk to you." She took a step closer, and I suddenly saw that her face was a mask of rage.

"Who are you?" I asked, taking a step back.

"Enough talk." She grabbed my arm and yanked me close to her. I struggled and she twisted my arm behind my back, making me call out in pain. "Shut up and listen to me," she hissed, jerking my arm up. I stopped struggling, desperately hoping someone would come in to the bathroom to help.

Seeing that I was momentarily cooperating, she let go of my arm, and I leapt toward the door. I almost had the handle, but she reached out and pulled me back again, slamming my stomach into the sink. I shouted, and she clapped her hand over my mouth.

"Shut. The. Fuck. Up." Her voice was a low growl from behind me. "If you don't stop, I'm going to have to hurt you. All I want to do is talk, and then I'll let you go. Nod if you understand me."

I nodded.

She kept her hand tight over my mouth and, with her other hand, twisted my arm up behind my back. She continued to hold me against the sink. She'd leaned over my back to give me less leverage, so I was effectively pinned. Despite her leanness, she was incredibly strong. I tensed my body, getting ready to fight as hard as I could. Turning my head, I could see her face a few inches behind my head, and I contemplated rearing back and smashing into her.

"I can feel you thinking about trying something, bitch, but don't test me." As if to stress her point, she twisted my arm back farther, hard, and I groaned. "I'm going to tell you something and then I'll let you go. If I don't get to tell you, I'll just track you down again. Do you understand?"

Reluctantly, I nodded again.

She grunted in satisfaction. "Here it is. Stay the fuck away from Amelia Winters. Break up with her tonight and never go near her again. In fact, quit your job. You can't have anything else to do with her after tonight."

She must have seen the confusion in my eyes, as she laughed, once. "Don't worry. You'll put it all together eventually, and even if you don't, Amelia Winters is not your concern—she's mine. I'm not giving you information here. I'm giving you an order. This is your only chance. If you don't listen to me, I'm going to have to hurt you." As if to make her point clearer, she yanked up on my arm and I screamed into her palm, my cries muffled by her sweaty palm.

She paused, and I turned to see her looking around for a moment, her eyes calculating and cold. "Now, I'm going to let you go and you're going to walk out of this room. I'll give you a minute while I clear out of here. If you try to follow me, I'll hurt you. If you call the police, I'll hurt you. If you do anything besides what I just told you to do, I'll hurt you. Press my buttons enough, and I'll hurt everyone you know, including that old lady you live with. Am I making myself clear?"

"Yes," I whispered against her callused fingers.

"Good," she said. I felt her hands relax, and I slithered away from her and toward the door. I turned to look at her, waiting for her to rush me again, but she just stood there, watching me leave.

Outside the bathroom, I rubbed at my sore mouth, the sweat from her hand tainting my lips. My shoulder and arm felt bruised and tender. I took a moment to review my options before doing anything. I could go straight to the bartender and get a bouncer to do something about her, or I could go back upstairs and tell Amelia. I looked back at the bathroom door, dreading the moment she would come out, and that made my decision for me. I raced back upstairs.

Amelia was pleased to see me, but she looked puzzled as I approached. She slid off her chair and came over to me, meeting me by the bar. I looked around behind me, waiting to see if the woman had followed for a moment, and motioned for Amelia to sit down next to me at the bar.

"What's wrong?" Amelia asked. "Why's your mouth so red?"

"There was a woman. Downstairs. In the bathroom. She put her hand over my mouth and twisted my arm."

"What?" Amelia asked, jumping to her feet.

Terrified, I pulled her back toward her seat, looking around wildly. "She might be watching us right now. She knows you. She told me to break up with you and never see you again."

Despite the dim light of the bar, I could see Amelia go pale, and she sat down on a barstool heavily. "It's Sara," she said.

"Who?"

"Sara. My ex. Was she tall? Slender? Dark-brown hair?"

"Yes."

"It's her." Her face was still white and shocked. "I can't believe she'd do this." She shook her head. "I never imagined she'd go this far…"

"Well, she has." I was angry now instead of frightened. "We need to call the police."

Amelia looked alarmed and was silent for a moment. "I think you're right." She sighed. "It's gone on long enough. I think she's actually lost her mind."

"What happened before? With your other girlfriends since Sara? I remember you said something about her being rude to them."

"She called them, left nasty messages. My last girlfriend swore that Sara was following her, but we never had any proof, and Sara seemed to stop after a while." She paused. "One time, she left a bag of cat shit on my doorstep, but that's as violent as she's ever been."

"Well, she's violent now." I rubbed my arm and shoulder. "I was afraid she would dislocate my shoulder."

Amelia's face fell and she embraced me, gently. "My God, Chloé. I'm so sorry about this."

I shrugged. "It's not your fault she's a lunatic. What happened between you? Was it a bad breakup?"

Amelia hesitated and then shook her head. "Not exactly. A lot of things happened." She paused, looking a little guilty, and then shook her head. "Anyway, we'd been growing apart, and when she got a job in New York, we just decided to end things rather than try a long-distance relationship. Things were quiet for a while on her end, and then she started sending weird messages to my new girlfriends and calling them at all hours of the night."

She didn't seem to be lying, but it was clear she was holding something back. There was plainly more to the story that she wasn't sharing. Deciding to talk about it later, I said, "I'll call my cousin Derek. He's a police officer. He'll know what to do. He might even be able to arrest her if she's still downstairs."

Amelia reluctantly agreed and we both got up, going into the upstairs bathroom to call him.

❖

After what seemed liked several hours, and after I'd repeated my story and given a description of the suspect what seemed like a thousand times, Derek finally let us leave the bar, escorting us back to the car. Several police officers had also grilled Amelia about Sara, and we were both exhausted. We sat there in the car, not moving or doing anything but looking out through the windshield.

When the police had shown up, Meghan and the others had looked stunned, but I didn't have a chance to explain anything to her. "Let me call Meghan real quick," I said in the car.

Meghan picked up on the first ring. "What the hell happened?"

Her usual bluntness made me smile. "It's a long story."

"Were you mugged or something?"

I glanced over at Amelia, whose face was a mask of weariness and exhaustion. "I had a run-in with a crazy woman in the bathroom. She threatened me and threatened everyone I know and then she let me leave."

"Are you hurt?"

"Not badly."

"I'm going to kill her!" Meghan shouted, and I had to pull the phone away from my ear.

"Anyway, I'm okay now. We're going to head back to Aunt Kate's. I'm sorry for interrupting your set."

"Jesus, Chloé, that's the least of my concerns. Tell me more details tomorrow, okay?" Meghan and Zach had been invited to Thanksgiving too.

"Okay," I said, not relishing the idea of reliving the story again. I hung up.

I rubbed my eyes, exhaustion crashing over me. "Let's go back and go straight to bed."

Amelia glanced over at me. "I had something to tell you, but all this interrupted me. Now it just seems silly."

"What is it?"

"This is your new car."

I blinked at her a couple of times, my brain foggy with fatigue.

"My car?"

"Yes. The paperwork is in the glove box."

I blinked a few more times to clear my head and opened the glove box. Inside, I saw the title with my name on it. I stared at it for a while.

"Amelia, what the hell?"

She shrugged. "You needed a car. I told you I was arranging to get you one two months ago. I'm sorry it took so long. I prefer the German-made engines, so it had to be imported."

"You told me you were arranging to get me a *company* car. This is completely different."

"Well, yes, but the function is the same. You need a car and now you have one."

I sighed, frustrated at her seeming obtuseness. "Yes—both of them are cars. But this one belongs to me. I thought I was getting a company car. One that belonged to the *company*. You know I can't accept it."

"Why not?" She looked genuinely puzzled.

I laughed. "Listen. I know you come from a place where giving someone a car is no big deal, but this is too much. It's way too nice and too expensive just to give me."

She still looked confused. "Would a cheaper car be better? I can trade this one in."

I sighed again. "Look. I like to earn my things, not have them given to me. I know that sounds crazy, but that's how *I* was raised."

She shook her head, still clearly baffled. "But you need a car."

"And I wouldn't mind *borrowing* one from the company, but you can't give me one."

She was still obviously struggling with the concept, and I shook my head wearily, sighing. "Let's not do this right now, Amelia.

We're both too tired to have this conversation. I just want to go home and go to sleep."

Resigned, she started the car. We were home in a couple of minutes.

After we'd peeled off our clothes, we squished into my tiny bed, spooning. Amelia drifted off almost as soon as we were down, but I continued to lie awake, staring into the darkness. Sara's warnings were still ringing in my ears when I finally fell asleep.

❖

Sara waited for them outside the bar, hoping to catch them together, but when the police showed up, she made herself scarce, crossing the street and spying on the action from Big Daddy's bar. She sat just inside the doorway with her cocktail, watching a few police officers appear and leave until only one policeman remained. She waited for him to go away, but he was clearly buddy-buddy with Amelia's new slag, as he actually escorted them back to their car a couple of blocks away. Sara followed all three of them, keeping to the shadows. She watched the cop leave and then the women sit there in the car for a while. The car had dealer's plates. She understood in a moment that Amelia had bought the car for that bitch.

Sara looked down and her clenched fists and made herself relax. She left tiny nail marks in her palms, drawing crescent moons of blood. How could Amelia love that woman? What did that little blonde nobody have that Sara didn't? She was clearly poor and from a poor, unknown family. She certainly wasn't prettier than Sara and was, in some regards, rather strange looking. She was much too skinny and gawky for Amelia's tastes. There must be something else. Amelia wasn't interested in being fucked, so Sara knew it couldn't be that. Chloé had to have some powerful control over Amelia somehow, or Amelia wouldn't be interested or stay interested in her for this long. Since she'd broken up with Sara, Amelia had slept around the City of New Orleans, and none of the women she was with had held her attention for more than a few weeks. This little blonde was somehow different. Sara just didn't know how. Yet.

When they continued to sit in the new car, Sara, knowing where they were going next, walked back to her rental and drove over a few blocks to where Chloé and her aunt lived. Sara had been staking it out for a few weeks now, following the aunt and Chloé around town every time she could fly down from New York for a couple of days. She kept expecting Chloé to come home in tears, devastated after Amelia fired her like the other "assistants," but she never did. Instead, Chloé spent half her nights at Amelia's place and always looked so self-satisfied that it was sickening.

Sara almost did something, said something, when they got out of the car in front of Chloé's place. Only God knew the next time she'd catch them alone. In fact, Sara pulled out the knife in her purse and had her hand on the inside handle of her car door, ready to get out, but then she stopped. Considering what she'd just seen at the bar, she was half-afraid the policeman would show up again just to make sure that they got home okay.

Instead, she was forced to watch them disappear inside the little house and do nothing. When she decided it was safe, she got out and stood on the sidewalk, staring at the window that had lighted up and gone dark after Amelia and that bitch went inside. As the sun started to brighten the street around her, Sara made her way back to her rental and drove toward the airport. Her flight back to New York didn't leave for a couple of hours, but she didn't want to be here anymore. If she stayed in New Orleans she might do something stupid, and she needed to be careful now that she'd shown her hand. Amelia was on to her now. Sara decided she had to let it go, at least for now. She'd wanted to resolve this before she left the country for a few weeks, but that apparently wasn't going to happen. Still, she knew she would have more opportunities to do something to that little bitch in the future if Amelia decided to keep her around.

The New Year was just around the corner, after all.

CHAPTER TWENTY-THREE

I woke to an empty bed and sat up, looking around in confusion. Amelia's overnight bag was open on my vanity, mostly empty. The light coming in through the window showed that it was already late in the morning, and a glance at the clock confirmed it. I would need to hurry if I wanted to be ready for Aunt Kate's early dinner. I stood up and stretched, then pulled on my heavier bathrobe. It was finally beginning to seem cold, and Aunt Kate always forgot about turning on the heat. We rarely needed it for many days in a row, even in the winter, so we often went without.

Jim greeted me in the living room. He was sitting on the couch, reading the newspaper, alone. Confused, I walked into the empty kitchen, wondering where my Aunt Kate and Amelia had gotten off to. I caught a glimpse of movement outside and saw them both sitting on the patio by the fishpond. They were hunched up next to each other, obviously in deep discussion. Not knowing if I should interrupt, I finally decided to take a shower and get ready. If they had a tête-à-tête, maybe Amelia could begin to help Aunt Kate get over her reservations about her.

I showered quickly, massaging my sore shoulder under the hot water. I spotted several finger-shaped bruises on my forearm, and my mouth was still a little red around the edges from Sara's hand. When I came out of the bathroom, Amelia and Aunt Kate were still talking outside. Starting to feel a little alarmed, I dressed quickly, wearing long sleeves and putting a little makeup around my mouth to cover the bruises and scrapes. By the time I came into the kitchen, they were both standing by the stove looking at the boiling cabbage. They turned and smiled at me.

"So sleepyhead finally decided to join us!" Aunt Kate said. She shook her head ruefully. "It's too late for you to eat breakfast now, sweetie. Dinner is in less than an hour. Maybe you could have some toast to tide you over." She pointed at the last of the breakfast baguette on the table.

"I'm fine. I just need some coffee."

Aunt Kate tsked but pulled out the little saucepan to heat up the milk while I got the coffee concentrate out of the fridge. As we waited for the milk to warm, Aunt Kate and Amelia chatted about the differences between Creole and Cajun cooking. They seemed relaxed, though not particularly warm. Ever since we started working together, I'd seen that Amelia was very good at finding topics for others to talk about in order to put them at ease, and it appeared she'd found one for Aunt Kate: food. Despite being a native, and a frequent restaurant patron, Amelia was completely ignorant of the differences in the local cuisine. Aunt Kate was more than happy to fill her in, explaining that our ancestry was French Creole, which was how she'd learned all her recipes. Amelia threw me a bemused look a couple of times as Aunt Kate lectured, but I was happy they'd found something to talk about. Kate was making Pompano en Papillote, and she had several loaves of bread baking in the second oven—one for each guest. We would also be eating several different kinds of cabbage salad, snails, oysters, and, in the one nod to American tradition, a spicy, candied sweet-potato casserole with cranberry garnish.

Meghan and Zach let themselves in, carrying two pies, a couple of grocery bags, and several bottles of wine. "I brought the most important part of the meal!" Meghan called, holding up the booze.

"Speak for yourself, missy," Aunt Kate said, sniffing with hurt pride.

Meghan laughed and put down her bags before giving her a quick hug. "You know I'm joking, Aunt Kate. Your food's always so delicious." She turned and rustled around in one of her bags, pulling out some fresh flowers. "These are for you." Meghan offered them to Kate as a peace token.

Aunt Kate seemed mollified and took the flowers over to the sink. As she ran them under the water, she turned and pointed at the table. "Meghan, you and Chloé should set the table. Zach, you open the wine. Amelia and I'll start getting everything together and in the serving bowls once I'm done with the flowers."

Twenty minutes later, we were all seated at the table, the food covered to keep it warm. Aunt Kate and Jim sat at opposite ends of the small dining-room table, and Meghan and I sat on one side together, across from Zach and Amelia. The setting was intimate and friendly and boded well for future holidays.

Aunt Kate held up her wineglass. "We're not a praying family. My parents stopped going to Mass when my sister and I were little. Still, the tradition in our household has always been to greet Thanksgiving with thankfulness. I am thankful this year for the return of my wayward niece and for the new man in my life. It's been a wonderful year."

"I'm thankful for the man in my life," Meghan said, looking at Zach. "And I'm also thankful that Chloé's returned to us."

"I'm thankful to be home," I said, "and I'm thankful for you, Amelia."

"And I you," she said quietly.

"I'm thankful I took another chance on women," Jim said, and everyone laughed. "Just so you know, you're never too old to find love."

"I'm thankful to have found such a wonderful, funny, gorgeous woman with such a lovely group of friends," Zach said. "And I'm thankful for this spread of food, too."

We all agreed and dug in.

❖

After dinner, we decided that a walk would help us feel a little less sloth-like and a little more human, so we went over to the new Crescent Park on the river. The views of downtown were spectacular, and since Amelia had never been here before, it was a treat to see her enjoy it so thoroughly. One positive outcome of Hurricane Katrina was the city's now-greater emphasis on urban beautification, and this park was part of that process. In the early days of the park, the neighbors had worried it would drive up nearby rents, and with some cause. The park's development had coincided with an influx of wealthier, younger renters, and almost the entire neighborhood had become more expensive. My aunt took this all in stride, however, as it meant that her property would bring a higher price when she was ready to sell, and crime had significantly decreased in the last couple of years. I'd been dreading the erasure of the rag-tag, rougher edges that had existed in the Bywater before this and could already see that gentrification was well on its way. Still, I appreciated that change could be a positive force, too. This park was an obvious example.

We climbed over the crescent-shaped bridge and walked along the short river walkway, all of us voicing the hope that it would someday link up with the Riverwalk, making one long pathway along the edge of the Mississippi all the way downtown. The day wasn't quite cold enough to make us uncomfortable, but we found it a little chillier closer to the river. Aunt Kate began complaining that she hadn't dressed warmly enough, so we turned around to go back home.

As we headed back toward our house, Amelia's phone rang, and she fell back a little to answer it after excusing herself. Meghan took the opportunity to pull me aside, a little apart from Aunt Kate.

"I've been dying to ask you about last night," she hissed. "I realize you don't want to talk about it in front of Aunt Kate, so now's the chance. What happened?"

Without revealing that Sara was associated with Amelia, I told her the story of my bathroom assault. When I finished, Meghan's eyes were huge.

"Jesus! She sounds like a complete nutcase! Do you think there's a reason she chose you?"

"Yes, but I can't get into that right now."

Meghan looked puzzled, but as we were near the house again, she didn't push me to say more. I was hoping I could avoid details altogether, as the idea of identifying Sara was a little daunting, particularly as it seemed Meghan and Amelia were really beginning to get along now.

I glanced back just in time to see Amelia hang up the phone and thought I saw a guilty look dart across her face when she saw me looking at her. She walked faster to catch up.

"Who was that?" I asked.

"Just work," she said, not meeting my eyes.

We all went back inside, Aunt Kate and Meghan excusing themselves to get the pie and coffee ready. As we waited, Amelia managed to coax Jim to open up about the construction business, and he talked more than I'd ever heard before. Zach was wrapped up in his smart phone, clearly avoiding an awkward conversation, so I sat nearby, quietly, my mind far away. The phone call Amelia had answered troubled me. She'd seemed strange about it for a few minutes afterward and had clearly been lying to me about whomever she was talking to. I was worried Sara had called her but didn't know if I could get Amelia to admit it. It disconcerted me that she might be lying to me. She was likely trying to protect me, but I hated the idea of her deception.

I returned to awareness when Amelia touched my arm. "So how about it?"

"What?" I asked.

She laughed. "You must have been thinking hard about something. Jim here has been praising your artwork. I just told him I haven't seen any of it yet. So how about it? Want to show it to me now?"

"No!" I said, then blushed at her shocked expression. "I'm sorry. I didn't mean for it to come out like that."

Amelia was still clearly taken aback. "Why on earth not?"

Something about showing her my artwork terrified me, and I wasn't entirely sure I could explain—to either her or me—why that was.

Embarrassed, I was relieved not to have to explain myself, as Meghan and Aunt Kate reappeared then, carrying plates of pie and a tray of coffee. Amelia looked at me strangely a couple of times as we ate, but I couldn't think of anything to say to make up for my awkwardness earlier. I squeezed her hand, hoping she would drop the subject, and she eventually did.

CHAPTER TWENTY-FOUR

I was surprised to find myself hungry again by the time we started driving over to Bobby's house for our second dinner of the day. I'd been afraid I wouldn't be able to eat again for the rest of my life. We'd spent the afternoon playing cards and drinking wine, so I was pretty sleepy, but I was looking forward to experiencing a traditional American Thanksgiving spread. I'd only seen one in movies.

Amelia insisted that I drive the new car, and I found the ride exhilarating. I hadn't driven much in the last few years while I was in Europe, and getting behind the wheel of a new, powerful car was an experience I'd never had before. I caught myself speeding several times, and found that when I tried to slow down, because the car's brakes were incredibly sensitive, I constantly slammed us into our seatbelts. Amelia laughed every time. My poor driving didn't faze her.

When we got Uptown, she suggested that I park in her driveway, since Bobby lived just down the street. After a short walk, we were at his house. The smell of turkey and side dishes hit us like a wave as he opened the door, and I handed him the flowers and wine I'd brought after giving him a quick hug.

"Man oh man, am I happy to see you guys. We've all been waiting for you," he said.

"I thought you said six," Amelia said, alarmed, looking at her watch.

"I did, but we've been here smelling that turkey for so long, I think we're all just getting impatient. Enough chitchat! Come in, come in!"

Bobby's house was a warmer, homier version of Amelia's. Instead of antiques and modern furniture, all of the couches and chairs looked well-used and worn. With three children in the house, it was functional as opposed to decorative, though I noted that the artwork on the walls was impeccable, likely provided by Amelia.

All of the kids were eating in the kitchen, and I could hear them shouting and laughing in there. An adult's voice came through as a murmur, apparently trying to convince them to calm down, and I pitied the poor servant put to that task.

I'd changed clothes and was glad I had when I saw the others. Unlike at my aunt's house, the Winters family got decked out for Thanksgiving. The men were in suits and the women were wearing dresses. Bobby excused himself to let the staff know the food could be served, and most of the family came over to greet us.

"I heard you guys had another meal earlier," Emma said after we'd hugged. "Billy and I did the same. I'm so full of turkey, I could burst."

"Chloé's family is Creole," Amelia said, "so I was treated to some of the best seafood I've ever had."

Dean asked me details about traditional Creole food, and I detected in him the same knack Amelia had for being comfortable making small talk with strangers. After a while, we all sat down at the long table, and two women in uniforms appeared, followed by Bobby, each carrying different bowls of food. I got up to help, but Bobby motioned me back in my chair.

"You're a guest here," he said. "Please don't worry about it."

"Bobby has been cooking all day," Michael explained. "His chef has been tearing her hair out watching him make messes in there, but he wanted to do it all on his own."

"Hopefully we won't all be poisoned," their dad said, winking at me.

When the table was finally laden with food and the bowls started making the rounds, I loaded my plate as high as I could.

While I'd had turkey before on Christmas once or twice, all of the traditional sides and trimmings were unfamiliar to me, and I wanted to try everything. There was a ton of food, so I didn't feel guilty about taking as much, or perhaps more, than most of the men. Ingrid and Amelia's mom both took miniscule portions of everything, a habit that likely explained their angular, almost desiccated looks. If I didn't know better, I'd think Ingrid was the woman's daughter, the two of them were so similar. This, I guess, perhaps explained why Dean had found his wife attractive: familiarity. Neither woman had said a single word to me since I arrived, and though I was perhaps projecting, I seemed to sense their clear disapproval. It was going to be tough going to get either one of them to like me. Dean seemed indifferent, which I could deal with more easily than the women's outright dislike. Luckily the rest of the family was warm and friendly, and as I was sitting next to the siblings and the parent that genuinely seemed to like me, I was comfortable enough despite my nerves.

As we ate, Bobby had to excuse himself several times to see to the children, a task I noticed that neither Dean nor Ingrid contributed to, despite having children in the mix, too. This was apparently a burden they left to Bobby, and no one but me seemed to notice the discrepancy. As the rest of the family and I shoveled in food, I noticed that his own plate went almost completely untouched, growing cold. He was simply too busy to eat. When he came back in and sat down for a fourth time, I stood up. Everyone at the table looked surprised, but I smiled at Bobby.

"Why don't you go ahead and eat now, Bobby?" I suggested. "I'll go watch the kids for a while."

He looked relieved, and as I went toward the kitchen, I saw Ingrid give me a dirty look. That's what you get for being so rude to your host, I thought, smiling back at her as nicely as I could.

The kids were actually well-behaved, if a little loud, and were all incredibly curious to see a newcomer in their midst. Being in a collective gave the shyer ones a little courage, and they all tried to talk at me at once when I asked them how they were doing. Two of the older ones remembered me from the anniversary party, but to the others, I was a stranger. I introduced myself to all of them, and they shouted their names back at me, almost in unison. I had so far managed to learn two names and was pretty sure the others would sink in eventually.

Amelia's parents relieved me of my duties after about half an hour, and I was pleased to see that my actions had gotten me a little further in her mom's estimation, as she smiled with something like genuine warmth when they came in. I'd been expecting Amelia to join me the entire time I was in there, but she never came. When I returned to the dining room, I was further surprised to find her gone. Seeing my confused expression, Bobby pointed toward the front parlor, and when I walked in, she was just hanging up her phone. For a brief moment, she looked surprised and guilty again, and my stomach dropped with dread.

"Who was that?" I asked her.

She came near and pulled me into her arms, kissing my neck lightly. "No one important."

I pulled back a little. "Are you sure?" I wanted to give her a chance to come clean about the phone calls.

She looked puzzled but still guilty. "Yes. It was work again. Why do you ask?"

"No reason." My heart sank. I knew she was lying to me again.

She seemed confused and opened her mouth, as if she were about to explain something, but right then, several of her siblings joined us. I caught what looked like relief pass over her face and had to quell a momentary surge of anger at whatever deception she was covering up. I would get to the bottom of this, I decided, just not now.

I helped Bobby and his staff clean up, and by the time we were finished, I couldn't find Amelia anywhere. Emma finally showed me that she was outside on the porch, her phone clutched to her ear. Her face looked stern and anxious, and, the entire time I watched her, she didn't say a word. I could only surmise that she was listening to someone.

Sick with anxiety, I excused myself to lie down for a few minutes, and Bobby showed me to his guest room. I paced around for a few minutes, literally wringing my hands, before something occurred to me. I dug around in my purse for my cell phone and then called Lana.

"I'm such a terrible person for calling on Thanksgiving," I said.

"No, no, no problem. Jess had to work today, so we're having our Thanksgiving on Saturday with her parents. What's up? You sound freaked."

I quickly explained the situation with Sara and with Amelia's behavior today. Lana whistled long and low. "Doesn't sound good, padre," she finally said.

"No, it doesn't, does it?"

"If I were you, I would nip that in the bud, immediately. No deception allowed—even if she thinks it's for your own good."

I felt strangely relieved. I had been half-convinced that I was overreacting all day. "Thanks, Lana. I'm glad to know I'm not crazy."

"Nope—definitely not crazy. Keep me in the loop, okay? Let me know what happens with that nutcase Sara, too."

"I will. Thanks again and Happy Thanksgiving."

"*Ciao, bella dama.*"

"Ciao," I said, chuckling. Talking to her made me feel about a thousand times better.

I took a couple of long, deep breaths to calm down. The last thing I wanted to do was to cause a scene, and we still had a couple of hours to get through with her family. I looked in the mirror and smoothed my hair before rejoining the rest of the party. Amelia was back inside, one of her nieces in her lap, and she smiled when she saw me. She didn't look the least bit guilty about anything, and once again I began to doubt my suspicions.

Amelia, her family, and I spent the evening chatting over wine and pumpkin pie, and by the time we decided to leave, I couldn't imagine ever eating again.

Before we left, Bobby thanked me again, hugging me close to him. "Thank you again for letting me eat today." He kissed my cheek.

I laughed. "No problem. When I was a kid I had to watch my little cousins, and I know when someone needs a break."

"What did you think of the food?" he asked. "I know it was different from your usual holiday fare."

"It was wonderful. I didn't know if I would like the stuffing, but it was incredible."

He looked relieved. "Cornbread and sausage make the world go round. Anyway, thanks so much for coming. Amelia explained that you haven't been home for the holidays for a long time, so I understand it was a sacrifice for you to be here today."

"Not a sacrifice at all. Not when the food was so delicious and the company so lovely."

Amelia laughed. "You're going to give him a big head if you keep talking that way, Chloé. Let's get out of here or he'll make you say more nice things about him."

Despite the chill, I enjoyed our brief walk back to Amelia's house. We were quiet, both of us reflecting on the day, but for perhaps the first time since I knew her, the silence was comfortable and companionable. We were joined at the elbow, and she steered me deftly over several bulges in the sidewalk I'd likely have tripped on in the dark. When we got back to her place, I retrieved my overnight bag from the car and followed her inside to the dark house. She'd once again given her servants the night off, and her place seemed strangely hollow and cold without anyone in it.

"How are you feeling?" she asked, pulling me into her arms.

"Full. Very full," I said, and she laughed.

"Well, we'll have to burn off some of those calories, then, won't we?"

Despite all of my lofty goals about making her come clean, her words gave me a strong jolt of excitement. I'd wanted to talk to her about the phone calls and the deception I'd sensed earlier today, but that suddenly didn't seem as important as it had. I'll do just about anything to avoid confrontation, and I let her lead me upstairs to her bedroom. We paused in the doorway, looking in at the scene she'd clearly prepared ahead of time. Rose petals lay scattered on the bedspread, and unlit candles were set out around the room. She let go of my hand, walking around quickly to light the candles with matches.

I stayed there in the doorway, watching her light them, then turned off the overhead light when she'd finished. She turned and looked back at me from the foot of the bed, and I started to undress. I slid my shoes off one at a time, moving them delicately together. My dress had a side zipper, which I undid one tooth at a time, gradually, evenly. Even from a few feet away, I could see her eyes darken at the sight of me, and her body tensed in anticipation. She took a step closer, and I held up a hand, wanting her to wait and watch. I grinned at the frustration on her face and slowed my pace even further until she backed away again. I slid the dress off my shoulders and let it fall to the ground, stepping out of it, then rolled down my stockings. Finally, I unhooked my bra and pulled it off my arms inch by inch. I kept my underwear on for several long moments before I slid them down, very, very slowly. When I stood up, completely revealed to her, her face looked hungry, anticipatory.

I pointed. "Get on the bed."

Without hesitation, she turned and climbed up on the bed, completely clothed, shoes still on. I walked over to the foot of the bed and looked down at her, wanting to eat her up with my eyes. I reached down and pulled off her shoes one at a time. Her eyes widened a little when I reached up under the hem of her dress to pull off her stockings, but she didn't stop me. Emboldened, I climbed up on the bed on top of her, finding the zipper of her dress and helping her out of it. While I'd seen her nearly naked a couple of times now, this was almost as close as I'd gotten to undressing her completely, and I wondered how much further I could take this. She tensed when I lifted her up a little and found the clasp to her bra, but she let me unhook it and pull it away from her body.

Her breasts were a revelation. As I had never seen them completely bare before this, I paused for a long time, just gazing down at them. Her nipples were darker and wider than mine, and they were hard. I looked up at her face to see her staring at me with a marked concern and anxiety.

"They're beautiful," I said softly.

She appeared uncertain, and I leaned down to kiss her lips. Our breasts brushed together, and I felt her body respond to the contact as she heaved upward a little, clasping me to her. We kissed for a long time, and I kept up the contact as long as I could, relishing the feel of her nearly naked under me. The softness of her breasts against mine was intoxicating.

When I broke away and held myself up above her, her eyes were dark and serious. I could sense her nervousness and didn't want to force her to do anything she wasn't comfortable with. Accepting her naked breasts as the day's accomplishment, I rolled onto my back, pulling her with me and on top. The uncertainty left her eyes, and she bent down, kissing and nibbling at my breasts seconds later. I sighed happily and arched up into her mouth, grasping the back of her head as she sucked hard on one of my nipples, which was still sore from recent encounters.

Too excited to pause to tie me up, Amelia wrenched my hands above my head with one of hers.

"Keep your hands right there," she warned me.

I left my hands where she'd placed them. She started kissing her way down my body, and almost by their own accord, my hands almost immediately moved downward, touching her hair. She stopped and propped herself up again.

"If you don't listen to me, I'll stop right here," she said.

Frowning at her, I moved my hands above my head again and grabbed the headboard, hoping that would help me keep them in place. As her lips moved farther and farther south, though, I could feel my hands struggling to stay where they were supposed to be, and my arms trembled lightly with tension from trying to keep my hands where she wanted them.

When her lips brushed the area just above my pubic hair, my hands betrayed me again and leapt down, clutching at her head. She sat up completely this time and moved away, looking at me coolly.

"What did I tell you?" she asked me.

"To keep my hands up here," I said quietly, moving them back into place.

"But you didn't listen." Her face was a mask of coldness, and it was hard to tell whether she meant what she was saying or how serious she was.

I swallowed. "I'll try harder. I promise."

She moved back toward me, sliding between my legs. My hands clutched at the headboard, and I dug my fingers hard into the metal, gripping with all my might. It was hard to separate the need to keep my hands in place and the sensation of her lips on my lower abdomen. Amelia's fingers were tracing up and down the inside of my thighs, and I let out a low moan when one of them flickered across the folds between my legs before moving back to my thigh. Amelia's kisses moved farther down, but this time she skipped over the parts I desperately wanted her to touch, kissing up and down my legs, pausing on my inner thighs here and there, nibbling and sucking. My hands clenched down, hard, but my hips rose to meet her mouth. I heard her chuckle, low, and wondered in a desire-soaked daze if she were trying to punish me by making me wait so long.

Finally, after she looked up at me once to meet my eyes, her mouth dove into my center. After the long anticipation, the pleasure was intense, overwhelming. I threw my head back and moved my body into her mouth. She pushed me back with her hands, moving me into position. She lingered on the outer lips for a moment before plunging in, deeper, making me almost shout in pleasure. Though I couldn't move my hands, my legs were free, and I wrapped them around her back, pulling her into me. She slipped her tongue over my clit and I felt a jolt at the contact. Two of her fingers glided inside me, deeper and deeper until she found the spot she knew my body craved. Between the anticipation and the precision of her technique, I couldn't hold on for very long. The orgasm made me forget everything, anything, the world going white and bright behind my eyelids as I screamed.

Afterward, she lay in my arms, still clad in only her panties, and I stroked her hair. Though she hadn't let me touch her any more than usual, getting her this naked was definitely progress. Some of the anxiety that had been building up with my frustration with her finally began to ease a little. Progress was progress, no matter how slow.

Suddenly, after all these weeks, it seemed as if things might be okay after all.

CHAPTER TWENTY-FIVE

Late the next morning, after a wonderful breakfast of custom-made omelets prepared by her chef, Amelia insisted on driving me home in my new car. I was still on the fence about accepting the car as a gift, but I'd decided that if I thought of it as a company car, the weirdness would be a little easier to accept. If I quit my job, or if Amelia and I broke up, I would simply leave the car at the warehouse and let her sort out the details of swapping the title. While our relationship was stronger than ever, particularly after spending the last couple of days entirely together, and the progress we'd made last night, it still seemed entirely too early in our relationship to accept something so expensive. Given that I'd rarely received flowers from past boyfriends, the idea of taking a car *ever* was very strange. That said, I needed one to get to work and for work itself. I was tired of relying on being driven around by Amelia and her driver.

"We should have taken separate cars," I told her. "You know I was planning on painting today, and we agreed that I could have a night for it a week. It's not a lot to ask."

"You'll have your night off. I just wanted to see you home—that's all."

She was acting a little strange, but I didn't think much of it until she made an unexpected turn onto Esplanade.

"This isn't how you get to my house," I said.

"I'm going the long way."

"More like taking a detour," I commented, but stopped myself from saying more. I hate backseat drivers.

A couple of minutes later, we pulled into a driveway by her father's rental. There were two parking spaces here—one for the other apartment and the one we'd just parked in.

"What are we doing here?"

"I'll show you." Her eyes alive with merriment, she got out of the car and left me there.

I climbed out my side after her. "Amelia!" I called after her, shutting the car door.

She turned and motioned for me to come nearer. "You'll love this. Just come with me."

She took my hand and led me around the side of the house to the front steps. A paper sign hanging on the door said WELCOME HOME! and a couple of blue balloons were tied to the doorknob. I paused and she turned back to me, looking elated.

"What's this?" I asked.

"You'll see." She pulled me forward.

Amelia opened the door and stepped aside so I could enter first. I held my breath and walked in, and Aunt Kate, Jim, Meghan, and Zach all jumped up from behind furniture.

"Surprise!" they shouted. Amelia followed me in and shut the door behind us.

I was too stunned to say anything. All of my furniture had been moved into the apartment. My armchair, my bookshelves, and a nice, new loveseat had been placed in here, almost exactly as I'd imagined it. A new painting hung above the loveseat, and the other pictures consisted of framed artwork and photographs from my walls at home. I slowly spun around, taking in the whole room. Everyone was smiling, looking incredibly pleased with themselves.

"What is this?" I asked.

"It's your new place." Amelia held up some keys.

"But—but—"

Amelia grabbed my hands and pulled me over to the couch. We sat next to each other while the others stood there, watching.

"I talked with my father and told him how much you loved the apartment. Since he owns the rental agency he uses for his apartments, he agreed to rent it directly to you without going through the agency. He took it off the list a couple of days ago so he could avoid the rental agency's fees. I asked Meghan about it once he told me he could, and she said the new price was exactly what you were willing to pay."

I looked up at Meghan. "You were in on this?"

She smiled and then indicated the others. "We all were."

"We worked like fiends after you two left yesterday to get it ready for you," Aunt Kate said, wiping her brow dramatically.

"You all did this?" I looked at each of them. They nodded. "Together?"

Aunt Kate laughed. "When your Amelia told me about the plan, I was thrilled. I knew you were disappointed about not getting this place. Jim and I wanted to help, so I called Meghan and Zach here to help us move your stuff."

My eyes were welling with tears, and Amelia pulled me into an embrace. "I wanted to surprise you."

"Is this who you were talking with on the phone yesterday?" I asked, pulling back a little.

"Yes. I also had to talk with some movers from work, so it wasn't completely a lie—I did call work. It was really hard not to give it away."

I laughed. "You're a terrible liar, by the way. I knew you were hiding something."

She shrugged, looking incredibly pleased with herself.

Aunt Kate was wiping her eyes.

"Thank you," I told her. "Thanks all of you." I looked around at all of them. "It's the nicest surprise I've ever had."

Meghan's eyes looked a little red as well, but she laughed. "Go look around, you ninny! We've been working our butts off."

I laughed and stood up, walking into the kitchen. A breakfast table had been set up in here, and I saw on the shelves a combination of some of my old kitchenware mixed in with some new. A new mixer stood on the counter, as well as a couple of other small appliances. Out the back door, I could see a larger table set up on my small patio, and a big garden box that looked freshly tilled. I glanced in the powder room as I walked back into the living room, and Amelia was standing by the stairs.

"Can I show you?" she asked, indicating the stairs.

"Yes." I was still fighting tears.

We climbed the narrow, steep flight, and she insisted on showing me the bedroom in the back first. It was small, but functional, with a new queen-sized bed and a couple of tiny night stands. A new, huge wardrobe stood near the wall by the door, which, considering the lack of a closet back here, was precisely what the room needed. The main bathroom had been done up with several shades of dark-purple linen, which harmonized nicely with the gray walls.

Apparently saving the best for last, Amelia paused in front of the final closed door. "This was the hardest room for them to move and set up. I had some people from the warehouse help move the artwork, and they kept all the covered paintings hidden. I haven't seen anything yet." She paused, meeting my eyes. "I know you wanted to show me your work on your own time, so I won't come in with you if you don't want me to."

I smiled widely and pulled her into my arms. "Please come in with me," I whispered. "You've earned it."

Her face lit up with joy, and I opened the door for us.

My new studio was perfect. The easel had been set up in precisely the spot I'd imagined it. A new shelving system had been installed along the far wall for my materials, which, I noticed immediately, had been added to, liberally. I saw extra canvases and framing materials I knew I hadn't owned before, and it looked like my paintbrush and paint set had grown twofold. My newest painting was sitting on my easel, still covered with a drop cloth, waiting for me to return to it. Also, my paint palette lay on a small table next to the easel. The sun streamed in through the large, nearly floor-to-ceiling window, and I could tell that the light in here would be fantastic for painting.

Amelia walked in and immediately started examining my older paintings, several of which had been hung on the walls already, just as they'd been in my studio at Aunt Kate's house. A selection of even older paintings were propped against another wall, again, just as they had been in my old studio. I watched her for a long while as she gazed at the work on display, holding my breath. After she'd seen the last one, she turned to me, her expression bright.

"They're wonderful."

"Really?"

She looked gravely serious and met my eyes. "You're incredibly gifted. Even the older ones are charming."

I relaxed finally, breathing out a long breath. "You're just saying that."

Her face became stern. "Not at all, Chloé. Your work is marvelous. I'm not saying anything to flatter you. I like it a lot."

I shrugged, not quite believing her, but the compliment pleased me. I'd been terrified to have her see my work. Now that the ordeal was over, I wouldn't have to worry about it again.

"So do you like it?" She gestured at the room.

My eyes flooded with tears again, and I rushed over, pulling her into an embrace. "It's the nicest thing anyone's ever done for me."

She rubbed my back for a while, shushing me, and then, almost simultaneously, we realized we were being watched. All four of the others stood in the doorway, watching us with identical, pleased expressions. They walked in, and I gave each one a hug, temporarily unable to speak.

"I take it you like it?" Meghan asked.

"It's amazing." I looked around at all of them, blinking away tears. "You're all amazing. I don't know how to thank you."

Aunt Kate walked over to me and gave me another hug. "You deserve it, honey. I want you to be happy. We all do."

I saw her share a smile with Amelia, and my heart swelled with relief and joy. They were finally starting to understand each other.

"I am happy. Right now, I couldn't be happier."

I hugged all five of them, trying my hardest to stop crying, but my tears were infectious. Amelia, Meghan, and Aunt Kate's eyes were leaking by the time I'd made my rounds, and even Jim looked a little red around the eyes.

"Okay," Aunt Kate finally said, making a cutting motion. "Enough of these tears." She wiped her eyes. "This is a happy occasion, and we should celebrate."

"Port of Call is just up the street," Jim suggested.

"Oh, man. I could go for one of their burgers," Amelia said.

We all looked at her, surprised to think that she'd ever been to that dive bar, let alone eaten a burger there or anywhere else. Seeing our shocked expressions, she laughed. "Well, it is an institution, people. I did grow up here."

I laughed and grabbed her hand, squeezing it. "A burger sounds perfect." My eyes were tearing up again in perfect happiness.

"We'll go grab our jackets," Aunt Kate said, steering Jim out the door.

"We'll come with you," Meghan said, grabbing Zach's arm. Both of them clearly understood that Amelia and I needed a minute.

Amelia and I were left alone, and she pulled me into a long embrace. I kept swallowing the lump in my throat, too happy to tell her how I felt. After a couple of minutes of simply holding each other, I drew back. I met her eyes and saw that they were wet and red, too. She knew how I felt about what she'd done for me without explanation.

"You go ahead," I told Amelia. "I need a minute to calm down."

"Are you sure?"

I nodded. "I'll be right down."

She left and I turned slowly around once more, looking at my marvelous new studio. Had anyone asked me to describe the perfect studio, I would have described this room exactly. Somehow, without even asking me, Amelia had known just what I would like. Even after our progress last night, when I'd seen her almost completely nude, I'd still been harboring a kernel of concern about our future together. Now, seeing this room, those worries were put to rest. Our sex life could only get better—that I knew for certain. And if our love for each other deepened along with it, I knew that everything would eventually work out. I was determined to show her how much she meant to me, even if it took years for us to get there.

Wiping my eyes for the final time, I made my way downstairs and rejoined the others. They hadn't heard me coming, and I watched as the five of them joked and laughed with each other as they stood in my new living room. Amelia and Meghan looked relaxed and happy, and Aunt Kate and the men were watching the two of them banter with big grins on their faces. Amelia and the people I considered my family were finally seeing eye-to-eye.

Seeing them there, I knew everything was going to just keep getting better and better.

About the Author

Charlotte Greene grew up in the American West in a loving family that supported her earliest creative endeavors. She began writing as a teenager and has never stopped. She now holds a doctorate in English, and she teaches courses in literature and women's studies at a regional university in the South. When she's not teaching or writing, she enjoys playing video games, traveling, and brewing hard cider. Charlotte is a longtime lover and one-time resident of the city of New Orleans. While she no longer lives in NOLA, she visits as often as possible.

You can find and contact Charlotte on her website, charlottegreeneauthor.com, or follow her on Twitter and Instagram @cgreene_writer.

Books Available from Bold Strokes Books

18 Months by Samantha Boyette. Alissa Reeves has only had two girlfriends and they've both gone missing. Now it's up to her to find out why. (978-1-62639-804-7)

Arrested Hearts by Holly Stratimore. A reckless cop with a secret death wish and a health nut who is afraid to die might be a perfect combination for love. (978-1-62639-809-2)

Capturing Jessica by Jane Hardee. Hyperrealist sculptor Michael tries desperately to conceal the love she holds for best friend, Jess, unaware Jess's feelings for her are changing. (978-1-62639-836-8)

Counting to Zero by AJ Quinn. NSA agent Emma Thorpe and computer hacker Paxton James must learn to trust each other as they work to stop a threat clock that's rapidly counting down to zero. (978-1-62639-783-5)

Courageous Love by KC Richardson. Two women fight a devastating disease, and their own demons, while trying to fall in love. (978-1-62639-797-2)

Pathogen by Jessica L. Webb. Can Dr. Kate Morrison navigate a deadly virus and the threat of bioterrorism, as well as her new relationship with Sergeant Andy Wyles and her own troubled past? (978-1-62639-833-7)

Rainbow Gap by Lee Lynch. Jaudon Vickers and Berry Garland, polar opposites, dream and love in this tale of lesbian lives set in Central Florida against the tapestry of societal change and the Vietnam War. (978-1-62639-799-6)

Steel and Promise by Alexa Black. Lady Nivrai's cruel desires and modified body make most of the galaxy fear her, but courtesan Cailyn Derys soon discovers the real monsters are the ones without the claws. (978-1-62639-805-4)

Swelter by D. Jackson Leigh. Teal Giovanni's mistake shines an unwanted spotlight on a small Texas ranch where August Reese is secluded until she can testify against a powerful drug kingpin. (978-1-62639-795-8)

Without Justice by Carsen Taite. Cade Kelly and Emily Sinclair must battle each other in the pursuit of justice, but can they fight their undeniable attraction outside the walls of the courtroom? (978-1-62639-560-2)

21 Questions by Mason Dixon. To find love, start by asking the right questions. (978-1-62639-724-8)

A Palette for Love by Charlotte Greene. When newly minted Ph.D. Chloé Devereaux returns to New Orleans, she doesn't expect her new job, and her powerful employer—Amelia Winters—to be so appealing. (978-1-62639-758-3)

By the Dark of Her Eyes by Cameron MacElvee. When Brenna Taylor inherits a decrepit property haunted by tormented ghosts, Alejandra Santana must not only restore Brenna's house and property but also save her soul. (978-1-62639-834-4)

Cash Braddock by Ashley Bartlett. Cash Braddock just wants to hang with her cat, fall in love, and deal drugs. What's the problem with that? (978-1-62639-706-4)

Gravity by Juliann Rich. How can Ellie Engebretsen, Olympic ski jumping hopeful with her eye on the gold, soar through the air when all she feels like doing is falling hard for Kate Moreau, her greatest competitor and the girl of her dreams? (978-1-62639-483-4)

Lone Ranger by VK Powell. Reporter Emma Ferguson stirs up a thirty-year-old mystery that threatens Park Ranger Carter West's family and jeopardizes any hope for a relationship between the two women. (978-1-62639-767-5)

Love on Call by Radclyffe. Ex-Army medic Glenn Archer and recent LA transplant Mariana Mateo fight their mutual desire in the face of past losses as they work together in the Rivers Community Hospital ER. (978-1-62639-843-6)

Never Enough by Robyn Nyx. Can two women put aside their pasts to find love before it's too late? (978-1-62639-629-6)

Two Souls by Kathleen Knowles. Can love blossom in the wake of tragedy? (978-1-62639-641-8)

Camp Rewind by Meghan O'Brien. A summer camp for grown-ups becomes the site of an unlikely romance between a shy, introverted divorcee and one of the Internet's most infamous cultural critics—who attends undercover. (978-1-62639-793-4)

Cross Purposes by Gina L. Dartt. In pursuit of a lost Acadian treasure, three women must not only work out the clues, but also the complicated tangle of emotion and attraction developing between them. (978-1-62639-713-2)

Imperfect Truth by C.A. Popovich. Can an imperfect truth stand in the way of love? (978-1-62639-787-3)

Life in Death by M. Ullrich. Sometimes the devastating end is your only chance for a new beginning. (978-1-62639-773-6)

Love on Liberty by MJ Williamz. Hearts collide when politics clash. (978-1-62639-639-5)

Serious Potential by Maggie Cummings. Pro golfer Tracy Allen plans to forget her ex during a visit to Bay West, a lesbian condo community in NYC, but when she meets Dr. Jennifer Betsy, she gets more than she bargained for. (978-1-62639-633-3)

Taste by Kris Bryant. Accomplished chef Taryn has walked away from her promising career in the city's top restaurant to devote her life to her five-year-old daughter and is content until Ki Blake comes along. (978-1-62639-718-7)

The Second Wave by Jean Copeland. Can star-crossed lovers have a second chance after decades apart, or does the love of a lifetime only happen once? (978-1-62639-830-6)

Valley of Fire by Missouri Vaun. Taken captive in a desert outpost after their small aircraft is hijacked, Ava and her captivating passenger discover things about each other and themselves that will change them both forever. (978-1-62639-496-4)

Basic Training of the Heart by Jaycie Morrison. In 1944, socialite Elizabeth Carlton joins the Women's Army Corps to escape family expectations and love's disappointments. Can Sergeant Gale Rains get her through Basic Training with their hearts intact? (978-1-62639-818-4)

Before by KE Payne. When Tally falls in love with her band's new recruit, she has a tough decision to make. What does she want more—Alex or the band? (978-1-62639-677-7)

Believing in Blue by Maggie Morton. Growing up gay in a small town has been hard, but it can't compare to the next challenge Wren—with her new, sky-blue wings—faces: saving two entire worlds. (978-1-62639-691-3)

Coils by Barbara Ann Wright. A modern young woman follows her aunt into the Greek Underworld and makes a pact with Medusa to win her freedom by killing a hero of legend. (978-1-62639-598-5)

Courting the Countess by Jenny Frame. When relationship-phobic Lady Henrietta Knight starts to care about housekeeper Annie Brannigan and her daughter, can she overcome her fears and promise Annie the forever that she demands? (978-1-62639-785-9)

For Money or Love by Heather Blackmore. Jessica Spaulding must choose between ignoring the truth to keep everything she has, and doing the right thing only to lose it all—including the woman she loves. (978-1-62639-756-9)

Hooked by Jaime Maddox. With the help of sexy Detective Mac Calabrese, Dr. Jessica Benson is working hard to overcome her past, but it may not be enough to stop a murderer. (978-1-62639-689-0)

Lands End by Jackie D. Public relations superstar Amy Kline is dealing with a media nightmare, and the last thing she expects is for restaurateur Lena Michaels to change everything, but she will. (978-1-62639-739-2)

Lysistrata Cove by Dena Hankins. Jack and Eve navigate the maelstrom of their darkest desires and find love by transgressing gender, dominance, submission, and the law on the crystal blue Caribbean Sea. (978-1-62639-821-4)

Twisted Screams by Sheri Lewis Wohl. Reluctant psychic Lorna Dutton doesn't want to forgive, but if she doesn't do just that an innocent woman will die. (978-1-62639-647-0)